Bygone Buffoonery

The Real Fake History

Jeff Charlebois

BYGONE BUFFOONERY
The Real Fake History
Copyright © 2019 by Jeff Charlebois

All rights reserved. No part of this publication may be reproduced, distributed, or transmitted in any form or by any means, including photocopying, recording, or other electronic or mechanical methods, without the prior written permission of the publisher or author, except in the case of brief quotations embodied in critical reviews and certain other noncommercial uses permitted by copyright law.

Although every precaution has been taken to verify the accuracy of the information contained herein, the author and publisher assume no responsibility for any errors or omissions. No liability is assumed for damages that may result from the use of information contained within.

Library of Congress Control Number: 2019912800
ISBN-13:   Paperback: 978-1-64674-011-6

Printed in the United States of America

LitFire LLC
1-800-511-9787
www.litfirepublishing.com
order@litfirepublishing.com

CONTENTS

Dedicated to: vii
Acknowledgements ix
Introduction xi

World History in A Nutshell 1
Mutiny on the Ark Cruise 14
The Greek Geek 35
An Emperor with No Horse Sense 53
Little Red Robbing Hood 64
A King, the Fling and a Knight who could Swing? 71
America in a Nutshell 105
From Little Pecker to Big Pecker 112
The Prancing Cowboy 126
Grinding to the American Dream 139
The Forgotten Vaudevillians 157
From Sauce to Riches 163
Menace of the Reich 182

EPILOGUE 200

When humor goes, there goes civilization.

—Erma Bombeck

DEDICATED TO:

Everyone who has come into my life and helped me…

and there are many of you.

ACKNOWLEDGEMENTS

I must first and foremost give thanks to God. Without Him I would literally be nothing. I think, but I'm still not positive, He blessed me with a sense of humor which I try and share with the world… whether they like it or not. I'm just hoping God's not up there saying, "No, no, no, you're not doing anything I created you for. Enough clowning around."

My parents, who are never far from me, provided me with an incredible childhood that consisted of a world of possibilities and vast opportunities. They instilled valuable work ethics, some wisdom and important values that have guided me through life. I have no words to convey the appreciation of the many sacrifices my mother and father made for me and our family. It never went unnoticed, nor forgotten. I'm just hoping I don't have to pay them back.

My brothers, Steve and John, were my right and left arms. In His infinite wisdom, God knew that I would need two brothers to bring me through a difficult period of my life. We learned and did everything together, from throwing a football to throwing each other. I could not have made it through life without them.

My sister, Lori, who somehow prevailed through years of brotherly torment. (And, she still was nice enough to make her siblings Betty Crocker cupcakes.) Very talented in all she does, she makes us all proud to have such an awesome sis with a big heart. She oversees her boys and has become the backbone of the family. If anyone can make it happen, Dimps can.

Jim Elliott, he's just fun to drink beers with and watch football. I'm thankful he's in the family. I'm going to need him down the line.

My friends, who are too numerous to list, put a lot of life into my life. They always saw me and not a disability. Each one has given me their own treasured memories. I know who the real friends are… the ones who buy this book. In truth, I am amazed at how many great friends I have had come in and out of my life, helping me in their own way. I love almost all of them. No doubt, God was watching over me placing these wonderful people in my world.

All my parent's friends.

All my history and English teachers.

Special thanks to Katherine Mahoney, my editor and proofreader, who made this writer look better than he is.

Diane Cisneros who freed up much of my time so I could write this damn thing.

Finally… Olaf and Musky are my attention-starved cats that flop on my desk and watch me while I write or stare at a blank screen. The book, most likely, would have been finished six months earlier had I not been summoned, all too often, for belly rubs and back scratches. (It did give me time to organize my thoughts.) At times the pesky cats would walk on my keyboard and a sentence would appear on the screen. Sadly, it was better than anything I could have written.

INTRODUCTION

For some authors, writing comes easy. Not me, which is why I spend much of my time wondering why I chose to be a writer. I don't know why they call it writing anyway. It seems all I do is think about what I want to write. But somehow, over the past year, I was able to put together enough words, on enough pages, to compile a book. And, with this manuscript now completed, I could finally look in the mirror and not have the words "lazy bum" pop up.

My third book and I felt an overwhelming reluctance to turn it into the publisher. The truth was that I had no confidence in the writing. My biggest hang-up, is it funny? Without the funny, it was meaningless. I perform stand-up comedy to audiences with a "whatcha got" look on their faces, so I know instantly if something I come up with is funny. Writing is a different animal - one hour it's funny and then ten minutes later the animal seems to have gotten worms and you're asking yourself how in God's name did you write such trash. I was nervous, afraid the publisher might read it then ask for the advance back. It seemed like only yesterday they were handing me a check. But I knew it wasn't yesterday because yesterday I was at racetrack spending the last of the publisher's advance. Where did all the money go? I knew some of it went on Lightfoot in the eighth who, incidentally, during his race, turned towards me and smiled while slowly walking by. All I could do was excitedly yell, "Go catch your friends! Go get 'em, boy!" I guess he figured whether he won or lost, it didn't matter, he wasn't getting a cut.

Panic rolled over me, believing they would hate the book. I take hate personally – especially when it's directed at me. What if they hated it so much that I'd have a better chance of curing Ebola then being bankrolled for another one? Insecurity attacked me with pounding fixated thoughts of what if I no longer had it in me? If, by chance, some form of dementia had robbed me of the silliness I used observing life. I wanted to avoid turning it in, having lost faith in myself. I thought about telling the publisher that my hacked computer had resulted in all my files deleted from the hard drive. Then I realized I'd look like an idiot for not backing them up. I considered skipping through a grocery store then suddenly flipping out, throwing vegetables, cans of soup, and claiming I was Captain Crunch. Being declared legally insane is not a bad go-to but then I thought of the endless hours of chatting with a shrink. I became a writer to avoid talking, besides, I don't need him delving into any of my personal sick fetishes. A little prison time crossed my mind until that whole rape thing popped up in my head. Sure, I get lonely and can use a hug, at times, but that's just a little out of my league. Mexico was a possibility but, what if I drank the water and died with my pants soiled? How embarrassing. The more I brainstormed, the more I realized I had no place to run. I was broke, anyway. Life and women have taught me you can't do much without money. Sadly, I didn't even have enough dough to buy a ski mask to rob a bank.

To tame the doubt demons lurking within me, I knew I needed some constructive feedback on my manuscript. By constructive feedback, I mean someone who would tell me, "I love it," or "I wouldn't change a word" and "you are amazing, big fella, and I love your smile." The problem was very few people read these days and, if they do, my stuff wouldn't be at the top of their reading list. A talented writer colleague of mine, Chip Jacobs, enlightened me of a dreary fact; ninety percent of people who buy a book don't read it. That told me people are lazy and like to piss money away. It's why I don't like to give out free books. If you're not going to read my stuff, you're going to at least pay me for it.

My close friend Buddha (so nicknamed because of his robust belly and not for his wisdom) reluctantly agreed to read it and give me his thoughts. I was grateful, ignoring his under-the-breath mumblings of "Like I don't have better things to do" and "I'm sure it sucks, anyway." (It's funny the way men show their friendship. It's never, "Hey, dude, your hair looks nice today." A real good buddy throws out, "Hey douchebag, your face looks like crap.") I had no choice but to trust him, even as I reflected on the times, he left me stranded at the airport.

The next day I waited at the diner for Buddha, anxious to get his critique. (I had promised to pay for his pizzas for a month, so I was pretty sure he'd post.) An hour passed with no Buddha, and I debated how long I would make a fool of myself waiting here. I decided I could handle being a jackass for twenty more minutes.

Suddenly, a mysterious man wearing unmatching clothes and sporting a scruffy beard approached my table. "Is your name. Jeff?" "It could be," I hesitantly replied, reluctant to admit it in case this dude was about to whip out a subpoena. (I felt safe, though. Groping a woman has only crossed my mind and never acted upon.) "What can I do for you, chief?" The man introduced himself as Marvin then reached into the satchel slung around his neck. Before I could dive under the table, thinking bullets might fly, he pulled out my manuscript. Holding it up, he said, "This book. I love it!"

I squinted towards the manuscript, making sure it was my book about which he was discussing. He hadn't handled my work of art with kid gloves the way it appeared torn and tattered with splotches of coffee stains; at least, I hoped it was coffee.

"You like it?" I perked up, quickly forgetting about the condition of my manuscript or who the hell this shady stranger was.

"You are one talented SOB," he blurted out. For a few seconds, I was speechless as I fought back the tears. This guy could be pulling some scam to rip me off or murder me. "Well, don't just stand there. Have a seat, my good friend," I gleefully said like I was talking to a long-lost twin brother who had been swept away in a tornado when we were toddlers.

"How did you get my book?"

"Some chubby guy named Buddha said he'd pay me twenty bucks to read it then said you'd give me fifty bucks to give you feedback on it."

I wasn't surprised. Buddha had spent his life avoiding work. Why would he take the time to pick up my book? There were no fold-out centerfolds in it. I looked at the man convinced anything he had to say would be trivial and meaningless. I rolled my eyes, sighed, then slid fifty bucks across the table. Hell, he wanted to talk about my book.

Buddha knew a lot of people from all different backgrounds. For all I knew this guy could be a college professor. Intellects don't always look the part. What did I care, anyway? The dude had read my book. For someone to tell me how much they loved my writing, ah yeah, I'll shell out fifty bucks for that. I had no idea what this man knew about literature, but trepidations quickly subsided when Marvin pulled out a pair of eyeglasses and put them on. Case closed. Only intelligent people wear glasses. If he were to put a spectacle's arm in his mouth while appearing to ponder, I'd be thoroughly impressed. That's a trick only used by a sheer intellectual. And, used in conjunction with some slow nods with some beard stroking thrown in, one can only assume you're amid genius.

"So, tell me," he began. "How did you come up with this stuff?"

"Well," I blushed, "when I was younger, my father got me interested in history. I guess I romanticize the past. Sometimes I think part of me wants to live in another time and place." Marvin pulled off his glasses and put one of the arms in his mouth. Just what I wanted. "The human spirit is a restless beast. It's never content in the place and time."

Wow, for someone with a scruffy beard and invading body odor this was one intuitive cat. I could tell his elevator went to the top floor, and the doors opened. Maybe from reading my book he could read me like a book. I liked him right away. This was a man I could trust for insightful feedback. "If you don't mind me asking, what was your favorite story?"

"Putting my feet to the fire. I like your style," Marvin smirked. "I wouldn't know where to begin. Each one is superb in its own way. What's your favorite?"

"Oh jeez, they're all like my kids. How do you pick a favorite?" I stammered. "I liked the one about the Roman Caesar, who married his horse." Marvin laughed. "Married his horse. Is that great or what?"

"At least you don't need a ring with carats. You need carrots," I quipped. We both laughed one of those fake laughs. I felt a connection with the guy. "Another one of my favorites," I continued, "is when Little Pecker went through all those crazy rituals." Marvin looked up then caressed his beard, uttering, "Little Pecker, Little Pecker" as if trying to recall.

"Remember, he was the young brave in the Poonani tribe? The journey into manhood? The perverted gold miner?" I rambled, trying to spark a recollection.

"Oh yes, that does ring a bell. Little Pecker. He was a… pistol."

"That he was," I nodded with another fake laugh.

"You got a lot of stuff going on up there," Marvin commented as he swirled his fingers around my head.

"That I do, and I feel compelled to get the insanity down on paper. But who appreciates it?" I sighed. "People like you Marvin are few and far between. You know what? I can tell you this. You get me. And I'm a better judge of character than I am a writer."

"What made you become a writer?" This cat was deep. Nobody ever asked me that before. I barely knew the guy, and he gave a damn about my life. He was genuinely interested in me. It was an awesome feeling.

"I don't know. I always hated it in school. I used to think it was an escape from the boredom of life but, as I get older, I'm starting to think it's more of an escape from the world. When I write, I create my own worlds."

"What's your favorite stuff to write?" he asked.

"You got the meat of it right there, big fella," I proudly stated. "I'm sure you could see the humor jump off the page. It's all about the laughs, baby. You… you laughed, didn't ya?"

"Sure. I'm sure I laughed," Marvin replied stone-faced, briefly leafing through the manuscript.

"Why do you like being funny?" The question seemed to come out of the blue and caught me off guard. I never contemplated why I felt I needed to be funny. It always seemed like it was just part of my nature. It was just there, perhaps filling some void in my soul.

I began to reflect. "For some odd reason, my seventh-grade teacher had this big cage in the corner of the classroom. I had no idea why it was there. Anyway, one day, the teacher went out of the room, and I climbed in that cage and began goofing around, acting like a trapped monkey. My classmates were in hysterics. When the teacher walked back in, he just sat down at his desk and laughed, obviously enjoying my little chimp show. And, it was then when I felt a calling to be the funny clown."

"So, after that, it became all about the laughs?"

"Pretty much," I surrendered. "Sometimes, I feel like a junkie chasing that first high."

"I can relate to that. I really can."

Marvin did seem to understand, and I could feel he sensed something deeper in me. In a way, it felt good not to be thought of as a wisecracking buffoon who found nothing serious in life. Damn, this little shrink was shoveling under the surface. He was making me think of things I never contemplated before. He was good. I found myself thoroughly enjoying what felt like a therapy session. "Being funny makes me feel good. I think every joke subconsciously reminds me not to take anything in this world too seriously. It's my buffer to depression," I surmised. "If I didn't have humor as my crutch, I would be swept under a tide of reality into a sea of sadness. I do what I do to keep my head above water. Plus, a good, funny, clever remark garners me a little attention."

"We all need a little attention."

"Why not?" I shrugged. "Enough about me. So, did you really like the book?" Marvin stood up to leave, then responded, "Shouldn't the question be, did you like the book?"

I sat in my car for a of couple hours replaying our deep and insightful conversation in my head. What a good man. Intelligent, knowledgeable, scholarly, and soothingly therapeutic. And, most importantly, the kicker was he loved my book. This wonderful man had impeccable taste. I wondered what he did for a living. Probably an English professor at some small college in a quaint town. I felt alive again. I was no longer apprehensive about submitting my book to the publisher. I could feel a budding confidence. I was excited and anxious to release my Pulitzer Prize masterpiece of history-oriented, funny stories to the masses.

I drove around with my head in the clouds. The feedback I received from Marvin was priceless. He was spot on with his critique, which meant there was no need to change one word. This man certainly knew what he was doing. What really impressed me was his ability to understand the inner me by reaching into my soul and pulling out the reasons of why I like to write. Why I desperately wanted to connect with my readers. And, why it was important for me to put some laughter into the world. Marvin hit nerves, providing me with introspection. He made me look at myself, my goals, my life's mission.

With new-found courage, I drove over to the publisher and plopped my manuscript on her desk. "This book. You'll love it!"

"What's it about?" she asked.

"Real fake history… with lots of buffoonery."

"Will it sell?" pressed the publisher.

"In these days of fake news, I don't see why not."

On my way back home, I decided to stop in at the diner, figuring I deserved some chicken strips and French fries after spending a year of my life pecking on a keyboard with an empty head while asking myself, "What the hell are you writing?" But I finally believed in me and my writing. Marvin gave me that confidence, along with a realization of why I do it.

As I began walking towards the restaurant, I heard some loud garbled ravings emanating from the alley. Curiosity got the best of me, and I ducked around the corner to see what the ruckus was. Slumped against the dumpster was a man, clutching a bottle of Johnny Walker, with his chin buried in his chest deep in conversation with himself. "I got a tattoo of my shoe," I think I heard him mutter. My first thought was this alley rat could use someone like Marvin to elevate his life circumstances.

I debated on just minding my business and walking away, but a sense of compassion gripped me. "Excuse me, sir, are you alright?"

"They're all around. Watching us," the bum mumbled then followed by, "There's a cat in my mailbox." He took a sip of booze then slowly looked up at me. I could feel my jaw drop on my feet. That face. That scruffy beard. It was Marvin, and he is plastered. Well, at least I knew my money went to a good cause. Next to the dumpster was a large cardboard box with the name Marvin's Place scribbled on the side with a pile of raggedy clothes on top of it. My keen intuition told me this could very well be where he resides.

My mind began to whirl. Then, as if slapped in the face by a half-frozen pork loin, it hit me. It all started to piece together; the scruffy beard, the tattered stained manuscript, his urine scented cologne smell. Marvin was not some college professor; he was a bum. Just a simple drunk homeless bum... who gave me feedback on my book.

"Marvin" I hissed, hoping to catch his attention in between the gulps of booze and the nonsensical rants. His glazed eyes finally looked up and locked on mine. "Do you remember me?" I huffed.

"Chummy, is that you?" he slurred with a smirk. "The city below the city of palms lies the pirate's treasure. Silver and gold." He pulled his bottle close to him," Chummy gave this to me."

It was strange that the rambling fool threw out that name. I think I had met a Chummy once who may or may not have been instrumental in helping me with my book. I just don't know, and the story is too long and probably too unbelievable to go into. Right now, it wasn't important.

"Marvin," I sternly stated while he sipped on his bottle staring straight ahead and making clicking noises with his tongue. I had now become deeply concerned. "Marvin," I calmly said. He looked up at me. "Did you or did you not read my book?" For a second, his eyes became coldly serious then mumbled something like "Zephendackyl" and started laughing. I didn't speak "loon" so I ignored him, even though the word sounded vaguely familiar.

As I sat in the restaurant, I replayed the whole lengthy conversation with Marvin in the diner. It dawned on me the scruffy louse took me for fifty bucks. He had never given me one tidbit of useful information on my stories. He nodded, asked questions, and coaxed me into just talking about myself. He knew absolutely nothing about my book. Maybe it was best. How much constructive feedback can you get from a homeless guy who enjoyed the bottle and laughed like a loon? If only I knew the laugh was a result of one of my stories. I could forgive him.

Buddha claimed he never gave the manuscript to anyone and was still planning on reading it. I didn't believe him. He once told me to meet him at a costume party. I went as the cowardly lion. The only problem was it was just a regular party and no one else was dressed in costumes. I had to try and convince everybody that dressing up as a lion just made me feel good about myself.

The publisher loved my book, claiming she peed herself several times. Uncontrollable urination is always the highest form of flattery for a humor writer. It was a real blessing to know my writing could have that effect. I received a ten-thousand-dollar advance for my next book. On my way to cash it, I reflected on one of my stories about an ancient Greek actor sent on an outrageous odyssey. It reminded me that things in life are just separate little journeys in hopes that we learn something worthwhile. The silly story made me chuckle. As a matter of fact, I was laughing all the way to the bank. (What? No drums and cymbals?)

I held up the first copy of my book, admiring the cover. After a brief proud smile, I leaned over and set it on Marvin's lap. It was a signed copy in which I wrote: "Marvin, thanks for helping find my purpose of spreading some laughter in the world." I hoped he'd at least read that. I also hoped he'd find the envelope tucked in the book with $5,000. I considered him a partner.

As I walked away, I heard the homeless man murmur, "King Artie and Dancelot." I would've chalked it up to intoxicated blather, but the reference was too obscure and had to have come from somewhere. I turned around and stared at him. He smiled, held up the book, then mentioned "Love that Little Pecker" adding "Very clever." And with that said he ventured back to the bottle, back into his world of conversing with a make believe friend.

That sneaky SOB had read my book, referencing my favorite chapter. Had I not met Marvin the manuscript would be sitting on my desk or possibly in a trash bin. I thought how funny it would be if I had thrown it away and Marvin found it in the dumpster, brought it to some publisher and made a million bucks. My mind thinks like that. It looks for the absurdity in life… like a homeless bum helping me to believe in myself.

WORLD HISTORY IN A NUTSHELL

Before delving into some amazing accounts of some extraordinary characters who are, well, characters, to say the least, it is vital that the reader has a grasp of world history. Well, it's not "vital" but, it is important to understand…, actually, you really don't need to know anything about past events that shaped the world. Hopefully and God-willing, the stories will speak for themselves. At some point in my life, I wrote this all-encapsulating humorous overview of how things came about in the world and who did what and when. The main takeaway is the piece made me seem like I was an intelligent guy. The truth of the matter is, it's a cute summary of events, and I just didn't want to see the thing go to waste. It took way too many hours, and vodka and sodas, to write it. I refuse to let my liver decay in vain. And, who knows, you may learn something. I doubt it though, but stranger things have happened. So, here is a tongue-in-cheek crash course on the history of the world. Buckle up.

A long, long time ago, somewhere along the Nile River, one of the first great civilizations to arise was the Egyptians. These were tan people who wore diaper-like outfits and drove around in compact chariots. Their big claim to fame was constructing giant pyramids so they could store dead pharaohs wrapped from head-to-toe in adhesive tape. They must have been extremely big rulers because their tombs were humongous. Nobody knows how they were built. Many believe it was aliens. My thinking on that is, a highly advanced group of people who have spaceships that travel at the speed of light are building a structure made of rocks. Come on, what about plastic or fiberglass? It doesn't even have automatic doors or what about duct tape used on the mommies?

They also came up with something called hieroglyphics. These were symbols and stick men often in pornographic positions. You got to do what you got to do to get the kids to read. They found scribbling on hard surfaces was too time-consuming, so they invented papyrus, and thus the first pornographic images were set down on paper. Forget how the pyramids might have been built; the bigger mystery was how the human body could contort in some of those positions.

For labor they used slaves, like the Jews, to build these monstrous monuments that took years to construct. The Jews were like, "We're tired of lifting big blocks and making large triangles." They thought it was all one big pyramid scheme, but their whining had no effect on the pharaoh, so they said, "Oi vey, we're out of here."

The pharaoh was like, "Oh no you ain't."

Moses stepped up and said, "You gots to let my people go."

"I ain't gots to do nothing," the pharaoh snapped back.

With God in Moses' corner, the Big Guy threw down a few plagues on the Egyptians. There was a famine, scores of icky swarming bugs, a bloody Nile River to name a few. Ra, the sun god, was of no help to the pharaoh so finally, he succumbed.

"Okay, I've had it," he barked. "I want all you crazy Jews out of here… and take your God with you because I'm so sick of sleeping with frogs in my bed and picking festering boils on my skin."

That sounded good to the Jews, so they fled north to a promised land, taking a shortcut through the Red Sea. They brought everything they could with them; food, tents, silver, goats, a golden calf, etc. The one thing they forgot was a map. Eventually, after forty years, they found a little plot of desert land with high hopes of just living there in peace and quiet. Location, location, location. If the Jews knew what they were in for they might have stayed in Egypt building pyramids. The pharaoh was left to cuddle with the Sphinx.

On the other side of them was a growing empire known as the Babylonians. They talked incisively in incoherent sentences. It is thought that all foreign languages came out of there. The poor drank beer and the rich consumed wine, which may explain all the babbling. They invented the potter's wheel most likely to hold their booze. They also created the seed plow which really pissed the ox off. They were responsible for the first system of writing and the earliest known codes of law. These two elements paved the way for "the attorney." This prompted them to go grab the Jews and enslave them because they made the best lawyers. So, in 587 BCE, the Babylonian king, Nebuchadnezzar's army captured Jerusalem, destroyed the Temple, and exiled the Jews to Babylon (modern day Iraq). The Jewish people were on the move again.

At some point, the Persians rose to power under Cyrus the Great who developed a unique form of governing. Everyone conquered could keep their language and their culture, but not their money. The taxes went to exquisite gardens where they trimmed shrubs into animal shapes. Then they would sit under fig trees and work on Algebra problems because they were good at math. They passed this knowledge onto the Jews, and many became shrewd accountants. The Jews exhausted Cyrus with their constant complaining about psychosomatic illnesses, so he released them because the elderly women often made him feel guilty. After arriving in Jerusalem, the Hebrews rebuilt their city and temple to thank God that all their troubles were behind them. If they only knew. But, for now, things were looking up for the Jews.

From Cyrus to Darius to Xerxes, Persian rulers continually amassed a vast kingdom. Eventually, their greed for more power would be their downfall as they attempted to expand their territory into Greece. It was a no brainer because the Greek girls were virgins with dowries.

In the Mediterranean, a teenage boy known as Alexander strolled on the scene. The famous philosopher Aristotle tutored him, and he would ponder questions like "Why? Why haven't I taken over the world yet?" Up until now, the nineteen-year-old was called only by the name of Alexander the So-So, but soon the hairy warrior would begin a snatch-and-grab mission in the civilized frontier. He started by uniting the Greek city-states and led the Corinthian League. It wasn't enough. The type A go-getter began to excel by becoming the king of Persia, Babylon, and Asia, and created Macedonian colonies in Iran. It was quite an impressive résumé for such a young man who may even have been gay. (He like to redecorate empires he conquered.) He changed his last name from "the So-So" to "the Great."

It had a better ring to it. Malaria struck him in 323 BC, and Alexander learned he could conquer a lot of things, but death wasn't one of them.

Athens had developed into a hub with hang out areas such as the Acropolis and the Temple. Renowned philosophers like Socrates discussed good and evil. While Plato pondered, "What it all about, Alfie?" And, Aristotle wanted to know "Who was Alfie?" These profound life teachers were respected and just wanted to know why. Was that too much to ask? Today, they would be considered unemployed bums with a worthless major.

On the other side of Greece, the city of Sparta was on the rise. They were known for their elite fighting force, and they did it in skimpy outfits. The soldiers were called hoplites because they could quickly hop around with their shields and spears. Soon these two great powers would butt helmets and wrestle in the Peloponnesian war. This action would bring about marathons and Olympics.

The Greeks had gods for everything, and plays were written about them. The characters lived in oceans, caves, mountains and hell, to name a few. They were gods of love, music, war, pleasure, drunkenness, and more. Those Greeks covered it all. These god creatures did silly things like go on odysseys, fight one-eyed monsters, kill siblings, sleep with their mothers and even turn people to stone. These gods were so confident that they refused to wear clothing when being sculpted. One thing is for sure; no one ever asked the Venus de Milo ever to lend a hand.

Off in the Far East, the Chinese were busy building a great wall in hopes of keeping invaders or pesky rodents out of their country. Dynasties from the Shang to the Ming to the Qing would rule. Many traveled by horseback but for some reason were very poor drivers. Chinese restaurants were popping up everywhere, and egg rolls were the rage. Kingdoms soon began warring because people were upset about the nonspecific lame fortunes in their cookies. The emperor was the only one whoever won. Monks started fighting each other with kung fu, swords, and chopsticks. At some point, they invented gunpowder and soon firework stands were popping up all over the countryside.

To the west, in the boot shape territory known as Rome was a republic supposedly created by the offspring of a She-wolf. As the people began to pull together as a community, they elected several kings which morphed into a senate body which then granted Mr. Gaius Octavius the "Augustus" title - which meant "divine." It affirmed his position as the most important man in the empire and brought the end to the Roman Republic. With a new emperor, a new empire could rise and let the orgies begin.

Julius Caesar climbed the corporate ladder from an infamous general to the Godfather of all Rome. As their leader, he would conquer more land, invent a salad and get busy with Cleopatra, who would later get busier with Caesar's best friend, Marc Anthony. "When in Rome…"

Eventually, the Roman Empire reached from Europe to Africa to the Middle East then reached in everyone's pockets. Sometime in the first century, over in Israel, the Son of God raised a ruckus by healing people and teaching folks how to love one another. Some didn't like that message, so they decided to show their philosophy of hating and crucified Him. The love your neighbor thing finally did catch on and began to resonate, and this new Christianity began to spread all over the world.

Everyone had their own ideas of how this religion should run so someone had to oversee the flock and thus the pope became the new emperor. The pontiffs of ancient times helped in the spread of Christianity and the resolution of various doctrinal disputes. It was their way or the highway; the highway to hell that is. Major decisions like being forgiven, going to heaven and how much money you need to give to the church would now rest in his holy hands.

Over the years, Rome began to weaken and was splitting into two empires. In 455 A.D., the barbarians, namely the Vandals sacked the city. It was like Revenge of the Nerds. The Germanic tribe looted what they could, snatching things like grain, pottery, candles, togas and lots of wine barrels, after all, it's not a party without the booze. The Romans were like "What the hell happened to the good life of decadence and debauchery?" The senator bribes would stop, the orgies would cease, and the pope got the hell out of Dodge and moved to Byzantium while the Jewish people would scatter around the world. In the other half of the hemisphere, the Aztecs in Central America were eating chocolate Acai berries and ripping out hearts to appease their sun god. The North American Indians were enjoying life hunting buffalo, smoking peyote and tickling each other with eagle feathers.

Meanwhile, the Byzantium Empire in the east started to flourish as Europe was coming into the light while still in The Dark Ages. The economy was among the most advanced in that whole neck of the woods for many centuries. The capital city, Constantinople was a prime hub in a trading network that at various times extended across nearly all of Eurasia and North Africa. It was the main stop on the Silk Road which would later become Route 66. They gave us mosaics, palaces, monasteries, and probably area rugs. The Muslims and Turks would often attack the Byzantines because they were stealing all their mathematics and astronomy knowledge and making claims like they invented the Pythagorean Theorem and discovered not only the Big Dipper but the little one as well. The Byzantines were a smorgasbord of people that spoke Greek, Arabic, Latin and maybe even some Pig Latin. They would flourish for over 1,000 years.

With the coronation of Charlemagne in the year 800 AD, the challenge to the authority of the Byzantine emperor as the legitimate Roman emperor became clear. He was crowned the new emperor by Pope Leo and thus began the Middle Ages, which occurred at the start and not the middle. This king, Charlemagne, united most of Europe, converting them to Christianity with mottos like, "You either love our God of love, or we'll kill you." Hey, whatever works. This attitude spilled over to the Crusaders in the tenth century. The Crusaders, who used Constantinople as a rest stop, had a mission to free the Jews from Muslim control and gain access to the holy sites in Jerusalem and to prevent the expansion of Islam to the near east. At times, they killed some Jews forgetting their goal of freeing the Jews.

Things reached a grinding halt in Europe when the Black Death emerged. This disease really plagued the people. Fleas carried it on the bodies of rats - and that's fur real. It was a valuable lesson in always brushing your rat before snuggling in bed with it. The Bubonic Plague wiped out over 100 million people. On an up note, it really opened the job market. You could not warn people of the dangerous epidemic by tweeting either, simply because no one could read. Because of the devastating disease, people reawakened to their immortality, and got in touch with their humanistic spiritual side and their world view began to change. The Renaissance was about to blossom. Can you say naked paintings?

In the 15th century, medieval knights hung up their lances and suits of armor in their castle closets. Chivalry was dead, and the Renaissance was born. It spread with great speed from its birthplace in Florence, Italy to the rest of Europe. Every region seemed to have its distinct take on humanism as there was a yearning to get back in touch with the ancient Greek and Roman cultures. Architects designed cathedrals and buildings like the Chateau de Chambord with columns, arches, and domes, oh my! Many of these beautiful, awe-inspiring structures are still standing and are almost as old as some of the jokes in this book.

During the Renaissance, philosophical reasoning took a backseat to the new scientific methods being discovered and now respected. You had to see it to believe it. Stars weren't held up in the sky by angels. There were now sound, logical explanations for everything. The Renaissance saw significant changes in the way the universe is perceived, and the methods sought to explain natural phenomena. Because of this, mathematics, astronomy, alchemy, and biology flourished. Illnesses could cure by reliable means of leaches and drilling holes in the skull to release demons. Science was on the move. Galileo and Copernicus were looking to the stars and expanding people's self-centered worldview. The sun didn't revolve around man, and the world wasn't flat. While Columbus was out proving these new ideas by sailing to new continents and dropping off a few European diseases; his peeps back in Spain began a grand inquisition where they put the Jews on trial and, through torture, asked them nicely to convert to Christianity. The Muslims, or Moors, would pack up and leave Europe and set up shop in Africa.

In the art world, Da Vinci doodled human anatomy sketches and painted a pissed off Mona Lisa as she constantly murmured, "Are we done yet?" Michelangelo would reach for the sky as he threw together a little something on the ceiling of the Sistine Chapel. As the Renaissance progressed, images of secular nature overtook religious artwork. Scenes from Genesis eventually became dogs playing poker. Off in England, the Elizabethan Era was in full swing, and Bill Shakespeare feather penned a few poems and plays. On the twelfth night, sometime during a midsummer's night dream, he wrote about kings, romance and betrayal – all the while taming a shrew. He made it big after his death, but at that time, it was much ado about nothing. Oh well, all's well that ends well.

Over in Germany, a theologian by the name of Martin Luther popped on the scene and didn't like the way the religious show was running, basically saying I don't like all your pope stuff and your pope rules and your popey-pope-church. As a matter of fact, there was a pope-potpourri of reasons why he wanted to break away from the church. His main beef is the sale of indulgences in which people would flip God a shekel, and their sins were wiped clean. The uppity monk nailed a list of demands to church doorways then told the pope, "Let's get ready to rummmmmm-ble!" Around this time, a dude named Gutenberg invented the printing press, and Luther was able to do a mass mailing of his grievances to surrounding villages, thus getting the word out quickly and ringing in the Protestant Reformation. Coupons would start be printed the following year.

Russia was a smorgasbord of fighting principalities but somehow pulled together to find a Tsar in the mid-1500s. Catherine and Peter would become great, and Ivan would just be terrible. The Ming Dynasty in China was at the peak of its expansion and was tinkering around with a powder that would fire projectiles through the air and into people's mushy heads. That was a game changer. The sword was put down, and the musket was picked up. England was fighting the Scots, while France was fighting England, which would only last one hundred years. During that brief battle, Spain and Portugal would parlay off Columbus' findings and send fleets over to the New World to grab some coffee. But they needed sugar for their coffee. Next, they realized they wanted to smoke on their coffee break, so they grabbed some tobacco. Their women demanded chocolate, so they went back for that. When they noticed their teeth were falling out, they confiscated all the gold in Central America to use for their fillings. Finally, they said, "Ah hell, let's just grab the land and colonize it." As a result of the colonial expansion, the European superpowers would slug it out for their piece of shepherd's pie. France would end up fighting Spain, but this time, it only lasted thirty years.

The Americas became a honey hole. With all the great goodies found over there, an industrial revolution exploded and made a mediocre Britain great. Factories and mills sprouted an upbringing about long workdays. The English put their profits into building ships and cannons, then sailed over to India and Asia to grab some spices and added a few more territories to their rapidly expanding empire, just so the sun would never set on them.

One of their big colonies was taking off. America had cotton, fur, snuff, and damn good whiskey. King George was like, "Hey, we paid for your trip over there, and we want our money back." So, he imposed a bunch of taxes on items like tea, stamps, and booze. The American colonists went crazy and rebelled. A bunch of highly intelligent men with white wigs got together and formed a continental congress and drafted a declaration stating, "We don't need you, pompous limeys, ruling us. We want our independence!" King George fired back, "That ain't be happening, govna!" Patrick Henry slurred, "Give me liberty, or give me a lager." Samuel Adams answered the call.

While Thomas Paine was making sense with "Common Sense" pamphlets, George Washington was sharpening his sword that had been dulled by a cherry tree. It was go time — the redcoats against the beaver coats. After an out-of-control tea party in Boston, the English loaded up their ships with cannon balls and crates of whoop-ass then set sail for America. The always-indecisive Paul Revere rode through the town yelling, "The British may, or may not be coming!" A revolution ensued. A general crossed a river, soldiers shivered at Valley Forge, battles won and lost, and a general turned traitor. And somehow, eventually, thirteen little colonies became one big country.

France was instrumental in helping the United States gain its independence. They liked the revolution idea so much that they decided to give it a whirl. Enlightened visionary philosophers; like Locke, Kant, and Voltaire, oh my, stirred up the French peasants to throw out the monarchy and crooked church scumbags who had been running the country. There was an attack on the Bastille, a march on Versailles, and terrible begat sword fights in the streets. It was raining a reign of terror and people lost their heads - thanks to the guillotine. When things calmed down, and everyone was tired of fighting, an unknown peaceful fellow stepped into power. His name was Napoleon. Unfortunately, this little poodle tyrant had a complex and would try to fix it by invading the European continent. Somewhere in Russia, his soldiers would turn into frozen mousse cakes, and the rest of his military tartlets would get a beat-down at Waterloo.

During the 19th century Victorian era, Beethoven was tearing up Vienna, Dickens was getting tale in two cities, and monarchs were marrying other rulers from every European country. Nobody could keep track if a queen were a niece, a sister, or a wife to another monarchy. It was noble incest gone wild. This situation would bring about family squabbles and a bunch of wars in Europe. Who doesn't like a good fight to clear the air? A treaty followed every battle, and another battle followed every treaty. But, while Dukes were duking it out, off to the west, a great power was emerging.

Hot off its independence, the American mindset was, "Whatever money I makes, I gets to keeps." The industrial revolution had made its way to the newly liberated country, and capitalistic ideals propelled people to be the best they could be. Entrepreneurs opened businesses, educated themselves, farmed, trapped, ranched, and invented anything that could make a buck: steam engines, cotton gins, mining tools, and textiles. The beautiful, spacious skies were the limit. Goods (and Bads) were transported around the country by horseys, canals, and railroads, oh my (never gets old)! Everything was rapidly on the move – even bearded old timers in the west, who were in search of gold. There were saloons in every town and cathouses in every saloon and horny cowboys in every cathouse. Slavery put a black mark on the label "land of the free" and, at some point, there was a civil war that wasn't very civil. Thousands lost their lives, while the ones who lived just lost limbs. Ultimately, slavery was abolished, and Rhett Butler told Scarlet he didn't give a damn.

Over in Turkey, the Ottoman Empire was mixing it up in the Crimean War with Russia. Islam encompassed the Middle East, and the Jews were still scattered. Africa had big purring, furry cats as of yet unendangered and a bunch of tribes with cool names like Zulus. (The Brits would fight this kingdom in 1879 and Alfie would be in a movie about it in 1964.) In Japan, Shoguns were enjoying kabuki and silk paintings but were shown no respect by geisha girls who walked all over them. By the turn of the century, the Japanese would put down their samurai swords, pick up rifles and attack Russia. Why not? Everyone else had. China was still hung up in the dynasty thing and wanted to remain ancient while hiding behind its Great Wall. The best way to do this was by massacring the foreign missionaries to keep outsider influence away. This massacre, known as the Boxer Rebellion, had nothing to do with dogs or Rocky Balboa.

At the turn of the 20th century, the rough riding American president, Teddy Roosevelt was whispering and carrying a big stick. Henry Ford was taking the horse off the streets and putting the horsepower in a Model T. Two Dayton dudes, Orville and Wilbur, were proving they had the "Wright stuff" by flying a winged bicycle over the dunes of Kitty Hawk, meowing at the friendly skies - later, Amelia Earhart would curse the duo on her way down.

Things were beginning to percolate in Europe, especially in the Balkan region where Serbs and Greeks were booting the Ottomans outta' there. Turkey was almost gobbled up, but, more importantly, this would be the opening act to World War One. Called "one" because one little assassin's bullet hit the archduke of Hungary causing a frenzy of countries to align themselves against each other. The main event would be Britain, France, and Russia, taking on Germany, Austria-Hungary, and the Ottoman Empire. America would roll the doughboys over to the party later in the game. Trenches dug, machine guns fired, and shells lobbed with a little mustard gas on the side. Millions of people died over nationalism. The League of Nations formed, and a Treaty of Versatile was signed. All was quiet on the western front. Finally, peace forever, or so we thought.

Everyone in the world needed a time out, except the Russians. Lenin stirred up a bloody revolution in which his Bolsheviks overthrew Czar Nicholas II and set up the first Marxist state. (No, Groucho was not in the picture, although movies were appearing for the first time in the US, along with flappers and prohibition, as happy days were here again.) A depressed Germany rolled wheel barrels of worthless money down its streets in search of a loaf of bread, as an angry unsuccessful artist with a funny mustache stewed. Soon he would rise to rescue the shattered Fatherland.

The roaring 1920s party came to an end, and people in 1930s had a hangover. The stock market crashed and greedy brokers high-dived from the forty-story windows. While the world was dealing with depression, Adolph Hitler was thinking about aggression. The new German dictator busied himself with producing a huge army, tanks, submarines, airplanes, some Hitler youth and a few concentration camps where the Gestapo could concentrate on extinguishing the Jewish race. Over in England, Neville Chamberlain, the prime minister, sat with some tea and crumpets confidently stating, "The Hitler chap is perfectly harmless."

World War II began with an opening number of Germany invading Poland. All of Europe and some of Africa would be next. Fascism was in, and Chamberlain was out, as Churchill vowed to fight by land, sea, or air. The Luftwaffe bombs would replace the London rain. With France and Italy under his stiff outstretched Sieg Heil arm, the furor, with a fury, decided to play Russian roulette by turning his panzers towards Stalingrad.

While America was doing the Lindy Hop, Japan was doing the island hop, grabbing lots of Asian landmasses. They would give a wake-up call to the "sleeping giant" by attacking Pearl Harbor. There was nothing to fear but fear itself - and bullets and bombs. From Saipan to Iwo Jima, to Guadalcanal and the Philippines, it was a jungle out there and MacArthur returned, and nipped it in the bud. The naval battle of Midway turned the Pacific tides of war and Tokyo Rose changed her tune over the airwaves.

Hitler's Nazi knees knocked as the Russians, along with their winter, froze the German advance. The allies would breach the Atlantic Wall, and Patton, with the greatest generation of soldiers, would slap his way to Berlin. They would come face-to-face with furry hat soviet comrades, the handwriting was on the Berlin Wall, and a Cold War would take center stage for the next fifty years.

In 1945, Japan was willing to fight to its death, but they had second thoughts after the second bomb mushroomed. They signed a peace agreement and the sun set on the land of the rising sun. The peaceful Gandhi curried the favor of the British by going on a diet of nothing until India was left to self-govern the snake charmers. That Hindu could do! A man named Mao started a revolution in China until it turned red. And, the United Nations gave the Promised Land back to the scattered Jews, and the pissed Arabs decided to hold the world over the oil barrel.

America confronted communism in Korea and drew the red line at the 38th parallel. They would try the same thing, valiantly, in Vietnam, but it was long and winding Ho Chi Minh trail, and the political will to win was lost. For the most part, civilized countries settled down to their private infrastructures. The Germans and Japanese were no longer making war, but great cars. Big band swing went to rock and roll, and the only major invasion was the Beatles in America. The Soviet Union challenged the U.S.A. to a race to space. The Arabs fought the Jews. Europe became more secular than in the past. Saudi Arabia was making a killing on black gold, and Pol Pot was making a killing in the fields of Cambodia. Reagan acted like a world leader, while the pope became blessed with a loon's bullet. The Jews fought the Arabs. Soccer became the main goooooal in South America. Australia built an opera house, and not much happened in Canada - ever. Islamic terrorists leveled some Twin Towers. A Malaysian airliner vanished, and David Copperfield had nothing to do with it. And too many crazy countries are on the verge of acquiring nuclear missiles to erase the past and the future. Yada, yada, yada, the rest, as they say, is history.

MUTINY ON THE ARK CRUISE

One day God spoke to Noah. "Noah, it's me, God. We need to talk." Skeptical, Noah looked behind the rocks and the bushes. Convinced that his sons weren't playing a joke on him, he yelled, "Yeah, what can I do you for God?"

"Noah, I want you to build me an ark," God requested.

"Sure thing, Lord," Noah responded. "Ah, quick question. What's an ark?"

"A big boat," replied God.

"When you say "big" what's your definition of 'big?' Cause "big" can also mean lots of time, work, aching back… I'm just saying."

God answered, "I'll have Gabriel swing by with some blueprints."

"Okee-dokey," Noah nodded, "But it may take me awhile. It's supposed to rain next week."

For forty minutes and forty seconds, Noah bickered with God on the design of the ark. "Three hundred cubits long and fifty cubits wide? Are you serious? I'm 462-year-old. I don't know how many more cubits I have in me." The old man scratched head as he looked over the scrolled blueprint. "Wow, this ark thingy's gonna be pretty damn big."

"What can I say," God responded. "I like things big. Have you seen the world?"

Noah, keeping with Jewish tradition, continued to whine and complain to God, disputing some of Gabriel's calculations. "Ou vey, how's this thing gonna float?"

"Don't worry; it'll float," God retorted in a stern voice.

"I just don't see how," Noah argued. "The bow's too short."

God released a frustrated sigh. "I said it'll float. Trust me."

"Float, smoat. I'm telling you it'll never float," Noah maintained.

God told him it was quiet time, but Noah had other issues. He thought the ark should be mahogany; God wanted cypress. After several grueling hours of quarreling, the Almighty changed his mind. Instead of twenty days and nights of rain, it was now going to be forty.

Noah started his workday later than planned when he couldn't find his hammer and saw. They were eventually found up in the kid's tree fort.

Hard at work, while sawing some wood in the hot sun, the townspeople stopped by to mock Noah. "Look at the crazy old man building a giant boat," one yelled.

"Yeah, and he has some breadcrumbs stuck in his beard," another one shouted as the crowd laughed. Noah just kept his head down and continued to labor until the boat was complete. A raven landed on his shoulder, and Noah took that as a sign that the big day was near. In retrospect, the raven just wanted to snack on the croutons left in Noah's snowy white facial hair.

One day Noah and God were conversing. "So, you need to gather up two of every all living creatures, and we should be good to go. Oh, and make sure they are on the ark by Tuesday."

"Excuse me?" Noah responded, taken aback.

"Just do what I say." God insisted without wanting to get into it.

"Are you crazy, God?" Noah snapped. "Do you know how many living creatures are out there?"

"I do. I created them."

"Why'd you put that hump on a camel, anyway?" Noah inquired then added, "It seems useless."

"I'm not doing this now, Noah. We're not going there," God retorted. "Just do what I say and have the animals on the ark by Tuesday… Wednesday the very latest."

For four days, Noah, with his sons, ran around trying to catch animals. The best they could do were a sloth and a couple of turtles. Then Noah had a grand idea. He posted some signs in the forest, deserts, and mountains that read ***"Want to get away? Free weekend cruise for you and your spouse. All you can eat."***

Creatures of all shapes and sizes appeared at the ark, excited for some fun and relaxation. Noah was there to greet them. Holding a stone clipboard, he checked off each species before allowing them to board. "Wombat, wombat, ah, here we are, wombat. Third stall, middle deck."

The animals unpacked and settled into their quarters. The rooms were tiny. It wasn't long before the hen sought out the cruise director, Noah's wife, and complained about the bathroom facilities.

"A hole in the floor. I don't think so," the hen loudly clucked as she pecked poor Noah's wife's ankle.

"Straw on the floor for a bed? You gotta be kidding me," a dingo joined in.

"Hey, you got some kinda watering facilities here, a pool, maybe a pond or something?" a rhino asked.

Some animals playfully ran around the decks, excited for the voyage to begin. The less active ones just curled up in a corner to rest up for party time. Others just passed the time grooming, licking themselves and chasing their tails.

As the ark sat on dry land, for what seemed like days (which it was) some animals became restless as they looked out their port windows, muttering, "Now what?" A whiny aardvark became disgruntled and demanded his money back. Noah reminded him that it was a free cruise, which helped calm him but threw a wrench into his plan to finagle some drink coupons. The mischievous chimps and hyenas, wreaked havoc with the other passengers by dropping banana peels on deck and laughing when someone slipped and fell. But, most of them, killed time, casually touring the ship and admiring Noah's meticulous craftsmanship.

Finally, it started to drizzle then shower then pour. Many of the animals foolishly hoped their nests and dens would remain dry while they were gone but figured a little dampness wouldn't hurt. At some point, the boat began to waver then rise and soon was afloat. The animals scurried to the decks and started waving and yelling "Bon Voyage" to the family members and friends that had patiently waited around to send them off. (Unfortunately, this unlucky bunch would never hear any wild cruise stories.) Noah stood on the upper deck and called down to the herd of travelers. "Welcome aboard 'Judgment Cruise lines.' We should be underway in approximately four or five days."

The animals that were lower on the food chain, designated as waiters and cocktail waitresses, were in charge of passing out cheese, vegetables and beverages. Noah's three sons Ham, Japheth, and Shem, oversaw the operation, making sure the bar was always fully stocked, and the service adequate. Entertainment was essential to keep the creatures occupied from attacking each other. Ling Loo, the dancing Panda bear, was scheduled for three nightly shows. Two seals, Whiskers and Slippy, performed twice a week doing a long, drawn-out paddy-cake routine that went nowhere. Tusca, a walrus that sang songs from the musical "Joseph and the Amazing Technicolor Dreamcoat" lulled audiences with his versatile vibrato. The Great Vegemite, a kangaroo magician, dazzled the crowd with stunning card tricks and illusions like pulling a rabbit out of his pouch. And, a thirty-year veteran, Hymie the hippo, who just finished a tour in the Serengeti, did a ventriloquist act with a puffin on his lap.

Passengers were continually complaining about the weather. During the day, Noah's wife, set up various activities to keep the livestock occupied and the monkeys off her back. Pin the tail on the donkey was oodles of fun until the ass got tired of being poked in the ass and kicked an orangutan. The younger creatures enjoyed shuffleboard using old cow paddies as discs. The older ones stuck with bingo and bridge, while a pseudo karaoke was big with the birds. (The hummingbirds would hum a melody while the parrots hammed it up by singing songs like "Hava Nagila," even when the birds were humming a different tune.)." The animals with a sense of rhythm took dancing lessons from "Hoofs" a well-known gazelle with the gift of glide. Noah fondly smiled when he saw a water buffalo waltzing with a wildebeest. They were far from light on their feet, but they knew how to rock the boat.

Several nightclubs catered to the nocturnal crowd. Raccoons and owls never missed the last call, and the possums were always the last ones on the dance floor. The cougars stayed late too, still keeping their eyes open for some young, fresh meat. These late-nighters usually slept through breakfast only to eventually rise with a pounding headache and, at times, in a puddle of booze-infested vomit. Many of them had no idea what they had done the night before. The penguins were also known for their all-night binges and dice games. One early morning, Noah found them next to a couple of cheap raccoons, passed out in the garbage. Their black and white feathers wrinkled and looking like they wore a tattered tuxedo. He scolded the bird lushes calling them "bums, riff-raff" and "two-bit critters." "Why can't you be like horses and hit the hay early? Don't you know the early bird gets the worm?" The penguins would mumble something like "we like fish" through their pounding headaches.

There was plenty of food on the Ark, except Noah had a golden rule "No eating each other." The carnivores huffed and rolled their eyes but obeyed for fear of being tossed overboard. The buffets were popular, as long as the rhinos and elephants weren't in line. The pigs made pigs of themselves. The turkeys gobbled down everything they could. And, the moose loved the mousse. One night was a vegetarian Luau with platters of carrot sticks, broccoli heads, melon balls, and wedges of goat cheese. Everything served on the vessel was of plant origin. Sure, this upset members of the cat family who were hopeful that pigs-in-the-blanket might appear or, at least, some veal. (They were always hungry—so hungry they could eat a horse or anything in that family.) But Noah was a fair man and politically correct. Any meat was off-limits. Besides, many of the wildlife had now become pals. They didn't want to jeopardize their new friendship by munching on someone's spouse.

The animals, figuring on a weekend vacation, had no idea that they had booked a forty-day cruise. After two weeks boredom set in and the creatures became anxious to feel land beneath their paws. One night, after the evening meal, Noah gathered the animals together. He paced the floor in deep thought as a herd of beady eyes followed him.

"I went to the pantry to get some strawberries and noticed six were missing.

"Now I know I only ate three. My wife had four and Japheth and Shem each had two while Ham had three," the patriarch suspiciously said. "There's only a quarter of the strawberries left in the barrel. I wanna know how that happened."

"I only had one," a mongoose spoke up.

"I had five," said a beaver, "but I traded the anteater two berries for six ants."

"I had two… but you said I could have two. You said it," an armadillo blurted out.

"Yes, I did. Now, what about everyone else?" Noah said interrogatingly, resulting in an irritated groan from the animals.

On a mission, Noah went around the room, getting a strawberry count from each of the mammals. Whatever number they said they had eaten the old man dropped that many into a wooden drum. His aimed to see if it all added up to a quarter of a barrel. The night wore on and, after several counts, he finally released the animals back to their pens. He was still unsettled and fully believed six strawberries were missing.

Scuttlebutt began to circulate throughout the ship that the captain was going crazy. That, maybe, Noah had no idea what he was doing or where he was even going. For all they knew, the vessel could wander the seas for years until all supplies consumed, and they would starve to death. Realizing this dire possibility, an errant honey-badger concluded he was not going down with the ship. In a stall towards the back of ark, he stood on a wooden bucket looking over a group of animals consisting of a weasel, lemur, chipmunk, wombat, hedgehog, otter, muskrat, gopher, and a koala bear, to name a few of the mischievous mammals.

"We're doomed, see," the slick badger spoke then continued. "This old man… he has no clue where we are or where we're going. He's gonna take us all down, see."

"How do you know?" the lemur questioned.

"I just know. I got animal instincts, see," the badger insisted. "Somethin' gotta be done."

"Are you saying "mutiny?" the chipmunk said as his eyes widened. The surrounding animals gasped in unison.

"I ain't whistling Psalms here," snapped the sneaky badger. "The old man's got to go… see."

The pounding rain pelted the roof of the ark. Although it was relentless, there was a certain peace contained within the drops. A candle shone in Noah's sleeping quarters as the old man knelt in a circle with his family. They praised the Creator for keeping them safe, for the food they had to eat but, most of all, they thanked God for stopping the manatees from snoring.

After the family had laid down for the night, Noah proceeded to do his nightly rounds to ensure that all the animals were still on the ark and nestled into their stalls. The last thing he needed was some sly fox slipping into the hen area for a midnight snack or a horny Tasmanian devil making whoopee with a beaver. It would be catastrophic. The offspring would build a dam then tear it down. Noah did not want to be held responsible for adding another species in the world, not without God's approval. He'd seen the big guy's wrath firsthand.

Up on deck two, Noah turned the corner to peek in on the rabbits to make sure they were sleeping in separate pens. He did not trust those cotton-tailed multipliers. Suddenly, from out of the shadows, the clan of treasonous critters bushwhacked the old man. Some dropped from the ceiling while others darted out of the woodwork. Before he knew it, Noah had an otter on his head, a chipmunk in his beard, a lemur on his shoulder and a gopher gnawing on his ear. And, if that wasn't enough, he had a koala and wombat nibbling on his toes, a hedgehog lodged in his robe and a weasel biting his tuchus.

The skirmish was full of screeching and howling as Noah did his best to fend off the attackers. There was a lot of scratching, clawing, and biting, but that was how Noah had to defend himself. The scrappy old man was peeling off varmints left and right, then heaving them out of harm's way. A curious mule peeked his head up over the stall to see what the ruckus is all about and was walloped in the side of the face by a flying, squealing muskrat. Noah fought like a wild animal himself, circling and ripping animals off his back. He flipped a baboon, wrestled a spider monkey, drop-kicked a wolverine, and stopped a charging ram dead in its tracks by chucking a porcupine and hitting the beast squarely in the chest.

The elderly patriarch, breathing heavy, crouched down circling with his dukes held high. He waved on an indecisive chimp, "Come on, monkey boy, you wanna piece of old Noah?" Like a nimble deer, the crazed prophet jumped on the back of an armadillo and pounded his chest. "You wanna dance with the prophet? I'll take the whole lot of ya!"

He let loose a loud, whooping battle cry as if he welcomed a good fight. By now, other animals had awoken to the melee. The badger jumped up on the back of an elk to rally larger mammals, hoping to enlist their help to bring down the feisty ark captain. "Rise, my friends! We must save ourselves, see! This ark is aimlessly wandering the seas, see! Our destiny shall not be death! We must seize the day, see, seize, see, seize!"

The speech seemed to spook the other animals who had, up until now, been oblivious bystanders. Soon Noah found himself surrounded by some larger prey. Circling his fists in front of him, he began to make odd noises like barking, growling and yipping hoping to scare the monsters off but only added to their suspicions that this guy is a loon. Noah knew he could go toe-to-toe with a gopher or weasel, but he was staring at lions and tigers and bears. "Oh my, this does not look," he murmured to himself. Thinking quickly, the prophet stooped down and began flapping his arms like wings and quaking like a duck. Noah's plan was to distract them, but the critters just watched in utter disbelief, unsure of what to make of the old buffoon. Noah soon realized that beyond his dog-and-pony duck display, he had nothing. As a matter of fact, he wondered why he even did it in the first place having nothing to follow it with. He vowed if it ever happened again, he'd make sure he had an exit plan but, for now, he was just concerned about saving face. Composing himself, he threw out a few light chuckles as if to appear that he was just clowning around. He nodded and smiled implying "ya got me." With no choice but surrender, Noah dropped to his knees and looked up to the heavens, "My Lord, my fate rests in your hands."

Noah was allowed to bid his wife and sons goodbye; after all, the animals didn't hate the old man; they just didn't like the idea of sitting on the bottom of the ocean. The rebellious clan brought Noah out on the deck. Through the torrential downpour, the honey badger spoke, "Ya shouldn't have plucked us from our homes, Noah, see. We were happy on land, see."

"I saved your lives, you ungrateful monsters," Noah sneered. "You'll certainly perish without me."

"That's crazy talk, see. We don't need nuttin' or nobodies, see. Nuttin' or nobodies!" the badger huffed, "And that's why you gotta go." There was a short pause. Noah stared down the badger then impatiently waved his hand, signaling for the mammal to finish his sentence.

"See," the badger complied. Noah released a defeated sigh. "So, you want me to throw myself into the ocean?" The animals bowed their heads in shame, refusing to look at the old man.

"It's the only way… see," the badger softly spoke.

Noah bravely lifted his head, then pulled his shoulders back. "So be it. What must be, must be. I do not fear raging waters, the darkness, nor death. I will face it with the courage of, not a cougar or ape, but that of a prophet of God. For my God is a good God, and he will see me through." Noah's pluck impressed the animals, giving many second thoughts over the mutiny. The brave old man turned towards the tumultuous sea, prepared to meet his fate. "I just wanna say…" Noah sighed, then perked up and pointed to the sky. "My goodness, is that the Big Dipper?" The animals turned and looked up at the night sky and, Noah, like a bolt of lightning, darted towards the back of the ark.

"Get him, see!" the badger screamed.

Feeling duped, the herd of animals galloped after the old man, stumbling over each other, muttering and grumbling curse words. Noah dashed through the wet, dark air, racing around the boat. With his life hanging on the edge, the old man dug down deep and ran like a wildebeest chased by a lioness looking for lunch. The creatures were hot on his tail, bellowing a whooping war cry. The feeble prophet, hauling ass, did his best to juke and zigzag in hopes of shaking the charging beasts. Although he was 436 years old, he moved like he was 324. After circling the ark sixteen times, Noah was running out of gas, as was evident by his wheezing, which he could blame on months of breathing in sawdust. Just as a jaguar was about to leap on his back, Noah spun around. "Stop!" he yelled, holding up his arms. The stampeding bunch froze in their tracks.

"Is this what it has come too?" Noah said, while doing his best to catch his breath. "I bring you all on a nice cruise with your lovely spouses, and this is how you repay me?'

"This cruise sucks," a camel commented.

"Yeah, the food is stale," a prairie dog spoke up.

"The entertainment's crap," a woodchuck butted in. "That Hoofs has got two left feet."

"And that walrus couldn't sing his way out of a clay grain vessel," added an ostrich.

"Also, if I may say so, the boat smells like a doo-doo hole," a skunk chimed in.

"You're one to talk. You're all ungrateful monsters," Noah seethed. "The Lord has made a grave mistake allowing you all to live and repopulate the earth. You will bring much selfishness, sadness, and sin into the world and that is a place I wish not to live." The badger stuck out his snout, "Well, we don't want you either, see."

"See! See! See!" Noah roared. "I see animals starving and dying and wishing they had their captain back."

"Not me, pops," snickered the badger. "Toss the geezer over."

All the animals in unison said "see" to finish the badger's sentence. The furry creatures reluctantly moved in. Noah threw his hands up and snarled, "don't you touch me, or I'll bite you." Then, he composed himself and straightened his robe. "I will gladly depart from the lot of you, and you can fend for yourselves." Noah moved to the edge and looked down at the raging ocean below. He slowly turned back to the rebellious wildlife. Surrendering, he lowered his head then quickly looked up and pointed to the sky. "Oh my God, is that The Little Dipper?"

And, just like animals, they turned and looked. Noah, fired off, like a meteor hurtling to the earth. The bolting prophet was on the move again.

"Get him, see!" the badger yelled.

Another chase ensued. Noah, resembling a spry reindeer, hoofed it, double-time, around the edge of the ark. The herd breathing down his neck, furious that they were hoodwinked a second time. Still tired from the previous chase, the 436 year-old-man felt like he was 642. He peeked over his shoulder to see the mammal mob bearing down on him. His trick knee began acting up, putting him into a limping jog. It opened the door for the sprinting leopard, who was inches from pouncing on him. Noah quickly spun around and held up his hands. "Okay, okay, ya got me. Ya happy now? Ya happy?"

The animals looked at each other and, after a moment of indecisiveness, nodded.

"Yeah, we are happy, see" the badger spoke up. "We're not falling for no more shenanigans, see. Tricks, see."

"What have I done to you to warrant my death?"

"You're an omen, see - a bad omen. You snookered us on this cruise, see. And you're taking us down, see; we're not going down, see. That's for suckers, see. And we're not suckers, see."

"Why did you look up at the sky when I said, 'Is that The Little Dipper?'"

"We thought we saw something else in the sky, see. Maybe like an owl, see. And we like running around, see. It's good exercise for us, see. Now can the chit-chat, pops. You gotta go, see. And that's that, see. Now, are you jumping, or are we throwing you in?'

"You're animals! Filthy stinking animals!" Noah shouted.

The animals nodded at each other in agreement while a silver-back ape sniffed under his armpit and murmured, "I don't smell."

"The Lord will not tolerate your insubordination. If me, His humble servant is harmed, He will surely bring down His wrath upon you."

"Can't get any worse than all this rain," the weasel sniped.

"It is not too late to turn from your sinful, wicked ways. For my Lord is good. The Lord will forgive. Forgive you for this mutiny, the strawberries, everything. But, if you want me to go, then I shall meet my demise with no anger in my heart. But, please, if you will be kind enough to afford me the courtesy, I would like to say one last thing…" Noah quickly pointed to his left and cried, "Is that Orion's Belt!"

None of the animals flinched or batted an eye. Sucker time was over. They just stared at the old coot.

"Maybe not. My mistake. Probably just a… a gaggle of geese," Noah shrugged then nervously cleared his throat. "I have a wonderful story I would like to share that I believe you will get a kick out of if you might oblige me. Once upon a time…"

"Yeah, yeah, yeah, see" the badger ran up and bit the rambling man's ankle causing him to yelp then slip off the ark. As he fell from the upper deck, the treasonous animals could hear Noah's voice slowly taper off as he yelled, "You rotten bastards!"

For two long days, the animals partied it up like the world was ending. They were singing, dancing and playfully chasing each other throughout the ark. They broke into the storeroom and, like a pack of hogs, chowed down all the food. Once again, the pigs made pigs of themselves. The sheep ate so much that they felt baaaahd. And, the cow so stuffed it could barely moooove. With bloated bellies, the glutenous creatures fell asleep as rain pounded down on the holy vessel.

The next morning the animals arose with hunger in their tummies. One by one they made their way to the food storage facility. Mouths went agape, beaks dropped, and snouts fell open as they realized not one grain of seed was left. The mammals flew into a panic. They raced around the ark searching for a second storage room. Surely the old man had back up provisions. Noah was meticulous and had planned each meal to a tee. There were precisely 120 portions for each critter and in two days they managed to wolf down every single morsel. It was close to an eight-course meal, give or take a few courses.

After an anxiety-ridden search, the animals amassed in the lower deck. The honey badger circled, thinking to himself. "We need to keep our heads together, see. It's all gonna work out, see."

"What are we gonna eat?" Hymie, the ventriloquist hippo asked.

"Yeah, I'm hungry... even though I eat like a bird," the puffin dummy appeared to chime in, but everyone could see Hymie's lips move.

"We should be reaching land any day now, see. Once we do, everything will be alright, see," the badger continued. "Ya hear me? Alright, see."

"What if we don't?" a skeptical capybara commented. Incensed, the livid badger ran over to him and grabbed his fur collar. "There'll be land, see. Any day now, see."

"Okay, okay," the capybara recoiled. "There's no need to badger me, see."

Furious, the heated badger got in his face and barked, "I'm the boss here, see. Only I use the 'sees', see."

"We're gonna starve to death!" a warthog cried out.

"Ahh shut up," a fluffy buff lion said as he swatted the cowering creature with his giant paw. "We ain't gonna starve to death so get dat outta your heads."

"Yeah, you heard the big cat," concurred the badger. "Nobody's gonna starve, see."

A giant tortoise slowly cleared his throat then gradually meandered across the floor as the animals watched. Thirty minutes later, it was halfway to its destination, which was the lion. The animals grew restless, releasing frustrated sighs until the sluggish turtle finally reached the king of the jungle. The shelled reptile cleared his throat again, which took another five grueling minutes, causing some animals to let out an annoyed grunt and sit down. He finally spoke. "Why won't we starve?"

"A wonderful question, my little hamster friend," the lion said with a smirk.

"Hey, you," the tortoise lethargically spoke up. "I'm not a hamster… why I'm a…

"Shut up, I know what you are," the lion interrupted. "I was cracking wise. Now, on this ark, there are many, many, many small animals. Where I'm from, we call them… snacks." Several of the animals let out a nervous laugh, suspiciously looking at each other in bewilderment.

"There is no need for most animals here to worry their itty-bitty heads about starving to death," the lion continued. "They will not be alive to feel the pangs of hunger." The smaller creatures quivered.

"Hey, hey, let's not talk crazy here, kitty cat, see," the badger jumped in. "We're all in this together, see. We're friends, see. Friends don't eat each other."

"Oh, no?" responded the lion. "I'm feeling a bit famished now, and there's nothing I enjoy more than a little honey on my badger."

"Sure, I get it. Honey… badger. Honey on the badger. Honey badger," the skittish varmint stammered as he slowly backed up with the smaller animals following in his steps. The bigger carnivores like the bears, jaguars, cougars, gorillas, wolves, and panthers, to name a few, shuffled over to the lion's side. And, like two rival gangs, they faced each other.

Outside the ark, water spilled out of darkened clouds like a breached dam as powerful waves battered the hull. Suddenly, there was a flash of lightning and a loud thunderclap. The sea opened up and out leaped a large fish, soaring high in the damp air and landing on the ark's upper deck.

The larger, bully-like animals marched towards the cornered little ones who trembled in fear, sensing their end was near. Soon there would be no small animals left on earth to repopulate their species; then the larger creatures would turn on each other and, eventually, only one left with a full, satisfied, and bloated belly. God's grand plan lay in jeopardy.

"You don't wanna do this, see. Maybe we can talk, see," the badger stuttered as he stepped back and moved a skunk in front of him to use as a shield… a stinky shield. As the chop-licking, meat-eaters were just about to pounce and enjoy a feast, a voice rang out from the upper deck, reverberating off of the cedar walls. "Stop the madness, you animals!" The creatures looked up and were shocked and amazed to find Noah standing there. "The Lord has brought me back to you, and you're in some big trouble… with a capital T."

Noah spent the next few days scolding the animals for their insubordination. For punishment, they were all given chores of cleaning out the stalls, KP duty, brushing each other, and swabbing the decks. The days of a nice, relaxing cruise were over. They had abused their privileges and were now paying the price. Every morning the Lord provided their daily meal with schools of fish that leaped from the ocean and landed in piles on the deck. (Ironically, the giant fish that Noah spent three days in, would have a great, great grandson that would do the same thing to a man named Jonah.) Over time, the animals behaved well and completed their chores, so the Lord blessed them with a heaping of tuna, salmon, lobster, clams, oyster, and squid. It was a holy buffet much appreciated.

"Yummy, this is good food, see," the badger beamed.

"Don't you mean "sea" food," quipped a hedgehog, sending all the animals in a laughing tizzy as they rolled on the floor for several long minutes. Noah nodded with a half, fake smile. Either he didn't think it was that funny or, he didn't get it.

At night, Noah would tell the creatures biblical stories, teach them about the Lord's commandments and the importance of repopulating the earth. Then they would all sit in a circle and play "duck, duck, goose." Coincidentally, the duck and goose always won.

Being cooped up for so long on the ark began to weigh on the animals, and they were anxious to get off the boat. By now, they were on each other's nerves. Several species were mysteriously missing. Among them were the Snozeatles, known for their annoying, high-pitched cackle. Also, the Finglecats who had an uncontrollable, swinging long tail that, all too often, would whack an unsuspecting head. And, the Bushwads, who exhibited a loud, grumbling snorting snore when sleeping. No sign of these annoying creatures was ever heard from again. Noah asked one of the lions, who slept in the stall adjacent to the Bushwads, if he had any ideas of what might have happened to them. "Yeah, I don't know, ya know. One minute I saw them and, you know, then they were somewhere else."

"That's very odd. I wonder where those animals could be," Noah pondered.

"Yeah, well, they were known for sleepwalking. Maybe they accidentally fell in the water," reasoned the big cat. "Hey, things happen."

"I guess it's possible," Noah surmised.

"Sure it is,' the lion assured Noah as he put his paw around the old man's neck like they were best of friends. "Anything's possible in this day and age. You know them crazy Bushwads. They're here. They're there. They're somewhere."

"I'm gonna go check on the Snozeatles," Noah stated.

"Yeah, I'm pretty sure they do the sleepwalking thing too," the lying lion shrugged. The Snozeatles, Finglecats, and Bushwads became extinct before ever disembarking the ark and were never heard of in history again.

One day Noah sent a raven out several times to search the area for land. But, every time Noah asked it if he saw anything, the bird would reply, "Nevermore." The prophet, tired of the nonsensical answer, sent out a dove. The snow-white bird returned and said to Noah, "Ain't no land nowhere, no how." Noah breathed an exhausted sighed and replied, "You cannot be serious."

"It is what it is," the dove responded.

The next day Noah sent him out again. This time he returned with an olive branch. Disappointed, Noah put the sprig in some boiled water. While drinking his tea, it finally dawned on him the tiny branch meant land was nearby.

Noah stood on a bale of hay and addressed the animals. "Soon, we will be reaching land."

"When?" asked a chinchilla.

"Pretty soon," Noah replied.

"Like, how long?" questioned the zebra.

"Pretty, pretty, pretty soon," the old man responded with a slow nod.

"Days. Weeks. Hours. What are we looking at?" inquired a donkey.

"What's the difference?" Noah snapped in an angry, irate tone. "We'll get there when we get there."

"Get where?" a jackal probed. Pissed, Noah got up in his face. "There. When we get 'there,' got it? 'There' is where 'there' is. Now let's enjoy the rest of the God damn cruise."

Six days later, Noah stood on the ark's upper deck in the relentless rain looking down at the ocean. Surrounding him were a bunch of angry animals weary of being at sea.

"It's that time again, see," the badger said then continued. "We're hungry, see. You're taking us all down, see. We can't have that, see. So, you need to go, see?"

"I understand," Noah solemnly nodded. "You must do what you must do. But before you follow through with your farewell plans for me, I would like to ask one question." He quickly pointed to the sky, "Is that

Sagittarius?" The animals all looked up in the sky, and Noah was off to the races.

"Get him, see!" the badger screamed.

Noah zipped around the deck like his ass was on fire with the huffing, slobbering animals in hot pursuit. At some point during the zany chase, his stubby aged legs began to tire, and a cheetah pounced on the running man's back. Noah, having already spent three hellish days in the belly of a fish, was determined not to go back into that pit of reeking bile and dead squid. The cheetah, clinging to his back, felt like dead weight but the feisty guy had a gut-check and plodded on, knowing he was running for his life. The big cat slowed the old fellow down enough to allow a jaguar to jump on the cheetah's back. Noah released an ailing grunt then gritted his teeth as he lumbered on with a fire in his belly. Now moving at a protracted pace, it allowed a panther to leap on the jaguar than a mountain lion to dive on the panther than a cougar to hop on the mountain lion followed by a snow leopard than a puma, a lynx and a bobcat, who sunk his claws into the lynx. The last one to climb aboard was a skittish meerkat who hung on for the ride. The tenacious prophet lifted his head and howled at the darkening sky, hoping for a burst of God-given strength. The stubborn old fool dug deep refusing to go down and did his best to keeping chugging. By now, he believed he had the world on his shoulders, and he wasn't far off in this belief. His speed had immensely decreased, allowing a few of the slower animals like a sea lion, orangutan and kookaburra to climb aboard and get their piece of the pie. Noah did his best to keep his legs churning, but it was nearly impossible with over twenty-three species of animals on his back, all screeching and scratching, doing their best to drag the wrinkled meat down. He began to putter to a slow crawl, his knees practically scraping the deck from the huge herd he was carrying. The breaking point occurred when a vaulting wallaby decided to hop on the kookaburra. The great patriarch reared his head up and bellowed, "Damn these beasts!" He summoned one last excruciating grunt before his body gave out. He resembled a wailing caribou being brought down by a team of ferocious hungry cats on the Serengeti plain. Noah collapsed in a heap with a slew of animals resting on top of him. Some of the smaller animals who were lagging, like the mink, lemming, and water shrew caught up to the stack and piled on, acting as if they were instrumental in bringing the old man down. On top of the animals, a mole jumped up and down screaming, "We got him! The day is ours! Others climbed on and began chanting 'dog pile on the prophet. Dog pile on the prophet' as they leaped up-and-down with a conquering joy."

The rebellious creatures wanted to hog-tie the elusive pesky prophet, but none of them knew how to tie a knot, not even the hog, instead, they hoisted him on their shoulders and carried him to the upper deck. The whole way up, Noah was kicking and screaming, "Wait! I just thought of something! I have a grand idea! You need to hear this - I'm serious! Listen to me! This is the best idea ever! Ever!" The animals just ignored the raving lunatic, after vowing never to fall for his tricks again.

Noah stood on the edge of the ark too tired to even speak. He had put up a noble fight, but his back didn't allow for hauling cats long distances.

"I don't know about you, see," the badger started, "but I'm getting one of those déjà vu feelings, see. And if you think we're looking up at the sky again, see, you're crazy. Bonkers. Loopy. Cause it's not happening, see. We're on to you, see."

"I don't have the strength. You want me to jump; I'll jump."

"You don't jump 'til we tell you to jump, see. You don't run this place anymore. You're not the captain, see. We're the captains, see. This is our ship now, see."

"So, you don't want me to jump?" Noah asked.

"Hey, don't think you can crack wise, see. We don't play games, see," snapped the badger.

"I remember when we all had fun playing duck, duck, goose."

"That was then, and this is now," the badger barked. "Times have changed, see. It's a different world now."

Noah was silent for a few seconds. "Aren't you going to say, "see?""

"Alright, you rubbed me wrong, pops. It's time for you to jump, see. Yeah, that time again, see. You pushed me too far, see."

Noah sighed, accepting his fate. He looked at the sky and called up, "My Lord, do with me as you will." There was a long, long silence.

"We're not looking up, see" insisted the badger. Noah looked back down at the badger. "Oh, damn you to hell. I thought I had one more in me."

Suddenly, the rain stopped falling. The dark skies lit up as the sun burst through the clouds. Abruptly, there was a loud screeching thump, jolting the wooden ship to complete stop.

"Haha, we have arrived, my friends!" Noah shouted. "Do you son-of-a-bitches believe me now?"

Two by two, the tired, grumpy and tattered animals sluggishly staggered off the ark, grumbling, and growling as they made their way past Noah.

"Hope you enjoyed your time with us," Noah half-embarrassed uttered.

"That's the last time we take that cruise line," clucked a hen.

"Weekend cruise, my ass," a buffalo sniped.

"There's forty days of my life I'll never get back," sneered a wild boar. Every animal had a beef, a snide remark, or wisecrack as they passed by the old biblical prophet who now felt like he was 872 years old.

"See this face. Take a good long look because you'll never see it again," a black rhino barked.

"Good. I never liked that face anyway. None of your faces, God dammit!" Noah shouted to the animals heading off into the wilderness. "Hell, go multiply and stay out of my life! Better yet, don't multiply! The world doesn't need more ungrateful creatures the likes of you!"

While Noah's wife and sons cleaned up the ark, the weary man sat on a rock, burying his head in his hands. It had been a long journey and he could use a nap.

"Ya done good old man, see." Noah looked up to find Mr. Badger in front of him.

"That a... whole... mutiny thing... I hope you don't take it personally, see," the ornery varmint ashamedly stammered.

"I guess you did what you had to do," Noah sighed.

"Sure, I did see. You get it. Sometimes ya gotta sacrifice one to save the many, see," the badger stipulated. "I had to make sure the animals would be around, see. What good is a world without animals? Besides, they're my friends, see except for that lion who ate the Snozeatles, Finglecats, and Bushwads."

"I had a hunch," Noah replied.

"You had a hunch, and he had lunch. There's always gonna be a few bad apples, see. A few bad apples," the badger commented. The little rascal then pointed towards the sky, "Now ain't that a beautiful sight. That cloud, see. It looks like an angel, see."

Noah turned and looked in the sky. He smiled to himself, knowing when he turned back, the badger would be gone, and he was.

"Yes, I see," the old prophet whispered under his breath. On the rock next to him were six strawberries. He smiled and ate one.

"Noah, it's me, you're ole pal God. How'd everything go? Did I miss anything?"

"Where the hell were you?" Noah questioned.

"I'm so sorry. Whenever it rains, I get so sleepy. How long was I out for?" God yawned.

"A good forty days!" Noah roared.

"No. Really? Did I miss anything?"

"Damn straight, you did. Quite a bit," Noah fumed, not wanting to get into it. "Next time you need a favor, leave me out of it. Go ask the honey badger."

"I love them little things. Sooo cute," God replied in an adoring tone.

"Alright, we all through here?" Noah said with a heavy exhale and roll of the eyes.

"Ya done good, Noah. I'm very proud of you," God commended. "You know I was thinking, I may have another job for you down the line."

"Excuse me," Noah replied, taken aback.

"Yeah, at some point I'm going to need somebody to lead a group of people out of Egypt. Sound like something that might interest you?"

"No. No way. I won't do it," Noah firmly stated. "I had enough trouble with animals and now you want me to deal with people? No. Oh hell no!"

"Okay, okay, I was just asking. Thought you might need the money. I can always get someone... I think. It's not easy finding good people," God commented then asked. "You gonna eat those strawberries?"

Noah snatched the fruit and holding them close to his body sneered, "Nobody touches my strawberries. Nobody, see."

"Wow. Touchy. See if I give you another all expensed paid cruise again."

THE GREEK GEEK

The year was 492 B.C., and Zotikus had just arrived in Athens to study philosophy under an astute philosopher named Euripides (so called because he used to work as a ticket-handler at plays and when theatergoers would hand him their tickets they would say, "You rip a these."). While Plato and Aristotle had stressed the mind and the body, individuality, and happiness, Euripides was less conventional. He found overthinking about anything was time-consuming and stressful. Socrates felt it important to lead a questioning life; Euripides, on the other hand, felt that the less one knew, the more with which one could get away. He surmised that claiming ignorance was noble. When an inquisitive student asked Euripides if man was meant to suffer, the lame philosopher paused for a few seconds, slowly nodded his head and replied "maybe." He felt by being non-committal he had less of a chance of being wrong. Students became disillusioned with the teacher. One even asked for his money back. After refusing to return the student's funds, the irate prodigy snippily asked the charlatan if he had ever read any accounts on ethics by Socrates. He slowly nodded then replied, "And Socrates is?"

As Zotikus grew older he developed a love for the arts. One night, the young man went to a musical written by Homer and Hammerstein, about an illustrious affair between Zeus and a peasant flower girl. It was called "Gods and Dolls." The plotline revolved around Zeus teaching an earthly simpleton to portray herself as a societal goddess. Throughout the second act, he would attempt to teach her proper Latin but…, it was all Greek to her. The show-stopping number was called "I've Grown Accustomed to your Pomegranates."

While at the play he met a beautiful actress named Kaliope who played a Cypress tree and was enamored by the way she gracefully moved her branches. The talented artist was the king's daughter and had landed the part as a result of Nepotism—the God of the Casting Couch. The couple fell head over sandals for each other, and it wasn't long before they began discussing the M-word, which was money. He wanted to know how much was in the dowry if they were to get married.

Before King Vasilis would allow this Greek geek to marry his daughter, he wanted to ensure that the fellow was worthy. So, he assigned Zotikus a simple task of going to the island of Crete and picking up a bottle of perfume for the king to give to his wife, Queen Gagaga. Their anniversary was just around the corner. Lately, she had been on a new fad of dabbing sheep urine behind her ears, a rage that had recently made its way out of the Persian Empire. (The cowardly ruler lacked the guts to tell her she smelt bhaaaaaad.) Besides, last year he had forgotten the date, so his wife punished him by sleeping with Hermione, the bath boy, and then Cymone, the garden boy and completed a tawdry trifecta with Thekla, the soldier boy. The king apologized for his forgetfulness. She forgave him by sleeping with Agathe, the sissy boy. You might say she liked the boys.

"Can't you get anyone else?" Zotikus pleaded. "I'm playing the lead in a new play called "The Odyssey", and it opens next week."

"You'll be back by then," the king shrugged.

"I hope so. It's a once-in-a-lifetime role," Zotikus responded.

"So is marrying my daughter," the king sternly replied.

"Let's hope so, she had me sign a prenup," he retorted.

The king had some severe reservations about his daughter marrying an actor. "They don't make any money," he stated. "Plus, they're always seeking attention saying 'Look what I can do.'" Deep down, he was hoping the wannabe thespian would get lost at sea or, better yet, perish.

That night, Zotikus met up with Kaliope to say his good-byes before departing on his journey the next day. She was worried. The previous night she had a dream that he had fallen asleep in some far away land and was being nibbled on by a hefty slobbering sea monster. Zotikus chuckled as he patted her head.

"Please don't laugh at me," Kaliope shyly whispered.

"I'm not. I was thinking how much that would tickle," Zotikus speculated.

Knowing it would be a while before he saw her again, he became amorous and began pretending he was a hefty slobbering sea monster and playfully licking her. At first, she giggled. He continued lapping. An hour later, her laughter began to taper off as she threw out a few "Okays" and "that's enough." Believing "no" actually means "yes" he kept the tongue action going to amuse her. Her "Please stop" became louder. The idiot seemed oblivious as he continued the licking frenzy. Drenched in sticky salvia, she had reached her limit. The spit had hit the fan. She grabbed his long hair and pulled his head back and bit his nose.

"I said knock it off, jackass!" she snapped.

He jumped back and said, "Look what I can do," as he did a clumsy dance shuffle to diffuse the peevishness of the girl.

Before the pair separated Kaliope gave Zotikus an emerald bronzed fibula. The gift was a safety pin to help keep his toga closed. She did not want him hanging out in faraway lands.

"It was my grandmothers," she smiled.

"A knife or a sword might be handier," he remarked.

"You have my love," she responded assuredly.

"Love doesn't kill Titans. You sure you don't have a bow and arrow, or at least a shield?" he suggested.

"Don't be silly," she laughed. "You're just grabbing a bottle of perfume."

"Here," he said, pulling out a small vegetable token. "Take this cherry tomato as a symbol of our commitment to one another."

"You don't have a ring or something?" she questioned in a perturbed voice.

"I don't have a sword or shield either," he retorted.

She reached out her hand and gently touched his cheek. "Will you promise…"

"To love you forever?" he interrupted.

"No. Will you promise to bring me back some olives?" she breathlessly smiled.

They stared into each other's eyes for almost an hour, gazing lovingly at each other. Suddenly Zotikus jumped up and shouted, "You blinked! I win!" He kissed her like he had practiced on an armless Venus statue, except this time he didn't use his tongue. He then patted her head and vanished into the darkness.

The young and lazy Greek's voyage would begin the next morning but before departing it was imperative that he swing by Mount Parnassus and get a quick fortune reading. Around 1000 BC, a goat herdsman in Greece came across what looked like a burning stream at the top of Mount Parnassus. It was a flame rising from a crack in the rock. Most likely, a lightning strike ignited the natural gas, but to the Greeks, it was sacred.

The ancient Greeks, believing the flame to be of divine origin, built a temple around it. This temple housed a priestess who was known as the Oracle of Delphi; the flickering flame inspired prophecies she claimed. Zotikus was curious of what fate awaited him.

In the dingy cave, he put a coin in a clay vessel, and then sat on a small boulder, waiting for the show to begin. Through the eerie smoke, the Oracle appeared. Gracefully dancing and twirling she made her way over to him seductively. Zotikus became excited and began stomping his foot while howling, "Take it off! Take it off!"

The mysterious woman slithered up to the panting man who smiled and said, "I'm feeling lap dance time." Her crazed eyes seem to pierce him like a toothpick in a meatball hor d'oeuvre. Feeling a little uneasy, he softly mumbled, "Lap dance." She reached out and gently teased his hair then, suddenly, slapped his sleazy face. Rubbing his cheek, he could only reply, "Or not."

"A perilous journey awaits you," she murmured. "You will go through many trials in many lands. You will be weak at times and strong at other times. Some days you will be dirty, and some days you will be clean. You will find love, lose love and, who knows, maybe find love again. But, and this is very important, no matter how you slice and dice it, it ain't gonna be easy."

"Good to know. One last thing. Will I make it back home alive?" he apprehensively inquired.

The Oracle's pupils grew big as her eyes penetrated him like a toothpick in a spanakopita hor d'oeuvre. "You will…"

"Yes," the eager Greek said, hanging on her words.

"You will…," the Oracle dramatically paused.

"I think you said that," sighed Zotikus.

"You will…" the bug-eyed woman continued. The anxious Greek leaned forward in anticipation then…

"I'm sorry your times up," the mystic snapped.

Zotikus leaped up, frantically checking his pockets for loose change to throw in the vessel. The Oracle slowly moved back into the thick smoke. "No! No!" he screamed as she vanished. "I take it no lap dance?!" he called out.

Zotikus had gathered a group of guys to go with him. He brought his best friend Syphilis, a well-known playboy who hated Trojans. Also, with him were a group of the artsy clan he hung with; Atropos the juggler, Funicius the comedian and Efimia the mime. Basically, they were all out of work and were looking for something different in life. Kicking a clay pot in the street was getting old, not to mention they broke way too easily. "Why not get away for the weekend?" they all agreed.

They boarded a ship called "Halkyone." Nobody knew that it was a Persian name that meant "Water Holder." The gang seemed to be lackadaisical regarding the voyage and tended to look at it as more of a booze cruise. They set sail.

That night, the boys broke out the wine and started playing drinking games. Below them was Poseidon, who was fast asleep on a seabed of sand when he woke up to a boisterous band of off-key drunks singing *Giati poli s agapisa* over and over again with belching sound effects and puking interruptions. The god of the sea was pissed. He had a lot to do the following day; a typhoon in the China Sea, throw a rolling tidal wave towards Lycia, then a series of rogue waves sent to the Italian coast in hopes of reshaping the land mass to make it look like a boot.

Angry over the loss of vital sleep, he peeked his head up over the smooth ocean surface and released a huff of hot air, sending the Halkyone in the opposite direction that it was supposed to go. The passed-out crew was unaware of the course change. The adventure would begin when the boys sobered up the next morning… and the headaches would begin.

The fellas awoke with their ship lodged on a sandbar. Two hundred yards inland lay a desolate island. They jumped in the water and, after a quick game of Marco Polo, they swam to shore. Everything was quiet at first, then from the green forest came the sound of a million meows. The crew had found Calypto, the lost island of kitties. A rumbling noise was soon heard growing louder and louder. They picked up the brown rocks on the beach to have something to throw at any would-be attackers. It was useless. The beach was a humongous litter box, and they weren't holding rocks.

Suddenly, a herd of kitties appeared from out of the jungle and were charging full speed at the bums on the beach. Zotikus, thinking quickly, pushed the juggler in front of him and jumped on the shoulder of Syphilis. Closing in, the kitties were in a full gallop. The men cowered down as they prepared for the worst. However, the rushing felines stopped dead in their tracks then, lovingly, began circling their legs, rubbing their furry cheeks on their furry legs. It was an ingenious ploy to put the Greeks at ease so they would gain trust and follow them peacefully to their hideaway.

The kitties led them into the multi-level cat condo that was about the size of the Acropolis. It had taken years to build the feline nest. Sitting on a throne and nibbling on a small sea bass were the leaders Andromeda and Desponia. He and she were an adjoined Siamese cat with two heads and one fat, fluffy gray body. Separately each would be a meek, docile animal but, together, they were both one powerful Peloponnesian pussy.

The kitties made the boys slaves. They were ordered to bathe the cats once a week. After the fellows were through licking the cats' bodies, they would cough up fur balls for several hours. The felines were ruthless. For three months the outsiders were made to catch fish, fill kitty bowls, carve scratching posts, make small decorative squeaky toys and provide round-the-clock belly rubs. The men knew that their survival depended upon escaping.

Zotikus approached the rulers one day and told him her that he and his colleagues would like to thank all the island kitties for their hospitality and wished to make them a great feast.

"What would be on the menu?" Andromeda inquired.

"The main dish would be fish gumbo stew served with sardine appetizers, a few gyros, a little baklava, and some lobster bisque…"

"I'm allergic to shellfish," Desponia interrupted.

"Then I'll make you a seaweed feta salad and some crunchy keftedes?" Zotikus suggested.

"May we also have a side of spinach phyllo dipped in a cucumber sauce?" Andromeda excitedly asked.

"I don't see why not," Zotikus slyly remarked. "After all, you are the king and queen kitty."

"That we are, you petty, worthless stinking Greek," Desponia snarled belittlingly. "Now get your no-good-for-nothing, insignificant, useless hairy ass a cooking. We feast by five."

The fluffy oppressors taunted and threw out cat calls at the slave boys as they slinked off to prepare the meal. Unbeknownst to the kitties, Zotikus had loaded the meal up with a potent catnip made from jungle plants, moldy banana peels and mushrooms. The kitty's bellies were full and extremely satisfied, as evident by the purring chorus floating in the air. But now, they were hungry for entertainment. The catnip was kicking in, and the kitties were becoming restless and playful. To settled them down, Atropos the juggler, stood before the cats tossing up coconuts and conch shells. The little animals were bored off their tails. High on their weed, they attacked the entertainer, clawing him to death and stealing his coconuts. The others stood mortified. These cats meant business.

To change gears, Zotikus launched into a clumsy Zorba the Greek-like dance. As he squatted and kicked his fuzzy legs up, the kitties rolled around, roaring with meowed laughter at the clumsy clown. They were now peaking on the catnip and primed for the planned escape.

Then, as planned, Zotikus pulled out a small pan flute he had carved out of a piece of driftwood. He began playing and the kitties became quiet, cocking their heads in amazement. He continued to play the sweet song as he marched into the jungle. The cats, mesmerized, followed behind him in a straight line.

Leading them up to the mountain, he brought them into a cave he had discovered while looking for coconut milk for a litter of kittens. The moonlight seeped through the opening as the sound echoed beautifully off the walls. The kitties, in awe, sat and listened. Zotikus stopped playing and said, "Whoever plays this flute will have the strength of Zeus and the agility of Mercury." He then threw it in the middle of the cat clan and an all-out kitty brawl ensued as they scratched and clawed each other for the musical toy. A few moments later, the cave was pitch dark. Zotikus had ducked out during the melee, and his men had rolled a boulder in front of the cave, sealing the felines in. The men doggy-paddled off the kitty island to their ship. They sailed away amidst, faint, rhythmic, high-pitched cries. Later, the island would be known as "The Land of a Hundred Purrs and a Thousand Meows." Safely on board, the adventurers settled in for a long cat nap.

The weary travelers had now been gone for over a year and needed to get supplies. They had no idea where they were or even in what ocean. There was enough food for two days but more importantly, no booze. Things were looking dismal. The next day they took a vote to see who would be eaten first when the time came. Everyone agreed that the world could go without a mime. Even the mime agreed although he didn't verbally state it. (Plus, they knew that once they started chomping on him, what's he going to say?) While they were buttering and seasoning him, Apollo took pity on the lost adventurers. He decided to guide them to the nearest port. (He had a side bet with Zeus that these clucks would somehow complete their mission.)

They awoke to find themselves in the port city of Dodona. As the fellows walked through the town, they ran into a blind Cyclops on the corner peddling some of his Spartan sweat in a bottle. Marketed as "Apoxyomenos", the slogan on the bottle read, "Just a little dab of EROS will do ya." In high demand, the concoction was meant to arouse the female, putting her in an animalistic mood in the bedroom. A tiny smear on the upper lip and the horny, young women would start howling at Selene, the moon goddess while stomping their feet in excitement. Sometimes, if the girl had a mustache, (which many did) the smell would linger for days causing her to remain quite busy… and extremely happy.

"Sweat here! Get your pure Spartan sweat here!" the Cyclops called out from the downtown square. Intrigued, the boys decided to try some.

"What does this stuff do?" Zotikus asked.

"Makes a woman love you," said the one-eyed man. "Love you like sheep on a cold night."

"Great. You get a free strigil with that?" Funicious inquired.

The blind man laughed, then paused, then laughed again. The guys just looked at each other then decided to join in with the laughter because there wasn't much else to do.

"How would you little pigs like to try some?" the Cyclops asked.

"Why not?" Syphilis snickered.

"I'm sure it can't hurt," Zotikus chimed in.

The mysterious perfume peddler smiled then splashed some on the crew. The scent grew heavy in the air. Zotikus and his colleagues became dizzy, and their heads began to spin. They started to fade in and out of consciousness. Images flashed before them. Zotikus saw himself pushing a boulder up a hill, rolling it down then pushing it back up again. Atropos was in a cave with three men staring at shadows on the wall, claiming this was the real reality. Syphilis was in a darkened temple making love to a woman. At some point, she held up a candle and he released a high-pitch shriek when he saw his mother face. (He would later develop an Oedipus Complex.) Efimia had a vision that he was in a stadium full of virgins cheering as he threw javelins at watermelons.

The strange hallucinations eventually subsided, and when the gang came out of their funk, they noticed their bodies had changed; all of them transformed into goat-like centurions. The guys were stunned as they examined themselves from head to hoof. Zotikus trotted in a circle, getting a feel for his new body. He looked at his gang and said, "Is this nuts or what? My fiancée is gonna be a little upset."

The one-eyed blind man had disappeared. The new centurions sat in a bar drinking sambuca contemplating what they were going to do next.

"This is not good," Funicious said.

"I think I got fleas," Syphilis snarled as he gnawed his back.

"We are not returning to Athens looking like half-ass goats. My beautiful little pita bread will kill me," Zotikus whined.

"We need a plan!" Syphilis stated. The mime stood up and pretended to climb up a rope.

"We're not stuck in a hole, Efimia," Zotikus snipped.

In the back of the room, an old drunken woman leaned over the table licking milk out of a small bronze bowl on a pedestal. With a mysterious aura about her, she looked up and with a rough, raspy voice whispered, "Down below is your answer."

Zotikus approached her. Her beady eyes followed him across the floor. As he neared her, the woman put her hands up and, like withered tree branches, her fingers curled like a claw to ensure he kept his distance. "Down below is your answer" she snarled.

"Do you know how we get back to who we once were, woman?" Zotikus queried.

"Three whacks of the emerald scepter of Omarosa. Three whacks on the ass," she murmured.

"Where is this scepter?" Syphilis asked.

"Through the fires in the Temple of Surely," she blurted out, then leaped up and galloped out of the bar on all fours, disappearing down the street.

"Something's not right with that lady," Zotikus philosophically remarked.

The centurion goat men gave up and headed to the Surely Temple several miles away. Trotting inside, they found a young, red-headed hetaera dancing in front of an altar of fire singing, "On the Good Ship Lysagora."

"How do we become men again?" Funicious snapped at the little girl.

She ignored him and said, "Look what I can do," as she threw out a tap dance shuffle, followed by an exaggerated toothy smile.

"We don't have time for this cutesy crap," Zotikus bellowed as he grabbed the tiny tot. "How do we go down below?"

"You're a bad centurion!" she huffed as she smacked his nose.

He grunted saying, "Look, you little gyro, you better tell us where…"

"No!" screamed the small tigress. She tore away then kicked him in the goatnads. When he doubled over, she giggled and pushed him into the fire. He vanished. The guys stood there in disbelief.

"What the….," Syphilis mumbled.

Suddenly, from the flames, they heard Zotikus voice, "Come on in, fellas. It's all good."

The three Greeks inched up to the fire. They looked at each other with a "hell no" gaze. Before they knew it, the little girl kicked each one of them in the ass and into the fire. From the fiery blaze echoed, "You little harlot brat!"

The centurions galloped down a long, darkened tunnel until they reached a river. A sign read "Styx." They knew they were in Hades and this was no grand illusion. They goat-paddled across the water then walked for what seemed like miles but was really kilometers. A screech owl whizzed by their heads scaring them half to death. Emerging from the darkness, they saw a large cave entrance before them. With significant trepidation, the half-wits entered.

They passed a group of lost souls who seemed to be doing nothing, stuck in limbo. As they descended further, they were accosted by a lustful naked gaggle of souls climbing on them, hell-bent on sexually violating them. Somehow, the souls were beaten off. The horny Syphilis urged the others to go on; he'd catch up with them later. They would never see him again. The next group of souls they met was all fat slobs sitting around a banquet table of food. All they did was eat and didn't want to be bothered. Continuing, they muscled through a bunch of spirits who stole everything they had, even the shirts off their backs. Things were looking dismal for the naked centurions.

Next, they ran into restless, irate spirits screaming things at them like "I hate your guts! Go to hell! I'll kill your titan baby!" This situation reminded Funicious of one of his typical comedy shows. They pushed on past souls who were heretics, violent frauds, and just treacherous beings. It was ugly and frightening. Hell was not just for children. The boys knew this place was serious and no divine comedy.

In front of them, were two large metal doors. They pushed them open. Fire encircled the room and in the middle were two thrones, inhabited by Hades and Omarosa, who was holding the emerald scepter they needed.

The king of the underworld looked up at the visitors. He took a drink from his horn then shot a wall of fire at them, singing their coarse goat hair, creating a putrid smell.

"Who is it that disturbs the dead?" Hades singeing.

"It's just little ole me, Zotikus, and my two friends," the trembling man replied. "We just wanted to swing by and give you a little comedy show. We figured you could use a few laughs down here," Zotikus said volunteering his pal.

"I'd like that," Hades said. "How 'bout you, honey?"

"I guess," Omarosa sighed.

"Well, what the hell, let's see what you got, kid," the beast snipped as he settled into his chair.

Funicious couldn't believe Zoticus just threw him under the chariot. His mind started racing for his best material. Stepping forward for his audience of two, he began sweating, and it wasn't because of the flames.

"It's great to be here at the…. Underworld," Funicious began. "Nice place you have here. The fire really brightens up the room. My guess would be… you're both in heat. It's hot down here. I said, it's hot down here."

Hades squirmed then uncaringly murmured, "How hot is it?"

"It's so hot even the flames are pleading for a drink of water," the comedian gasped.

Hades had yet to smile. While his friend joked, Zotikus slipped around the side and crept up behind Omarosa's throne. While she half-heartily giggled, the sneaky Greek was able to snatch the scepter. It was just in time because Funicious was bombing, "A sturdy iron spear!" That's how you separate the Greek boys from the Greek men."

Hades jawed tightened. "Before I wrap up this laugh fest," Funicious continued. "Please remember… To do is to be. Socrates. To be is to do. Aristotle. To do, be do be do. Sinatra." Hades had reached his breaking point. Enough was enough.

"I thought you were a comedian!" Hades screamed.

"Well, my material always goes over big at the Acropolis," the comic nervously retorted.

"Silence!" Hades bellowed.

"He stinks. Kill him," Omarosa demanded.

"Wait! Wait! I do impressions," he pleaded. Try and guess who this is?" Funicious hunched over, acting like he was holding something. "Help me I got the world on my shoulders. Help me."

Hades just blankly stared at him.

"That's Atlas," the comic beamed. "You know that guy? See where I going?"

"Is that it?" Hades shouted.

"I'm still working on… Dionysus… on a street corner," he groveled.

Hades took a drink from his horn and shot a wall of fire at Funicious, who now stood there blackened and charred. "Wow, when you die at the underworld, you really die at the underworld," he wheezed as he crumbled into a heap of ashes.

Sadly, Zotikus had only his mime friend left. He grabbed Efimia and raced towards the exit. Breathing down their backs was Hades. They ran out the big doors and slammed them. Zotikus quickly raised the scepter and whacked Efimia three times in the ass. Poof! The mime became human again. The mime took the scepter and whacked Zotikus in the ass three times. Poof! He was back to being human. Hurrying, they slipped the scepter through the door handles just before Hades was about to barrel through. It stopped the beast and bought precious time.

The two Greeks retraced their path and made it back out through the fire at the Temple of Surely. They rushed outside where they found a horse lingering in the streets. Without a second thought, the pair leaped on his back and darted down the road. The next thing they knew they were soaring in the air. Much to their amazement, they were on a winged horse. Zotikus and Efimia were elated to be alive, and yet sad that their friends were dead, but probably they were happier to be alive.

The wind whisked through their long hair as the horse climbed higher and higher. Excited, Zotikus laughed out loud. Efimia just moved his mouth as they relished the view. Suddenly feathers on the horse's wings began dropping off. A few at first, then hundreds. Little did they know the horse's owner had glued the feathers on with bee wax to sell to some unsuspecting dupes. The sun was now melting the cheap concoction. It served them right for stealing the horse, who was just a cheap knock-off of Pegasus built by a greedy Italian entrepreneur. They began to descend rapidly; Zotikus screamed, and Efimia joined in by just moving his mouth.

The horse flipped over twelve times as they came in for a crash landing on Melina, a mountainous stretch near the northern Balkans. Somehow, they were alive. Inhabiting the area was Halitosis, a territorial, giraffe-like creature with eight legs and the head of a duck. The beast had breathed fire into the womb of Walriseris, a three-legged monster who lived in a volcano east of the sparkling dunes of Sisaloona. (It was a reclusive, skittish creature that, when approached would throw dead fish with his short stubby arm to ward off trespassers. She was deadly accurate. After plucking off her on-coming victim, she'd manically giggle while dancing a victorious jig around them, with one leg completely out of rhythm.)

Halitosis had taken Walriseris eight little offspring monsters that she had borne him and was now raising them. They were known as Halitoids, and they scurried on the ground releasing an eerie shriek, filling the surrounding air with a filthy, foul stench. Whatever they breathed on would shrivel up and die, disintegrating into a mound of green, smoldering ash. They always circled their father like whining brats. Deadly whining brats.

"Where the hell are we?" Zotikus questioned out loud as he tried to clear his head from the brutal fall from the sky.

Efimia just mimed a long, drawn out, exacerbated shrug.

Suddenly, from out of a rock pile, the eight screeching creatures swarmed in.

"Halitoids!" Zotikus screamed.

Thinking quickly, Efimia jumped in front and lay on the ground in a tight ball. The Hallitoids stopped in their tiny tracks. Curious, they circled him. The mime began to move one finger at a time slowly. Little did the little ones know, he was launching into his "man stuck in a clay vessel" routine that he had perfected in the bathhouses of Thebes when he was a teenage boy. Gradually, he uncoiled as he placed his palms on the inner portion of the invisible container, pretending like he was trapped. His exaggerated facial expressions made the little buggers laugh. Moving ever so slowly, he continued as the mesmerized creatures watched in awe.

Efimia excited to be performing to a live audience, instead of a room of marble statues, as usual, began to ham it up; this would be his demise.

The Hallitoids uncontrollable giggling released toxic fumes from their mouths. When it reached the mime, he made an exaggerated disgusted look then disintegrated into a mound of ash. He never made it out of the clay vessel and went down in history as the first urn.

"Holy Hermes," Zotikus mumbled. He thought of his girlfriend back home. How he wished he was back with that nice piece of ash too.

The Hallitoids turned their attention to Zotikus who stared at them and said, "Look what I can do." The little beasts went into attack mode, and the Greek was on the move, darting down a rocky pathway. He heard pattering feet, and high-pitched shrieking breathing down on his Achilles' heels. He couldn't believe what he saw up ahead. As fortune would have it, in the distance was a marathon runner holding a torch. He knew if he could catch that guy everything would be alright.

With the Hallitoids closing in on him, Zotikus reached down and, like Mercury, dashed to catch up to the jogger. As soon as he did, he jumped on the man's nappy, curly-haired back. (The unsuspecting jogger was unfazed, since this was not unusual for a Greek at the time.) He accomplished his goal of dislodging the torch. Quickly picking up the flaming stick, he turned it on to the oncoming monsters. As soon as they released their loud shriek, Zotikus held up the torch. The gassy, bad-breathed creatures exploded with eight booming bursts in the sky. Some say the flames reached the chin of Zeus on Mount Olympus.

Zotikus was able to get a piggy-back ride from a marathon runner who had told him that the only reason he was carrying a torch at the time was that his mother-in-law's oven fire had gone out. Zotikus told him the only time he would run twenty-six miles for a mother-in-law was if she needed a lift to catch a ship going to another continent. They both fell in a heap on the side of the road, laughing.

Zotikus hopped on a ship leaving a nearby port. He was now seven years older than he was when he left Athens and minus four semi-talented friends. Much to his chagrin, the boat stopped in Egypt to pick up some papyrus, then was almost sunk in a typhoon and then finally sunk in a Spartan naval battle. He was picked up by another ship where he was thrown below, chained and forced to row the three seas for three years. He was not happy sailor.

Eventually, the tenuous Greek somehow found his way back to Athens. Because of the Peloponnesian War the gates were locked, and no one was allowed in. Zotikus spent the next six months building a small wooden hollow donkey. He spent another four months pushing it up to the gate. The savvy man hid inside the belly and risked capture when a guard called out, "Bring the jackass in" and Zotikus yelled back, "I am not!" He was finally brought into Athens, two months later because, at the time, there was a command to be wary of any Greek bearing gifts. Once inside the gate, he realized he had built the thing with the latch on the outside. He spent another month chewing himself out of the back end of the wooden structure. A few city on-lookers watched the tattered man slide out from under the tail of the donkey but said nothing. They just walked away, disgusted.

Free at last and with a few splinters in his gums, Zotikus hailed a taxi chariot. It wouldn't be long before he was with the girl he loved… he hoped. On the way, the Persian cabbie with a gold tooth asked, "Hey, my good man, you want something good? My good man, you want to please woman. Hey, my good man, I have crazy stuff. So good. So good. Hey, my good man, you want to buy some perfume from Crete?" Zotikus' mouth dropped realizing he could've saved about ten years of life if he had just asked a local chariot driver.

"How much?" Zotikus sighed.

"For you, my good man," the cabbie smirked. "Only eighty-five drachmas."

"Sure. Why not?" Zotikus replied in a surrendering tone.

"Okay, you wait here, my good man," the cabbie assured as he pulled over at a nearby alley between the "Cronus' Yogurt Shop" and a "Troys'R'Us" kiosk. "I'll be right back. You wait here, my good man."

Zotikus decided to wait patiently, after all, he had come this far so what was another five minutes. The driver ducked around the corner. Hidden behind a dumpster of sheepskins, he pulled out a beautiful decorative ceramic bottle, slipped it under his toga and pissed in it. The cabbie came back with a beaming smile holding out the little container. "Your lucky day, my good man," he said. "Only seventy-five drachmas."

"Really," Zotikus was amazed. "You saved me ten drachmas?"

"Of course," he smirked. "You special friend."

"Thanks, big fella," an appreciated Zotikus replied. "And you're sure it's from Crete?"

"Buddy. Good man. My pal. Come on, I always get real thing. Always."

"You know what?" Zotikus laughed. "I trust you. Besides, what am I gonna do? Go back out there and get another bottle. Not in my lifetime." They both broke out laughing. Zotikus would later ask himself what was so funny.

Zotikus made it back to the palace to make his delivery as promised. The king accepted the perfume and gave the Greek errand boy a little pat on the buttocks.

"Ya done good, Zosime." he proudly said.

"It's a… Zotikus" he reminded him.

"Yes, well I'm sure the queen will love it," Vasilis said as he opened it and took a whiff as his eyes crossed. "Hmm, that is good stuff." He didn't have the heart to tell the little adventurer that several messengers had already come back with a couple of crates from Crete. He guessed the boy probably had a long day anyway.

"So, where is she? Zotikus asked excitedly. "Where is my sweet little Kaliope?"

Right as he finished his sentence, the woman entered the room. She was no longer a petite young girl. As a matter of fact, she had packed on about two hundred pounds. Her rosy cheeks were as a plump as giant Roma tomatoes. While awaiting his return, she had sat around the palace eating grapes wrapped in pita bread smeared with chocolate and numerous bales of hay. He thought that his heart was anxiously pounding to see her, but it was the sound of her footsteps galloping towards him.

"I missed you," she softly said, wrapping him in an unflinching bear hug.

"And I, I, I…" Zotikus squirmed as he turned to the king "Forgot the olives. Don't wait up for me."

Many that day claimed they witnessed Mercury, the speedy, fleet-footed messenger of the gods, dashing down the city streets like a bolt of lightning, but it was just Zotikus high-tailing it into the hills.

AN EMPEROR WITH NO HORSE SENSE

Somewhere between the rise and fall of Rome, there reigned a Caesar named Clymustus. He was the second son of the emperor Galba and was a product of a palace orgy that had shot out of control. He was an odd, chubby child who often spent his days reading Virgil poems and discussing Greek philosophy with an olive tree. One of his favorite past times was to sit on his father's lap and nibble his toes. Even though his son was just shy of his eighteenth birthday, Galba enjoyed the foot licking so much he promised the strange kid that, after his death, he would succeed him as the next ruler of the Roman Empire. Enraged, the first son, Uno, devised a plan to avenge the old man's decision. One night, he slipped into his father's bedroom. While he was sleeping, the bitter heir placed his father's hand into an Egyptian clay vessel of warm water. Galba awoke in a soiled toga. After the slaves had bathed, oiled and powdered the emperor's bum, they dressed him in a fresh sheet and left. Galba, with fire in his eyes, looked up and began to curse Peepeephilia. The disrespecting, profanity-laced tirade angered the goddess of bed-wetting, and the emperor died three days later from a urinary tract infection.

In 69 AD, at the age of thirty-two, Clymustus was sworn in as emperor of Rome. He was very different from the other Caesars that had preceded him. His actions were unorthodox, and he was thought to be missing a few spokes in his chariot wheel. Never knowing who his real mother was, an Ethiopian brothel belly dancer named Navalus raised him. She was warm, sweet, and had a reputation of lying with everyone in the palace, including the statues. As a pudgy young boy, Clymustus would go out to the marketplace and run around in circles and bark at the fruit. Then, he would skip off to the garden, sit under a tree, and count his toes for hours - arriving a different number every time. Sometimes, he would run over the Seven Hills, twirling and singing a Latin rendition of "The Sound of Music." However, his favorite activity was to venture down to the Coliseum and feed the lions his sandals, then entertain them with a barefoot belly dance. (Even the jungle beasts were too afraid to eat the oddity.)

Clymustus' first point of order was to change the existing Roman currency. Instead of coins, he required the people to pay in grapes. He surmised a plump, juicy grape would be worth twice as much as a raisin. When the Senate told him he was nuts, he replied, "Five nuts equal one raisin." Insanely, he also wanted a picture of him stamped on the grapes. After this was attempted the new currency became wine. Secondly, he requested that all water fountains filled with volcanic ash from Pompeii. He thought the dried lava would please Apocoliptis, the playful god of astronomical catastrophes. The insane Caesar ordered that the Roman numerals X and I always be written upside-down or face crucifixion. He also requested a census be taken of all pottery plates. But, perhaps the strangest Clymustus decree, was having the gladiators fight to the death using only stale loaves of bread from Macadamia. The baked batter bashings were held in the Coliseum every Saturday and, for the most part, raised a lot of dough for the city of Rome's highway system.

One day, a funny thing happened to Clymustus on his way to the Forum. A soldier, standing in a chariot, was talking to a pretty woman who had a stunning pair of jugs. (She had just returned from the city well and was holding a set of decorative clay vessels.) Looking at the sight, the emperor decided that he had never seen anything so beautiful. In a Rome minute, Clymustus had fallen head-over-sandals in love with the soldier's horse. Batting his eyes, he sashayed over to the mare and seductively fed her a carrot that he kept near the front of his robe to give the appearance that he was well-endowed. The animal chewed it down and began to shake her head back-and-forth while flashing her pearly white chompers, unaware that some hay lodged between a tooth crevasse. The promiscuous playful display made the emperor giggle uncontrollably as he feverishly petted the velvety beast uttering, "Who's your Caesar? Who's your Caesar?" Love blossomed as Roman candles exploded in his head. He brought the smelly creature back to his palace where he dined with it that evening. Several servants overheard him singing a seductive love ballad about a horse with no name. Attempting to impress his hairy date, he served the best wine. It was a French Chardoneighhhh. Later in the evening, the intoxicated emperor was seen belly dancing on a table attempting to woo the shy mare. Love seemed to have blossomed because, the next day, a decree was sent out, declaring that he was marrying a horse.

Sensing a possible uprising by the unruly people, the Senate secretly convened. The pressing topic was how to oust the loony dictator without upsetting Roman rule. For hours the pompous Senators bantered and bickered on how to reign in the reigner. They even sang songs like, "Who'll Stop the Reign" and "Reigning Days and Mondays." Some wanted him exiled. Some wanted him dead. Some just wanted a good old-fashioned sex bacchanal and if a horse was part of the orgy, so be it. After the hardened deliberation it was agreed that they would assassinate the crack-pot ruler. The plan was, on the night of the wedding celebration, an extra potent wine would be served to render Clymustus incapable of fighting off his assailants. (They had once seen him in a scuffle with a Macedonian slave girl and knew the pipsqueak could scratch and kick with the best of them.) He would then be dragged into his bedroom, flogged with wheat stalks, his eyebrows shaved off then stabbed in his royal, mushy flab by daggers. It would later be known as the "Ides of June." Elated over the insidious plot, the Senators summoned the teenage boys to celebrate.

The marriage ceremony was spectacular and was the talk of the empire. People had mobbed the streets in hopes of catching a glimpse of the adoring mare draped in a white, flowing blanket and veil, with colorful beads cascading down her mane. During the vowel exchange, Clymustus had broken out in tears three times, struggling to express his love for his horse-bride as he promised to love her until death or, at least, till she was put out to pasture. The Roman elite also cried, realizing how quickly their society was decaying because of the union between their leader and the long-nosed empress. At the end of the nuptials, Clymustus placed a gold horseshoe on his newlywed's hoof, fed it a sugar cube, and then was hoisted onto the equine's back as the crowd cheered. Perhaps out of joy, the mare reared up on two legs, throwing the chubby groom into a group of Christian bystanders. They helped him up, brushed him off, placed the flowers back in his hair and then blessed him. To show his appreciation, Caesar invited the kind-hearted zealots to the reception to enjoy some beverage and entertainment. When fed to the lions, it dawned on them that they were the entertainment.

The night was a fury of festive activity. Leaders from every province attended, bearing gifts of all shapes and sizes. Some Venetian leaders showered him with blinds for his windows. A Persian prince gave him a long-haired fluffy cat, which the emperor stuffed into the lower half of his toga, causing him to explode in an hour-long giggling delirium. However, his favorite gift was a talking Julius Caesar doll that when its string pulled said "Friends, Romans, noblemen, lend me your wives." Even his generals were present with presents. General Philatio, the great orator and often requested orgy guest, presented the emperor with a large hand-crafted Gaul bowl made of wood from the Argon forest. Carved on the side, in meticulous detail, were the words, "Ito magnus igneous como san lada ignoramus." It meant "May fungus never grow between your toes." The Latin proverb so touched Clymustus that he stood in the decorative bowl, placed lettuce leaves around his feet, had his servants sprinkle Parmesan cheese in his hair and then pour olive oil over his head. "From this day forward," he called out, "this will be known as a Caesar salad."

As the evening progressed, the wine flowed generously, and the guests became more and more sloshed. Clymustus was not far behind them. Throughout the evening he had been pounding vintage wine spritzers like there was no tomorrow. Little did the chunky emperor know that if all went as planned, there would be no tomorrow. The Senators watched him closely for any sign of drunkenness. It was difficult because, even in a sober state, the ruling buffoon would do unusual, silly things - hopping around like a bunny while reciting Greek poems was just one of them. Throughout the evening, Clymustus divided his time slow dancing with his mare, playing dice games and wrestling a chicken. Later, he devised a drinking game where he laid on his back and had gladiators tickle his lumpy belly. Once he laughed, everyone had to drink.

Sometime around midnight, a sloppy stewed Clymustus climbed up on top of a buffet table. He guzzled down a goblet of wine then carelessly threw it over his shoulder. It hit the unsuspecting eunuch in the head, rendering him dead. After trying to make love to an armless statue, the plastered Caesar ordered the band to play as the attendees observed him belly dance. During the jerky, spasmodic display, the aghast audience watched with a disgusted sour-look as he disrobed. (One vomited into a plundered Mesopotamian vase.) He staggered around pointing from his hip and winking at his male guests, slurring, "Hey, you're da Ro-man!" At some point, the bumbling Clymustus lost his balance and slipped, falling into an ornamental fountain where little statue men surrounding the ceramic container had water flowing out of their tiny penis'. The stream splattered on the emperor's head. The Senators felt the time was right for the assassination.

Clymustus lay wet on the floor in his tattered, wine-stained toga mumbling nonsensical sentences. Five Senators bent over and picked up the sloshed limp spectacle, dragging him by his leg into his bedroom. As the emperor passed his bride, he reached over and blindly petted her nose, murmuring "I wuv you, horsey." The mare-bride exhaled as her lips flapped in adorning ecstasy. She then stretched out her head and lapped his alcohol-numbed face, causing him to giggle.

Once in the sleeping quarters, the Senators yanked the half-dressed plastered lump across the floor and hoisted him on to the bed. "What has our empire come to?" they thought. After placing a bouquet in his butt crack and joking, "Looks like our Caesar's in full bloom" they placed wagers on how many minutes it would take until the tulips died. The underhanded politicians summoned the Praetorian Guards to complete the plan.

Upon entering, the guards pulled out sharp daggers, hovering over the sloshed emperor who lay passed out in bed. Inside his head, thoughts of younger days danced around like a pantomimus acting out a lascivious tragedy. His vivid dreams recalled him as a small boy swimming naked in the hot baths with his imaginary friend. The invisible companion was a mountain goat named Useeme - and he could swim laps around him. They would frolic about, laugh, and wrestle with each other in the warm water for hours. (Onlookers would see a deranged, chubby child chuckling alone as he playfully splashed himself in the face.) Eventually, his father banned him from the hot pools for annoying bathers by playing "Marco, Polo" with his pseudo alpine playmate. Eventually, Useeme tired of the clingy kid and ran for the hills in search of peace. Only later would the goat deduce he didn't exist. Unfortunately, Clymustus never reached that stage of realization, still placing bowls of milk by the back door hoping for the return of his beloved invisible goat.

The treasonous hired hands raised their daggers in preparation for the plunging. The soused Caesar rolled over, incoherently mumbling as he drowsily licked an Ethiopian silk throw pillow. Suddenly, without out warning, the limp mound let loose a series of loud flatulent rumbles. Flowers shot up in the air, and the noise sent reverberating shock waves rattling throughout the palace. The people still in attendance at the reception assumed Mars, the roman god of war, became angry. In a panic-stricken stampede, the naked attendees broke off from their orgy and made a beeline towards the door. The elite guards, hovering over the foul-smelling emperor, were soon encompassed in a musty gas cloud. The foggy-minded bunch, choking, dropped their knives and, with tear-welded eyes, began to gasp for clean air. One of the larger guards crawled to the far end of the room and mustered up enough strength to kick open the French doors leading to the balcony. Fresh oxygen poured in but not before Eurectus, the spindliest guard, had collapsed into unconsciousness. When the air finally cleared, the dizzy assailants regrouped for another attack.

Clymustus was now peacefully snoring as rivers of saliva dribbled from the corner of his mouth. With fire in their eyes, the angered guards threw a blanket on top of the disgusting sow and began to pummel him. The stench-ridden, hefty oaf rolled over but did not wake up. (Giggling in his sleep, caught amid a dream where a team of horses trampling him in a chariot race. For some strange reason, he always enjoyed that feeling.) As the guards raised their daggers for one more assault, the gassy, crude Clymustus ripped another blast, punching a hole in the back of his toga which was now smoldering. This flatulent bomb was so hideous that it made a nearby Venus mosaic blink her eyes – twice, then shake her muddled head to clear the fog. The image, now frozen in time with the goddesses' eyes crossed. In terror, the guards fled to the underground to huddle in the Catacombs until the coast was clear.

Upon entering, the Senators were shocked to see the emperor rhythmically snorting as he serenely slept. Doubled over and gagging, they quickly summoned a servant to bring in several bottles of myrrh to help fumigate the room. Incense was lit and the incensed senators pulled out their daggers to finally end the long, wretched ordeal. They tipped-toed to the edge of the bed.

Groggy, the hazy-headed Clymustus opened his blurred eyes to see the malicious, conspiring officials standing over him. Suddenly, knives were thrust downward causing the emperor to release a high-pitched shriek and roll off the bed. A reverberating thump sounded as he hit the floor. The daggers sliced through the air, barely missing the flabby lug and plunged into the mattress, sending feathers fluttering everywhere. Quickly sobering up, the frightened, frantic Caesar leaped to his feet and began shrieking as he scampered around the room like a scared squealing hog knowing he was about to be butchered. The senators chased him around, fumbling over each other, anxious to get the first stab in. A yelping Clymustus jumped on the bed and started bouncing as lethal daggers swiped at his feet. Globs of perspiration poured through his olive leaf headband and gushed down his forehead onto his blotched, rosy cheeks.

"Wait! Wait!" he cried. The Senators paused and looked up at the heavily panting emperor. Holding up his arms and catching his breath, the sweaty buffoon began to speak. "Please my fellow Romans, must we kill each other because one is different from the other? It's my wedding night and should be a time of great joy. I married a sweet, beautiful, loving horse. Does that make me unfit to rule the empire? I implore you, my dear friends, give me life, and I vow that with all my heart and soul I shall bless all of you until the end of time." The plump Caesar gave a warming smile then proceeded to belly dance. He seductively batted his eyes at the perplexed onlookers who watched the hairy mound of mid-section flesh roll back-and-forth as it flopped and swayed as lodged crumbs and grapes fell from his flabby crevasses. The agitated Senators were utterly astonished at the shameless exhibition.

"What in Zeus' name is that fat idiot doing?" Senator Herminia called out.

The hostile traitors then became angrier at Clymustus' behavior. "Kill him!" they screamed. Then, reason seems to prevail as they feared an assassination could cause a civil war throughout the empire. They decided to parade him before the citizens and make a public spectacle of the lunatic - then kill him.

They hauled the pleading emperor out on the streets, throwing him down on the steps of the Amphitheater. A crowd gathered as they watched the roman officials' shackle Clymustus to a team of chariot horses. They planned to drag the crazy slob to his death. The Senators positioned the stallions to run in full stride down a winding, rocky road. As they were about to command the horses to gallop onward, a deafening "Neigh!" was heard from above. Everyone looked up to see the emperor's bride mare standing on the balcony. She neighed again as if to say, "Enough of the horseplay." Unfazed, the Senators hit the horses on their rear ends to get the show on the road. They refused to move, so they beat them again, but harder. They remained still. Frustrated, they turned and cursed the empress who was flashing a cocky smile and nibbling on a carrot stick, knowing full well the horses would listen to her.

The senators huddled. Clymustus lay on the street wailing and kicking his chunky stout legs as if he was a tortoise that had been flipped on his back. Devising a new plan, in no time, the Senators had the dumpy emperor tied to a pole. Stones of all shapes and sizes were passed out to the hostile crowd. Since there were no gladiatorial games that day, the people were excited about doing some rock pelting. Hell, to them, well, it was something to do. They cheered and broke into a Latin rendition of "Everybody Must Get Stoned." Through his sniveling, Clymustus pleaded with them in a Woody Allen-like fashion. "Please, I beg of you, don't throw anything at me. I bruise very easily. I'm also a bleeder, not to mention, I have severe allergic reactions whenever granite touches my body. It makes my skin break out." The crowd was indifferent to the groveling, growing antsy as they awaited the "fire" command.

"Time out" a voice cried out from the drove. Stepping out from the herd was Uno, the emperor's long-lost brother. He had a scruffy beard, and he reeked liked he hadn't bathed in three months – one month was the norm. The filthy, unwanted sibling banished from the empire for once trying to poison his brother with a salmonella infected chicken, entered the fray. When the clueless Caesar found out, he was enraged and ordered that they give Uno the dark meat while he taunted him by eating the white strips.

Uno, exiled to Alexandria, became a well-known drunk. His days and nights were spent drinking and snacking on rats that couldn't run fast enough. He made whatever money he could on the streets by pantomiming great gladiatorial fights, often adlibbing wrestling maneuvers that never actually happened. Rolling around in the gutter, while putting himself in a half-nelson chicken-wing as he grunted and groaned, was usually good for a few Lyre. The hack street performer was forcibly asked to leave when it became clear he was throwing his fights by betting against himself. The city council also had received numerous complaints about his body odor which had been known to knock the head off of a Cleopatra statue. Knowing he had overstayed his welcome in the ancient city and, upon hearing about the despicable and embarrassing way his brother was running the empire into shambles, he decided to return to Rome, rather than head to Cairo and start up his promising venture of a pyramid cleaning business. He deduced that he could rightfully step in as the new and improved Caesar.

"It is I. The brother of the emperor," Uno slurred as a result of drinking on his travels, all the way from Alexandria.

"Are you the worthless, no-good-for-nothing, meaningless, insignificant street-performing bum who tried to poison our emperor?" someone called out from the crowd.

"That… is just one side of me," Uno reassured.

"Is the other the drunk side?" another yelled.

Uno attempted to calm the mob, "There's no need to take cheap shots."

"Looks like you've been taken 'em all morning," an old widow cried out sending the crowd into uproarious laughter.

The woman wasn't far off. Uno had not only been drinking all morning, but he also began when he left the port of Alexandria, six days earlier. Doing his best to come across as sober, he continued, trying to gain the people's trust. "Anyhoodle, my unstable brother, Clymustus, has disgraced and defiled this… umm…"

"Place?" a young boy screamed.

"No, I was thinking…" Uno stammered for the right word.

"Homeland?" a soldier guessed.

"No, it's right on the tip of my tongue here…" Uno pondered as the crowd remained silent, some of them looking up, pretending to think. "Has disgraced and defiled this… it's coming to me… defiled this…"

"Great Metropolis," an elderly demented craftsman yelled.

"That's it! He has become an embarrassment to our citizens, and our enemies no longer fear the once and powerful Roman empire. We are the laughingstock of the Mediterranean."

"Is it because Caesar married a horse?" another person bellowed.

"That's part of it," Uno nodded. "A pretty big part. However, it is time for a new leader, and I am he who stands before you." The crowd stood completely silent with blank faces. "As that guy… who is him," he added. With that said, Uno smiled but, then his cheeks puffed out as he attempted to hold in a burp. It was of no use. He ripped out a loud belch then leaned over and threw up on his sandals. The crowd sickened by the display felt they had no choice but to stone him to death. The first rock sailed over Uno's head. Perhaps feeling a little cocky, the drunken lush crotched down and wagged his bum back-and-forth, pointing his finger as if to say, "shame on you." Pushing his luck, he stuck out his tongue and, in a sing-song taunting voice "Ya missed. Ya missed. You're all a flask of piss." The next stone clocked him in the temple. He stood there for a brief second, dazed, peering out at the riled-up crowd. The elderly woman who just hit him flush in the head was sporting a toothless grin and shrieked, "You're a flask of piss!" Through his blurred vision he noticed arms rocking back with rocks. In a child-like voice he muttered "Momma." A barrage followed and Uno's days of drinking ended.

While the frenzy heightened, Clymustus' wife used the distraction to gnaw her way through the binding ropes and freed her sniveling husband. He climbed on her back as she let out an agonizing groan. "You stop. I'm not that heavy," the Caesar huffed. Tearing through the city, they galloped to safety in the countryside. Lying in a desolate haystack, they cuddled and rested for the night. The next day they stowed away in a spaghetti and meatball trading ship bound for the Island of Stromboli.

Constantine, now elected as the new Roman emperor, declared his first order of business as overturning everything enacted during the reign of Clymustus. Horses would once again pull chariots instead of oversized hogs. Roman legions would no longer be required to defend the country using loaves of Italian bread as swords and burlap spice bags for shields. (However, they were still subject to wear a Fuller Brush atop of their helmets.) The aqueducts would now carry water deficient of pickled herrings as they did before the reign of insanity. And, centurion hemlines would be dropped back down three inches to subdue creepy ogling and unwanted groping. The Senate could now get back to making ordinary laws, taxing, lavish feasts, and wild orgies. All the things that had previously made the empire great.

Clymustus spent a few years in exile brushing his wife, daily, and kissing her with a carrot in his mouth until, during "The Great Pasta Famine," she died of mysterious causes. (Coincidentally, the day after the ostracized Caesar had complained to several town folks that he was so hungry he could eat a horse.) He did return to Rome in his later years and became quite successful as a chariot test dummy. He would marry once again. Having suffered through the humiliation of being married to a horse, he learned his lesson and settled down with a donkey. Before his death, the once-emperor wrote his autobiography called "They're Coming to Take Me Away." In 1986, archeologists dug up various ancient Roman artifacts and among the trove was a book by Clymustus. When scholars examined it, it was found to only contain a compilation of barley recipes, a doddle of a puffy sheep juggling tomatoes and a chapter on the art of belly dancing.

LITTLE RED ROBBING HOOD

A carriage pulled by a team of white horses weaved its way down a dirt path cut through the dark woods. A band of soldiers surrounded the coach, protecting its cargo. Inside was a chest full of gold coins, jewels, and some juicy plums to snack on. A heavy man, known as Humpty Dumpty was in route to deliver the goods to King Cole. Mr. Dumpty worked for the king and oversaw collecting taxes from the counties that surrounded Sherbet Forest. He was mean, hard, and would boil when a tax payment didn't get made. He was simply a rotten egg.

An old Hickory Dickory Dock tree had fallen and blocked the pathway causing the caravan to stop. "Why are we not moving!" Dumpty bellowed as he spits out a plum seed.

"There's a tree blocking our route," a timid soldier answered.

"Well move it before I come out there and give you salmonella!" Dumpty ordered.

The king's men jumped off their horses and began to lift the giant log as they whistled a happy ditty laced with profanity for having to exert themselves. They were hired to kill, not for manual labor.

Suddenly, a "whoosh" was heard as an arrow soared in the wind and embedded into a soldier's back. Little Boy Blue blew his horn and arrows filled the air as the military entourage began dropping like dead soldiers - because they were. The trees brimmed with a band of hooligans. They were outcasts of every shape and size. There was Jack Sprat who was wanted for licking plates. Little Miss Muffet who was up on charges of stealing curds and whey. Peter Pumpkin Eater for spousal abuse. And, Georgy Porgy, booted out of town for making girls cry. (Sexual harassment was not tolerated by any means.) These were just of a few of the notorious felons who had found refuge in the forest. These merry fugitives led by a tiny outlaw named Little Red Robbing Hood - a young rebel who had gained notoriety by splitting a big bad wolf's skull with a picnic basket, hitting him right between the great big eyes.

Humpty Dumpty grabbed his treasure chest and waddled as fast as he could through the dense wood side. Huffing and puffing, he soon got cornered by Jack Horner. Humpty pulled out a dagger. Jack, realizing he was walking on eggshells, knew he had to be nimble and quick. He was an expert with a candlestick and threw it at the rotten egg. Dumpty attempting to dive out of the way had a great fall. He was found in pieces, still clutching his gold and jewels. They knew they couldn't put him back together again, nor did they want to. That night the group feasted on a giant omelet and danced to the music of the cat and the fiddle until the wee wee hours.

Little Red Robbing Hood began tormenting the king after escaping from the royal dungeon. She had been arrested for refusing to pay taxes and for illegal tiddlywinks' gambling. Laying low in a shoe with an old woman named Hubbard, Red blended in with her children and, whenever the leather domicile got raided, Hood would hide in a cupboard filled with dog bones. At night, she would sneak out and linger in the town pub. Skipping around and twirling her skimpy cape, the wily scamp would entice drunk soldiers into the back alley. In the darkness, she would sneak up behind the unsuspecting lush and clunk him over the head with her picnic basket and steal his satchel of coins. The confiscated loot would get distributed to the poor; folks like the humble Sow family who consisted of three little pigs that had recently lost their house in a highly suspect, freakish windstorm.

The word about the hooded Samaritan began to spread through the township of Hill and Dale. On the run, she escaped into the forest and found refuge in a tiny house made of candy, owned by a chubby German couple named Hansel and Gretel. They were more than happy to hide the little girl. Once upon a time - during The Great Banger and Chip Famine - Red had raided the king's food supply coaches and delivered some Bratwurst, Wiener schnitzel, and Jarlsberg cheese to the starving twosome.

Ole King Cole was growing more frustrated by the day over the little bandit. He ordered a decree stating that "whomever so bringith in - dead or alive - the head of Little Red Robbing Hood, shall receiveith six hundred pence and a blackberry pie." The hunt was on for the trouble-making vixen.

Partisan sympathy was on the side of Hood. Criminals about to be arrested would flee to Red's hideout where she would teach them the art of robbing and pillaging. Mary, a kleptomaniac, was on the lam for stealing a lamb from Bo Peep - the king's mistress. Hood welcomed the recruit, finding her quite contrary. Some of the other gang members included seven dwarfs, three bears, and Rapunzel, a rebellious little run away who refused to have her hair cut to the king's specifications. Disobedience meant death and Rapunzel did not wish to wind up like her dear friend Goldilocks.

The band wreaked havoc over Hill and Dale. Taking from the tax collectors, Hood's hoodlums distributed it back to the poor population. Jack and Jill finally had a nest egg to get married, and a brand-new pale to boot. The three men or "domestic partners" could buy that tub they had their eye on and rub-a-dub all day long. And Mildred, a neurotic cow, could now afford psychoanalysis for her grand delusion of wanting to jump over the moon. Little Red Robbing Hood had brought oodles of happiness to the countryside.

The king sat on his throne, tapping his bony fingers. Anger had seeped into his merry ole soul. Then, as if slapped in the face with a buggy whip, a cunning idea emerged. What if he could somehow lure the little trollop into a trap? "Yes, a trollop trap," he mumbled to himself as he giggled. The bait would be a chili cook-off. He had learned of Red's fondness for the culinary arts from an eensy weensy spider that had briefly befriended Muffet, a member of the elusive gang.

While Red was in the middle of a ring-a-round-the-rosy session, Jack Sprat sprinted into the camp with a royal flier. "Hear ye! Hear ye!" Jack cried.

"We hear ye loud and clear," Peter Pumpkin Eater snapped.

"Go lick a platter clean!" Georgy Porgy quipped causing the troupe to explode in laughter.

Sprat continued, "Saturday, the king is having a 'Silly Chili Cookin' Dilly.'"

Red snatched the paper from the messenger's hand. Her big blue eyes widen as they beam full of excitement. "Hmm, first prize is 3,333 shillings and a set of Ugly Duckling teacups and saucers. Enticing. Very enticing." she said as she curled her hair with her finger.

"You can't show your face there, Red. They'll kill you. They'll kill you, I tell you," Mary pleaded as she nibbled on a lamb chop.

Red smiled, "I'll be fine Mary. My chili is scrumptious. Now, go grab me some silver bells and cockle shells from your garden."

The beautifully decorated castle grounds were abuzz that Saturday morning. Damsels in colorful ballooning dresses paraded around, teasing the men in tights. Horses trotted about, also teasing the men in tights. Various games got scheduled throughout the day. Activities like jousting, stake burnings, and Dodge Ball. But, most of the people were there for the big event, "The Silly Chili Cookin' Dilly."

King Cole perched himself in the balcony overlooking the crowds. Next to him was Tweedle Dee and Tweedle Dum - his right-and-left-hand men. Below, on hundreds of tables, were pots and kettles of chili brought from every town in the country. One of the Tweedles bellowed, "Let the tasting begin!" The tasting judges had been hand-picked by the king. They were three bears who had gained notoriety for their succulent porridge dishes.

Scouring the contestant pool, the king mumbled under his breath, "She's here. I know she's here, but where?" The bears made their way down the long chili line. Using a fork, they dipped it into each container. (They could not use a spoon because the night before it had run off with a dish.) A glob of chili was swished around the mouth then graded on taste, texture, and the length of time it remained on the pallet. For the most part, the bear tasters found the chili either too hot or too cold. However, two recipes were just right. One of them was made by a Peter Piper, who used a peck of pickled peppers that he had picked to add zest and flavoring to his spicy concoction. The other prepared by a hunched-over elderly woman whose face was concealed by a knitted shawl.

"We have a tie for "The Silly Chili Cookin' Dilly," the pudgy bear called to the king. Thunderous applause rang out. King Cole made his way down to greet and congratulate the lucky winners.

"Bravo, my loyal chefs," the king said with a smirk. He plunged his bony finger into Peter's crock then rub it on his non-bony tongue. "Yummy" he replied. He slithered in front of the feeble woman and took a sample of her chili dish. "Now this one," the king paused. "This one leaves a bad taste in my mouth. Don't you think, Little Red Robbing Hood?" the king sneered while ripping the shawl off the petite girl's head.

"My, what a big ugly face you have," Red exclaimed.

"Seize her!" the king yelled.

Red leaped on the table and kicked a bowl of chili into the king's eyes. A pinto bean lodged in his nose and the spices burned his nostrils, causing him to release a blood-curdling scream. Red scampered across the tables giggling and doing cartwheels. Soldiers frantically chased the nuisance. They cornered her in, of all places, a corner. With swords drawn they moved in on the thieving tyke.

From the tower above, the sweet sound of a horn reverberated. It was Little Boy Blue. Suddenly, Red Hood's gang of merry men and women emerged from the crowd. Losing their disguises, they began to assault the soldiers. Georgey Porgey whipped pudding pies in their face. Muffet flung tuffets. Sprat heaved fat. And Peter could spit a pumpkin seed sixty paces with the force of a kicking white stallion, rendering a man unconscious.

The bamboozled royal army was an easy target for the forest felons. They began to drop like a glass slipper. The ones who survived the onslaught ran for the hills. The Jack and Jill clan would eventually capture them.

The panicked king witnessing the debacle ran to the stables. Red, during hand-to-hand combat, finished off her foe by biting his ear. (A move she had learned from Sir Tyson of Ringside.) She began to rush after the king but blindsided with a Tweedle Dee and Tweedle Dum body sandwich, she lay on the ground gasping for air. The pair started to taunt and tease her. Flashbacks of her older brother danced in her head. With the strength of three kittens and a rabbit, she leaped up and whirled into a tantrum. Kicking and screaming, she knocked the two bullies to the dirt and then unmercifully beat them with her trusty picnic basket. It wasn't pretty, but she knew her grandma would be proud.

The king had managed to climb on a horse, of course. As he emerged from the livery, his heart jumped when he saw her - the notorious Little Red Robbing Hood. Flashing an icy cold stare, she stood before him, panting, with her hands on her hips. "Leaving so soon, Cole?" she mused.

"You pesky little tramp," muttered the king.

"I'm rubber, and you're glue, whatever you say bounces off of me and sticks to you," Red said as she stuck out her tongue.

"You're nothing but a meddling brat," the king snapped.

"Sticks and stones may break my bones, but names will never hurt me," Red sang out while dancing in a circle.

Furious, the king dug his heels into the horse's side. In a full gallop, the beast darted forward towards the sassy little princess in hopes of breaking her bones. A high-pitched scream reverberated throughout the castle as the stallion raged over the hood of Hood.

Sensing the end had finally arrived for the little girl, King Cole charged towards the forest. Oblivious to him, Red had managed to climb up the horse's leg and was now gripping tightly to its tail, her legs flailing in the wind. With the determination of a hungry wolverine, she pulled herself up and over the horse's rump. Steadying herself, she pounced on the king's back. She buried her tiny hands into his royal scalp and tugged on his stringy hair. He cried out in pain and profanity. He reached back and attempted to release the pest. It was too late; Red had wrapped her legs around his neck and was playing patty cake on his head. The speeding horse had now entered the woods. Choking and turning blue, the king, in a last-ditch effort, was able to free the vice-like grip of the menace. He lifted Hood in hopes of slamming her to the rocky ground below. His plan quickly terminated when a tree branch collided with his nose—

dislodging a pinto bean. Cole tumbled off the horse while Red hung on by the long, coarse mane.

Robbing Hood eventually brought the equine animal under control. Looking over the motionless body of the king, she noticed he had fallen and broke his crown. After a sigh of relief, she took his silver, jewelry, and gold fillings, then covered his face with her hood. Heading into town, she was greeted by a cheering crowd chanting You go girl! You go!"

The church recognized Red as a martyr, and after her death, she would be canonized as a saint, Saint Hood. The kingdom abolished; a socialist government put in place. People would still have high taxes, but instead of the funds going for a king's toe manicure, the money would now go towards education, healthcare, and welfare. The government would soon go broke, and a worse tyrant, named Rumpelstiltskin would rule until his untimely death from eating a bowl of chili containing poisoned cockle shells. After that, everyone lived happily ever after.

A KING, THE FLING AND A KNIGHT WHO COULD SWING?

During the twelfth century, England was a country split by northern and southern tribes living in various counties and villages. Times were hard as people struggled to support themselves with meager crops, fearing raids by power-hungry kingdom grabbers and, for most, justice was just a flavor of the day. But soon, a Bretwalda (one who wields great power) would emerge and bring light into The Dark Ages. Artie was a small boy with dreams of someday becoming a shepherd because he loved the feel of soft, fluffy wool on his cheek. He was an orphan who never knew who his parents were and was now being raised by an older blacksmith named Pelican who had found little Artie wandering in the forest of Whitaker. The ornery man had a mind that would jump in and out of reality, often pretending to be a brave knight who battled Saxon barbarians which were, in fact, small birch trees. "Slew another one, my boy!" he'd yell, sticking out his chest. But, through the disillusionment, he was always a good father figure for the boy.

Young Artie would spend much of his days exploring the hills of Aneda and the banks of the rivers of Joan. It was in the Woods of James where he stumbled upon an old man dressed in a wool robe and a pair of rabbit-fur slippers. His deep blue eyes hid behind a wrinkled face covered with a long, snow-white beard.

"Hello, Artie, my boy. I've been expecting you," the old man said with a sly smirk.

"How do you know who I am?" Artie questioned.

"You might say a little owl told me," the old man replied.

"Who?" Artie answered back.

"Very cute. I get it," the old man responded as he rolled his eyes. "Have a seat on this log. I'm going to tell you all about your future while I feast on this jug of wine."

And throw down the wine he did. Coincidentally, his name was Merlot, and he was known as the greatest sorcerer in the land. His red wine stained beard wiggled as he enthusiastically revealed to the small child that someday he would unite all of England when he ruled as king. The boy loved the story but, down deep, he just figured it was the booze talking, after all, he'd seen Pelican after a snoot or two.

Merlot reassured Artie that Matilda foretold all as the maiden of the lakes of Rikki. "You must trust me, my boy. You will be king," the magician slurred as his booze breath almost knocked Artie off the log.

Using his magician skills, he taught little Artie about life by changing him into different animals; a woodchuck, raccoon, horse, snake, fish were just a few. As another form of life, Artie learned good and evil, just and unjust and, most of all, how human beings should elevate themselves above simple animals. He thoroughly enjoyed each lesson and grew in wisdom. His only beef was dealing with the fleas.

It was a cold, rainy day in the village of Peeples. The hillside scattered with town folk who circled a large overgrown potato that had become petrified over the centuries. Buried deep within the mutated vegetable was an old sword known as Exotica. The jeweled handle protruded out, glistening, without the help of any sunlight.

For nearly two centuries, it had become an annual event where folks would come from miles around to do their best to pull the sword out of the great potato. Oral accounts told of a King Rodney, severely injured in the Battle of the Saxes; a barbaric tribe of Scottish women, known as the Gaelic Gals, who had pummeled the Britannia Boys on the Fields of Salley.

Rodney crawled out of harm's way to a remote area, northeast of the Rikki Lakes, and, lying helpless, mumbled his second to last words, "Damn, this hurts." Then, he thrust his sword into the ground and, with his last dying breath breathed his final words, "May all thy royal powers pass unto the next possessor of thy sword Exotica." His blood seeped into the soil, blessing the sacred land. Later that night, under a red moon, a wayward warlock tripped over the sword protruding from the ground, and swearing, he cast a spell over the sword. By dawn the next day, a plump, delicious potato had fully grown, encasing the weapon. And so, a legend was born.

Standing amongst the on-lookers, Bishop Elvin unraveled a scroll and began to read, "Let it be known that thou who free thee thy sword of Exotica from thy grips of thee thy great potato shall be deemed thy new king to ruleth over the lands of Britannia." The crowd murmured with excitement over the possibility that one of them could become the next king. Raising his arms, the holy religious leader tried to calm the raucous bunch, "Stop with the murmuring!" he exclaimed. "Murmuring is a sin in the eyes of God, along with mumbling and muttering."

One after another the peasants stood in front of the jumbo tater, attempting to yank the sword out. As in years prior, each contestant failed but was at least given a stale carrot as a parting gift. It looked like the sword would remain where it had sat lodged for the last 200 years.

Suddenly, from out of the group Merlot the Magician staggered forward. He smiled as he held up his arms. "There is one more," finishing the sentence with a bubbly burp. Then, stepping out from under the great magician's robe, stood a timid, young boy. It was Artie from the Forest of Whitaker. With both tiny hands on the handle of Exotica, the small boy stood trembling in front of the skeptical townspeople, sporting smirks on their faces as if they were viewing a court jester preparing himself for the afternoon's amusement.

The steady downfall of rain pelted Artie's face as he stood there shaking doing his best to ignore the jeers of the peasant folk anxious to witness the sideshow of buffoonery. Hoping to get it over with quickly, little Artie swallowed hard and then, with all his might, pulled on the sword. Nothing moved. To save face, he tried again until one of his hands slipped off, and he fell back on his tiny bum. The mocking and laughter told him to end his feeble attempts of unlodging a sword cemented in time. With his head held low, he began to shuffle away. Merlot's hand fell sternly on Artie's shoulder as he turned him around back towards the sword. The youngster knew that he had to try one more time, fearing the old wizard would vomit on him again as he had done so many times before.

This time Artie gripped the sword tightly then planted his feet on the giant potato. Strangely, he felt a sense of courage. He looked at Merlot who radiated an all-knowing smile. And just as the boy pulled on the sword, the sky opened with a flash of lightning and a burst of thunder. It startled the people, causing them to cover their heads and fall to the ground. When they looked up, the rain had stopped falling, and a young little Artie stood before them, holding the sword Exotica high above his head. A loud cheer reverberated throughout the countryside and, thus, a new king emerged.

Twenty years passed, and Artie had settled into his destiny as king and built a promising kingdom known as Camelrot. The fair and just ruler was beloved by his people, who were well fed and protected.

On a May day an anxious King Artie paced the castle floor, gnawing on a long baguette, peering out the window every five minutes. Pelican, who is now his counsel, did his best to console him.

"Ootie" he reassured, calling him by the nickname he had coined when Artie was a boy, "They will announce her when she arrives. You're moving around like a scared fox."

King Artie set his bread on the throne, nervously running his fingers through his hair.

"What if she's pretty, Pellie? What if she doesn't find me… attractive?" he said plopping down on his throne, causing the long baguette to pop up between his legs unknowingly. Pelican's eyes bugged out as he shot a glance at the protruding loaf.

"I'm sure she'll find you quite… gifted, sire," he bashfully responded.

King Artie noticed the bread between his legs. Frustrated, he yanked it out, then broke a piece off, sloppily dunked it in porridge and then chomped on it. "Now, what if she's hideous? We will need a plan."

"Yes, yes, yes, Oootie. Good thinking," Pellie jumped with excitement.

"I know. If the girl is a sheepdog, you nimbly sneak up behind her and clunk her over the head with this bread," King Artie proposed.

"Ooo, that's a great plan. I love it, love it, love it, your majesty," Pellie concurred. "And it rhymes. Bread. Head."

Lady Chandelier sat in the carriage with her assistant, Flameer, who had a feminine way about him but kept a close watch over her none the less. On their way to Camelrot, they had journeyed from Wales for an arranged marriage in hopes of uniting the two warring countries.

"So, what do you know about this thing... the king... thing... a ling?" Lady Chandelier inquired.

"Woof! Totally hunky," Flameer said as he brushed her hair. "I saw him in the town of Cankersore about six years ago. A jousting tournament. Such a long lance... and could his buns fill a saddle."

"Really? Did he whip his horse gently or slap it?" she inquisitively asked.

"Whatever do you mean?" he questioned.

"Never you bother, pig. Your mind is in the loo," the lady snapped. "We need a signal. If I do not like him, I will cough four times. After that, you will say, 'You will have to excuse my lady; she has a tickle in her throat.' Got it?"

"You bet your frizzy curls," Flameer replied.

"Perhaps, we should practice," she said.

"Yes, yes, wonderful idea, my lady," Flameer perked up. "A little test tickle."

Lady Chandelier clears her throat then lightly coughs. Flameer seems preoccupied, checking out the countryside scenery. She coughs again, louder while her assistant continues to stare out the window. She releases a gurgled hack then elbows him. Flameer snaps out of his fog, "Oh... yes... Excuse me, your majesty, my lady has a test tickle in her throat." She wallops him in the head, "Oh, forget about it."

King Artie shifted several times in his throne as he attempted to find the best pose where he would look confident and composed, knowing any minute his bride-to-be would come through the doors. Pelican did his best to calm the nervous king by pantomiming an old Greek tragedy in which a Spartan warrior, Demitrus, dreams of someday having Zeus turn him into a mountain goat that dances for Aphrodite - the goddess of love. While Pellie pranced around, holding his fingers up by his head to act as goat horns, the doors swung open and in marched Lady Chandelier and Flameer.

The King leaped to his feet. Pushing Pellie out of the way (who was amid a goat gallop) he approached the royal princess. Artie eyes her from top to bottom. Taken by her radiant beauty, he releases a soft growl as his right leg shoots out and shakes. He subdues the limb, then murmurs "Hubbada."

"Welcome to Camelrot, my lady," Artie bowed then kissed her hand. "I so hope your ride wasn't too treacherous."

"Only through Rottsdale, Pottsdale and Scottsdale. I never cared much for the dales. I find the dales dull and dreary," she snottily responded. "Anyhoodle, I brought you a basket of fruit goodies," she politely replied, grabbing the basket from Flameer, and holding it up in front of her chest.

"You have lovely melons," the king stated.

"Thank you. And they're real," replying as she tapped the fruit. "Oh, Flamer, bring this up to the good king."

"It's Flameer," he said, rolling his eyes. With a short, exasperated sigh, he grabs the basket and prances up to the throne. After a quick dainty curtsy, he smiles, and then hands the basket to the king.

"Thank you, my good ma… person… thing." the king stammered. "I enjoy a little fruit."

"I enjoy you too, sire," Flameer blushed. King Artie pays no attention to the little assistant. He grabs two cups of wine and saunters over to Chandelier. "Some muscadine, my lady?"

"It is a bit early for cocktails but… well, it is a special occasion. I'll have a… snippet," responded as she snatches the goblet from the King's hand. "I very rarely drink. Rarely, really. I mean, really rarely, alrighty?" Flameer nods assuredly. King Artie turns his back, and Chandelier guzzles down her wine, staining the corners of her mouth.

Artie looks over at Pellie, on all fours, still caught in his pantomime world. "Chandelier. That's a unique name."

"Yes, well, my father was crushed by a ceiling fixture, three days before my birth. My good, good, good-for-nothing mother thought it appropriate to honor him and…, yada-yada- yada, and thus the name. I'm just lucky a horse didn't sit on him."

"Sad, but very interesting. So, what are your impressions of Camelrot?" the king inquired.

"I find the weather drab. The people a tad aloof. The animals, stinky. And this castle quite drafty. And was certainly not fond of the cat call from your town cobbler," she complained.

"Pay him no heed. He was hit in the head with a shekel loafer by an irate customer," Artie shrugged. "Is there anything you like about Camelrot?"

"The drapes!" Flameer spoke up. Chandelier hit the back of Flameer's head to quiet him then circled the room. "There is a subtle warm, mustiness in the air. Perhaps, Camelrot will grow on me. Perhaps even, you shall grow on me. King Artie smiles as he holds out the bottle. "More wine, my lady?"

"I couldn't. I wouldn't. I shouldn't," coyly responding then holding out her cup. "Just to the thumb." As he pours some wine, she slides her thumb to the top of the cup. Approaching Chandelier, the ruler asked, "So, tell my lady, what is the secret to your enchanting beauty?"

"Oh, you stop while you continue. You don't think I look… plumpish?" she asked.

"Most certainly not, but if you were, say chunky, I'm sure I would find that flabby mound ravishing," he said, gently touching her face. "Your skin has a radiant glow. Smooth as the bum of lamb." Chandelier stood frozen and starry-eyed. "You bahhh'd boy." The two are face-to-face, almost kissing. She smiles then daintily takes a sip of wine. It goes down the wrong pipe, causing her to begin coughing. Flameer, checking out the drapes, rushes over and jumps between the two. "Excuse us, sire. The lady has a test tickle in her throat." Flameer pulls her away as she resists him. Through her coughing bout, she hoarsely croaks, "No, I don't." The servant is unsure of her meaning, crouching to look in her eyes, "Do you or don't you… do?" Chandelier holds up her hand, attempting to catch a breath. She pauses, then starts coughing again. Flameer is completely baffled. "So, you do?" he probes, gently tugging on her arm.

"I don't do... have a... tickle," she says with a slight cough.

Confused, the helper stares at her trying to figure out what she wants. "So... no tickle?"

Chandelier fights not to cough, waving her hand. With her mouth closed, she stifles a cough, and her cheeks puff out. Flameer springs into action and grabs her. "We're outta here!" The testy woman pushes the little fellow over a Pelican, who is still acting like a goat, then quickly composes herself as she gracefully sips her wine. "So, tell me a little about yourself, hot stuff."

It was a lusty autumn day when King Artie married the woman of high-maintenance, Lady Chandelier from Dinglebury. With Pellie playing the part of best man and Flameer hamming it up as a bridesmaid, the royal wedding became the talk of the decade as the townsfolk were excited to finally have a queen that would provide an heir to the Camelrot kingdom. The reception included the peasants and the nobles, and wine and ale flowed freely throughout the night. The new queen stumbled around, flirting with every gentlemen guest she could find that could tolerate the slurred stories of her worldly travels to lands where sheiks rode on camels, slanted-eyed people ate with sticks and dark-skinned villagers made clicking noises when they talked. The king began to have second thoughts thinking he had wed himself to genuine booze hag who loved attention but soon chalked it up to an innocent evening of celebration.

Camelrot had enjoyed almost twenty years of peace and prosperity under the reign of King Artie, but the territories in the north had not been so fortunate. Over time, the insidious Duke of Wayne had been ransacking, pillaging and snatching up land from terrified villagers.

"The winds of tyranny have set Camelrot in its sights," Merlot informed Artie as they walked along the hill of Jonah. "The Duke will not be content until all that is and all that shall be is under his rule."

"The Duke has been a wart on the nose of England since I was a boy," Artie continued. "And nobody likes a hideous lump of scabby flesh. But how, oh tell me how, great Merlot, how can I deal such a festering wart?"

Merlot bent down and picked up a pebble. He dropped it in the river, causing ripples to swell outwards. Through the tiny waves, a vision could be seen on the glassy water; a sizeable triangular table in the center of the King's planning chambers and around it sat a variety of recognizable knights who were dutifully serving their ruler. Their right hands were on the bible as they chanted a Latin oath, stating their undying allegiance to King Artie. Next to the holy book was the skull of Saint Augustine, who was thought to encompass the four virtues of Justice, Prudence, Temperance, and Fortitude.

As the hazy image faded, Merlot tossed another pebble into the water that brought a new vision. It showed King Artie standing in the garden next to Queen Chandelier and kneeling before them was a muscular man with his head bowed, sporting a tiny, feather-like, Frenchy mustache. In knighthood dubbing fashion, Artie touched his sword Exotica down on the warrior then placed his hand on the man's head, and Chandelier followed suit, placing her hand on top of the King's.

Just then, the sky opened, and rain began to pour down, shattering the water apparition. Puzzled, Artie began to question Merlot through the driving rain. "Who were those knights? And why were they sitting around that big wooden table? What oath were they swearing? And what about the man who was kneeling? Who was he?" Lightning flashed accompanied by a crack of thunder that echoed in the atmosphere. Artie turned to Merlot, but he had vanished.

Later that night, king Artie tossed and turned in bed, mumbling a dirty Irish limerick as he unconsciously kicked the queen who was fortunately passed out from the goblets of wine thrown down after the glazed duck dinner. Suddenly, the king sat up in his bed, awakened by a dream.

"By Jove, I got it," he exclaimed. "A dream has revealed my purpose as a king. I can make Camelrot the greatest civilized kingdom in the world. A society built on justice and righteousness for all. From the poorest peasant to the wealthiest prince. Where all people have self-worth no matter what their status might be. My dear, would you like to hear my wonderous plans?" The queen stirred for a moment then went back to snoring as droplets of drool dribbled out of the corner of her mouth. As King Artie reached over to stroke her hair, she loudly snorted a snore, scaring him. He gently placed a pillow on her head then went back to sleep.

Upon rising bright and early in the afternoon, the king ordered a large triangular table built. He then brought in the fittest and toughest men in the country and trained them as great fighters with a sword and lance. Later, he dubbed them all knights. Gathering them around the table, he began to explain his grand vision for Camelrot.

"Congratulations, my brave knights. You have proved yourself worthy on the field of battle. You are my chosen ones who will fight evil and venture out into the world on noble quests."

"Quests?" inquired Sir Cumcise. "What kind of quests?"

"Good question, Sir Cumcise," the king answered. "These quests will consist of helping the poor, sleighing dragons, saving a damsel from a tyrant and most importantly... finding the Holy Grail." The knights excitedly began to bark like dogs and pound the table with their hands. Then, Sir Render stood up and addressed the king. "Hold on, your majesty. These quests, well, they seem like a, well, a lot of work."

"Yeah. Can't we hang around the castle and do other stuff?" added Sir Cumference.

"Like what stuff?" asked the annoyed king.

"I don't know. Sleep," responded Sir Render. The knights agree loudly with each other.

"Do any of you know what a great knight is?" King Artie probed.

"Yeah! A bottle of wine and two wenches!" bellowed Sir Prise. The knights roared with laughter as they reached over and high-fived Sir Prise.

"A great night. I get it," the king nodded. "Listen, my courageous knights, we have a calling. A calling to find the Holy Grail. With this relic, the people of England will have a sign from God to unite under one banner. They will no longer be under the tyranny of the Duke of Wayne. We will be a bright beacon on a hill. We shall bring justice into the world. To right the wrongs. Help the feeble peasant who has had his shoes stolen off his feet."

"Couldn't he just buy a new pair? Dragon hide wing-tips are in," exclaimed Sir Real.

"I think you're all missing the point, my foolish knights," the king stated with a defeated exhale.

"The king is right," a voice resounded from the back of the room. Everyone turned around to see a young, cocky, muscular man posing with his chin up and his hands on his hips. His small, pencil hair-lip wavered as he spoke, "We were all born with a great gift. A gift to make this world a better world. We are the chosen ones. Our minds must be clear, our hearts pure and our souls cleansed."

"And to whom do we owe this honor of gracing ourselves with thy presence?" asked the king.

"The name is Dancelot." As soon as he said his name, he did a twirl, followed by a two-step shuffle. He finished with a quick soft-shoe routine then held out his arms for some adulation. The knights clapped, nodding their heads in awe.

"Dancelot, I have seen a vision of you that foretold of your coming," the king beamed. "Camelrot welcomes such a brave, nimble knight with a cute, tiny mustache."

Dancelot himself had received a prophetic message while in his summer cottage in southern France. He was approached on the street by a natty-haired, bug-eyed hag, telling him he must make haste and travel to the kingdom of Camelrot to serve a mighty king. At first, he didn't believe her and tried to distract the old woman by waltzing with her. Wishing not to be fondled or groped, she slapped the brash man, causing him to whimper, then sternly sneered "Eee gads, get your derriere over there now, you cowardly petite tulip."

Dancelot prided himself on righteousness, purity, and living a healthy lifestyle of cheese, vegetables, tofu, and hours of physical training. The other knights despised him for his arrogance and snotty French accent that came across as degrading. Not only was he disliked by the Triangular Table knights but also by the queen who found him pompous and his cologne a bit fruity. However, the king loved Dancelot; his work ethic and, most of all, his undying loyalty towards him.

The knights trained for months, sword fighting, jousting, and daily checker matches to help their finger dexterity. One day, a messenger arrived at the court. Bent over, with his hands on his knees and completely out-of-breath, he stood before the king.

"Your majesty," he breathlessly exhaled. "I have a message."

"Where are you from, my dear boy?" asked King Artie.

"Yorkshire," the messenger responded with some wheezing.

"Ah, the pudding capital. Quite a long run," the king stated.

"It could be, sire, but I was just at the pub across the street for the last two days. It was the walk over here that killed me. I got asthma, scurvy and a little gout," he said, then dropping to one knee and singing, "And that's what it's all about."

"You're an odd messenger boy," Artie sneered as he snatched the message and began reading. "Two plump hens, six loaves of rye bread, paprika, goats' milk...,"

"That's me mum's grocery list," the boy interrupted. "The message is on the back."

King Artie grunted and rolled his eyes in frustration, "No yogurt?" He flipped the scroll over and began reading to himself. When he finished, he angrily tossed the message over his shoulder, ignoring the "Hey" blurted out by Pelican as the flying scroll bounced off his head.

"It appears the treacherous Duke of Wayne is on the move again. He has overtaken Potsdam, Rotterdang, and Hilterdarn."

"Damn. Dang. Darn," Pellie exclaimed.

"Exactly," the king barked. "And not only that, he's pillaged villages, towns, and barns and there have even been accounts of, dare I say, goat raping. We cannot have our goats in fear. Milk and cheese are necessities. Gather the knights. We leave tomorrow around sunrise-ish."

Early the next morning the knights had assembled, some on their stallions while others on oxen, donkeys, and sheepdogs due to their fear of a horse running too fast and scaring them.

Only one knight was not present, and that was Sir Rohis, who was still in bed, hungover, after a wild night of binge drinking. Dancelot, even in his silk pajamas with purple dragons, confronted the king. "Your majesty, I do not think it is right for me to remain back at the castle. You must certainly know that I am willing to fight to the last drop of your blood."

"I do, Dance," King Artie assured, patting the knight's head. "You are very loyal and always smell nice but, I cannot take the chance of leaving the queen unprotected. I know as sure as the swamp owl hoots that I can trust you."

"Hooty-hoot, sire. Hooty-hoot," Dancelot replied, with his chin up and chest out, unaware the trap door of pj's had flapped open.

That night, Queen Chandelier stood on her balcony overlooking the courtyard. Through the darkness, she secretly watched the nimble Dancelot, dressed in skimpy tights, gracefully dance through the garden, holding a broom, gliding and sliding around trees and bushes. The fluidity of movements mimics that of a London brothel dancer. Leaping on an ivy-covered wall, he continued his dance repertoire against a full moon. "And one, two, spin, look right, keep it tight, and kick, three, four, five to stay alive." The swan-like knight finished with a spin dropping into a split. With his arms up in the air, he dramatically released a heavy sigh as if awaiting applause from a non-existent audience.

Chandelier made her way down, emerging from the shadows. The rhythmic clapping of her hands startled the knight, causing him to let go a girly shriek.

"My, my, my, you got some jiggy moves there, slugger," uttered the queen. The comment made the knight nervous and uneasy. "Excusez-moi, moi lady. I thought you had retired for the evening."

"I couldn't sleep," the queen stated. "I've been having ungodly nightmares about witches and warlocks along with battling restless legs. Why were you fox-trotting in the midnight hours?"

Flustered, Dancelot looks at the broom in his hand. "I, I was... I was... I must prepare myself for battle. Dancing helps my agility. One day, it may make the difference between life or death. Rhythm is everything."

"I concur. Rhythm is good. I always thought that dance was a prelude for... romance," Chandelier affirmed.

"Yes, that's what the weak use it for," the knight retorted. "I learned to dance when I was a small boy. My mother was a renowned ballet prodigy, and my father was black." She flirtatiously walks towards him, eying him up like a golden huckleberry pie.

"I've always liked a little black in a man, especially if it's in the right place," she declared. "So, they tell me that you have never lost in a battle or a game?"

"Never. The shame would be all too shameful. I could no longer live with myself, and I don't plan on moving back in with my mother. I left that life months ago. My existence has been a longing struggle for perfection, and I have not fallen short," Dancelot assuredly replies as he hikes his leg on a nearby chair and stretches.

The queen shoots a quick gander at his crotch, responding, "Yes, short is indeed a pity," as she starts to circle him. "You're a boastful basket of poppy-cockiness. I might find that unattractive if you didn't have abs of iron and buns of steel, but I digress. What makes you think your shaved armpits don't stink like a barnyard pig? Are you so much better than everyone else?"

"I have the strength of six elephants, three hedgehogs plus two lion cubs, and the agility of a prancing fox. I also have the mineral enriched hair of grain-fed Gelding pony. Not one split end."

"My, my, my, somebody thinks his tights don't dirty," the queen snapped back.

"Why should they?" the confident knight responded. "I wash them myself. Pickle juice and cinnamon; knocks out the grease and grime, not to mention pesky grass stains. My own concoction. Thank you very much."

"Well, well, well, aren't you just the cow's meow," she jabbed.

"Excuse me, my lady," ignoring her. "I must adjourn to my chambers and polish my steel."

"Is that what you knights call it?" responding as she slurped her wine. "I've only heard it referred to as "husking the corn."

"I have no idea what you speak of, but I really must shine my hauberk," the proud knight said with a glare. The queen leaned into him, "Can you and your ego fit in the same suit of armor?"

"Of course," he replied. "It isn't as big as your... liver."

Infuriated, Chandelier tosses her drink in his face, yelling "Swine!" then quickly composes herself. "I like your style." She moves in and then playfully seduces him. "I take it you've never been in love... except with yourself. Have you not experienced the warm sensation of soft, tender lips pressing against your wet sloppy lips?"

"Of course, woman," he sniped. "I used to raise sheep."

She begins stroking his broom handle until smoke comes off it.

"Hubbada. Enough, my lady," Dancelot pushed back. "I lead a pure life. I step on such devilish feelings. They do not affect me." The queen walks her fingers up his shirt. "Then you shan't have a qualm in providing me with one meaningless dance - unless that frightens you?"

"I fear nothing," he calmly stated.

"What about male pattern baldness?" she asked.

"Hold your tongue, lady" the knight gasped then settled himself. "I'm sure the king would have no objections to an innocent waltz."

Chandelier claps her hands, and a violinist emerges on the balcony and starts playing. She takes Dancelot's hand, and they begin dancing.

"You have exquisite hands," she remarks. "Strong, yet soft, like a pile of mushy manure." The nimble knight twirls her as he responds, "I soak them every night in a bowl of warm goat's milk. It prevents chaffing."

"The word 'chaffing' turns me on," she comments, pushing her pelvis into him.

He pushes her back, "Please, my lady. No grinding. I am sure the king would not approve of such dirty dancing."

"The king," the queen huffs. "Maybe if I had the body of the Grail, he would look at me."

They both spin around. Facing each other, as if part of the dance, the couple slap opposite hands in patty-cake fashion then touch elbow to elbow, followed by a light slap to each other's face.

"The Holy Grail is an important relic," Dancelot continued. "It is said that whoever possesses the chalice will have youth and godly power."

"I don't believe in the black arts," she shrugs. "It's all pig poo."

Continuing the dance, they both squat down and duck walk, circling each other, and flapping their arms.

"My lady, please, I beg of you, watch thy potty language," snaps the knight. "You should always keep an open mind. You may be surprised." The pair stand up, placing their arms behind their backs. They touch nose-to-nose, growling at each other.

"Why do you intrigue me so?" she questioned, sizing him up. They briefly run in place, then abruptly stop. They cross their eyes and tug on each other's ears.

"Perhaps because I lead a life of perfection," he confidently states as they turn around and bump rear ends.

"And are you perfect at everything?" she asks as the music stops.

"I believe our dance has ended," Dancelot remarks as he releases her. "Unfortunately, I have surpassed my bedtime by seventeen minutes. Tomorrow, I'll have to punish myself by plucking a nose hair." He bows and kisses her hand, "Good night, my queen." He starts walking to the castle.

"It's very cool tonight," she calls out. "I'm going to slither out of this cumbersome dress, very slowly, and take a hot, wet steamy bath, naked, then slip on my see-through nighty and slink under my silk sheets. It helps me sleep like a rabbit. Nighty-night, knight."

Dancelot stops in his tracks, quivers, as he mumbles "Hubbada" then continues into the castle.

Several candles dimly light the queen's bedroom as she stands by the window in a sexy negligée. Her back is turned as her hands slowly move up and down in front of her. She releases several moans. It appears she is massaging her breasts but then turns around and is squeezing a Teddy Bear. She holds it up and asks, "Teddy, does this negligee make me look fat?" Moving over to the bed, she fluffs the pillow then gently lays the stuffed bear on it.

Suddenly, a knight, fully armored, appears at the doorway, startling Chandelier. "Who are you? What are you doing in my chambers? Get out! Get out, I say!" She leaps on the bed and seductively lays there. "Brute! I will scratch you if try and have your way with me. I'm alone here and very vulnerable. You hear me... vul-ner-able," emphatically stating as she hikes up her negligée to the top of her legs. Sir Dancelot lifts the flap of his helmet. He looks troubled and ashamed for entering her chambers. Chandelier jumps off the bed. "You monster!" she screams then quickly composes herself before sashaying over to him Flirting, she softly caresses his armored chest. "I could use a cock... tail." She starts to walk away but Dancelot grabs her, spins her around, and does his best to kiss her through the small armored flap opening. Struggling, she frees herself then slaps him across his helmet. "Get out, you beast, or I'll scream! Do you hear me? I'll scream." Dancelot begins to walk out. "Don't you dare walk out on me, you selfish pig!" Chandelier grabs him, spins the knight around then kisses him, her lips puckering through his steel hood. She suddenly pulls away, slaps him again, and shouts "Wretch!"

Later that night, the fluffy stuffed teddy bear bounces on the pillow as the sneaky couple rocks the bed. Chandelier's screams grow louder and louder. The candles flicker. The night table rattles. The mirror cracks. One last cry ends the love session. The queen's head pops up from under the covers followed by Dancelot's head, still wearing the helmet. "You weren't kidding about the screaming."

The following day King Artie and his Triangular Tabled knights returned to Camelrot. They had been successful in gaining their way into the Duke of Wayne's castle by posing as a traveling troupe of actors. Their plan was to leap off their hijacked wagon during their show and hold the Duke at knife point until he released the queen's sister. However, while performing their play on the fly, which was called "Of Monks and Men," the knights became so enwrapped in their roles that they had forgotten what they were there for. Sir Cumcise rolled into a forty-five-minute humdrum monologue while Sir Loin hammed it up singing catchy religious hymns, often making up words or whistling when his mind went blank, which it often did. He pissed off the other knights by weaseling his way into every scene, claiming he was the lead. The musical tragedy dragged on for six hours until the audience fell asleep, enabling the knights to snatch Sledge and flee. The biggest problem the knights encountered was getting the attention-starved Sir Loin off the stage. Fortunately, Sir Render was able to construct a makeshift long hook with his lance and yank the over-the-top actor off the pageant wagon.

Chandelier was elated to have her sister Sledge back safely. Dancelot had spent all afternoon preparing a feast to welcome his fellow knights. The meal was glazed ham, creamy potato scallops, buttered brussels sprouts, and chocolate mousse to top off the evening. As they all sat around the table, King Artie raised his wine glass to make a toast. "May truth and justice reign throughout the country and may the Duke of Wayne's wanker swell and fall off."

The knights clanked their glasses with silverware as they hooted and howled like owls and wolves. "Oh, and one more thing," the king continued. "I wish to thank my good, wonderful, faithful friend of all friends…, Sir Dancelot, for watching over the queen while I was gone. Now, tell me Dance, and be honest, did you two go to bed…" Caught off guard, Dancelot chokes as he spits out a brussels sprout.

"Did you two go to bed at a reasonable hour?" the king said, finishing his sentence. The French knight cleared his throat and composing himself replied, "Indeed sire. Early to bed, early to rise."

"Well stated, my noble, trustworthy knight," Artie nodded. "I'm glad to hear it. The queen can, at times, be a little bit of a nighthawk but, look at her. Is she the most beautiful woman you've ever laid…" Flustered, Dancelot spits out a mouthful of wine as beads of sweat dribbled down his forehead.

"That you ever laid eyes on?" the king added. Dancelot stopped squirming and perked up. "Oh, yes, yes. She's quite lovely. A fine catch, your majesty." The king threw down his napkin. His face turned deadly serious. "Don't play me for a fool, Dance. I know your secret. Shall I say it? Here. In front of everyone."

"It wasn't intentional, my king. I… didn't, I tried to, I was…," the French knight stammered unable to take the pressure anymore.

"Goat's milk!" King Artie blurted out.

"Excuse me, your highness," Dancelot gulped in oblivion as he dabbed his face with his purple silk hanky to stop the perspiration.

"You sneaky dog. You used goat's milk to make the chocolate mousse so rich and yummy?" the king responded, flashing an all-knowing smirk.

"Oh, yes, yes, yes, my king. I can't fool you," Dancelot quickly fired back with a sigh of relief and a nervous, hysterical laugh.

King Artie then addressed his guests, "If everyone is good and finishes their vegetables then, perhaps, after dinner, we shall partake in a game of 'Hide the Sword.'" Silver spoons clinked glasses as the knights whooped, turning to each other, beaming with excitement. Quieting them, the king carried on, "My brave knights, with the Duke on the run, we may now finally turn our efforts towards finding the most sacred relic in the entire world." Sir Render leaped to his feet, excitingly responding, "The Beowulf comic book!" Unaware, a thin, deathly-looking, pale young man, dressed in black tights and a puffy shirt, slithered in the room, lurking in the back. He steps out from the shadows.

"I believe he means the Holy Grail," uttered the pale man. A gasp reverberated from the curious dining group.

"And who might you be?" Artie questioned. "If you're the plumber you were supposed to be here at noon. The queen's bucket is in dire need of plunging and will need a good scrubbing."

"I assure you I'm not a plumber. My blood is of nobility," declared the sickly man with a dry, cocky tone.

"You look like you could use some blood," Pelican spoke up, causing the knights to roar with laughter.

"And pray tell, lad, of which nobility line do you descend from?" inquired the king.

"Why yours, sire," he stated with a smirk. The king looks amused as everyone snickers. "You have a morbid sense of humor, my dear boy. What's your name?"

"Morbid. Son of Morgan da Lay," he replied. The king's face turned to stone as he heard some eerie suspense music play. He angrily glares over at the band playing music in the corner of the room. They slowly stop playing, one instrument at a time tapering off.

"Who is this Da Lay?" the queen asked.

King Artie slumps in his chair as his mind rolls back to the past. "As a teenage boy, I spent a summer as a lifeguard at the palace of Prince Albert. I never saw much of him - he was always in the can. Poor chap battled nasty explosive diarrhea. It was best to always keep your distance from the noble boomer. Not only could he stain a pair of tights but blast a hole in his legwear the size of a red fox. Anyway, I was a simple pool boy in search of manhood..." The king recounted his childhood story and how the Lady Morgan da Lay had seduced him one sweltering day, how she deflowered him in the haystacks of the royal barn. And, how awkward he felt losing his virginity to an older woman in the presence of a team of laughing horses.

After he finished his story, Chandelier stormed out of the room, and the knights sat in disbelief. It had become evident that there would be no "Hide the Sword" game tonight.

The illegitimate son was welcomed into Camelrot, although not well liked by most. For several months business went on as usual as Artie spent much of his time trying to bond with his pansy bastard and avoid fighting with his wife about the sexcapade he had had earlier in his life.

One night, while Sir Dancelot was in his chambers muddling through a series of stretching exercises, a woman with a shawl over her head slipped into his room. The brave night grabbed a pillow and held it in front of his chest and shrieked, "Don't you touch me, or I'll scream." The woman pulled down her head covering, and he could see that it was the queen.

"My lady," he gasped. "You shouldn't be here."

"Oh, shut up. There's no time for chitchat," the queen responded while quickly undressing.

"Take me and make it rough. But do it quickly. If the king should awake and find me gone, he may grow suspicious. We must hurry if we wish to get in a spanking session."

"We mustn't," the knight exhaled. "There is already much talk and scuttlebutt and scuttle talk butt within the Camelrot walls. There are whispers of your infidelity."

"Lies! Filthy lies!" Chandelier insisted as she leaped onto the bed. "Now, drop them breeches, hot stuff."

Dancelot turns away from her and folds his arms. "I think you should leave, my queen."

My mind has been in torment since our first embrace. I cannot go on deceiving the king and tarnishing the honorable code of the knights of the Triangular Table. Oh, if you only felt the pain that pierces me, like daggers to my..." He stops in mid-sentence as he turns to find the lady seductively lying on the bed in a skimpy, sexy teddy. His head quickly shakes back-and-forth in surprise, causing his cheeks to flap as his eyes bug out and he mumbles, "Sacré bleu. Woof!" He rips off his shirt, revealing a glistening oily chest, then dives into bed with her. A minute later, Chandelier is lying in bed with a glazed look on her face, smoking a pipe.

"That was amazing. Where did you learn that last move?" the relieved knight said as he nibbled on a carrot.

"I call that the "cream puff squeeze," she casually stated. "It was taught to me by the dessert chef of Windsor. My God, did he have a nice rolling pin and pastry bag."

Suddenly, the door is kicked open. Morbid and a group of knights rushes in with drawn swords. Morbid holds his sword to Dancelot's neck who timidly pulls the covers up to his chin as he mutters "Mommy" in a high-pitched voice.

The following morning, a somber, distraught King Artie sits on his throne next to Pelican. Chandelier and Dancelot stand before him, accused of treason and adultery. A teary-eyed Dancelot sniffled then spoke up, "Your majesty, it's not what it appears. We, us, were playing a game. You jump on the bed, and one person says a letter then, the other says the name of an animal. For instance, if I said "R" you would say..."

"Rat. Lying cheating rat," Pelican bellowed from the corner.

"Pellie, please," the king solemnly stifled. "Dance you were found naked in bed with the queen who was smoking… a pipe. What does that say?"

"She doesn't like a fine cigar," the nervous knight guessed. "But sire, we were carelessly jumping about, like innocent school children, our attire became loose, and in all the pure, clean frolic our clothes must have dropped off. It could happen to anyone." The people in the court erupted in disbelief.

"Is this true, my queen?" Artie asked.

"Yes, yes, it was all quite innocent," she stated through her hung-over headache.

"I want to believe you but…" the king jumped to feet and pointed at her, "Liar! Liar! Pants on fire!"

"Sire, if I may intercede," Morbid stepped forward. "You are known throughout England as a fair and just king. Your laws, written for righting the wrongs, to be applied to everyone... including the chivalrous knights of the Triangular Table. Serve justice or chaos will certainly ensue, and Camelrot will be tainted with the smell of, shall we say, favoritism. The law is the law. And, sadly, adultery carries a sentence of death." Everyone yells "Here! Here!"

Troubled, King Artie puts his head down in his hand as he contemplates the dilemma. "Pellie, what kind of death?" Pelican snaps his fingers, calling out "The Book." Seconds later, a chubby bishop enters with a dwarf monk, who is holding a large book. Flameer, standing next to Chandelier, whispers "Must be a short story." She elbows him.

The bishop sets the book on the midget's head and opens it. He begins reading with a speech impediment that causes him to slur all his S's. "Let's see. Stealing a saddle is a stoning. Smoking in a restaurant is a slow scalding. Slandering a soldier renders six ass slappings. Whispering sacred secrets is seven scratches to the scrotum..." Flameer flinches, covering his mouth in fright as an irritated King Artie interrupts, "Oh, get to infidelity crimes!"

"Yes... certainly, sire... sir," the bishop slurred as sprayed droplets of spit into king's face. He began turning pages. "Sex, sex, sex... here it is," then reading "Whomsoever conspires to sleep in the arms of another man's wife shall be sentenced to swing from the gallows. The cheating spouse shall join him in the solemn swinging."

"Do either of you have anything to say in your defense?" the king said exasperated.

"Does anyone have any aspirin root?" Chandelier murmured.

"I'm of the queer kind! I like the boys!" Dancelot cried out.

"And I'm a dragon slayer," Flameer quipped as he powdered his nose. Panicking, Dancelot started groveling, "The queen raped me! It was all her idea! I was asleep when that, that wicked harlot attacked me."

"Something was awake," the queen remarked, causing Flameer to giggle. The brave French knight dropped to his knees, pleading, "Please, don't kill me! I'll take the slapping or a spanking, yes, a light spanking for my treachery. Whatta ya say, my king, ole chum?"

King Artie and Pelican confer in a whisper, hoping to find an out for the sniveling knight. The royal leader stood up, "The law is the law is the law." The ringing words caused Dancelot to break down and cry.

While Dancelot and Chandelier were locked in a prison cell, the king brooded while slumped in a chair with a glass of brandy. Sledge did her best to lift his spirits by doing some indigenous bird calls. His mind was too foggy to even venture a guess between a finch or a sandpiper. She eventually stopped chirping and found herself massaging his neck.

"I wish there was a choice. But the law is the law is the law. If I could save their lives, I would," the king sighed. "But, my loyal knights would certainly overthrow me, and Morbid would take the throne. My hands are tied."

"I've spent the last three days in the royal library," Sledge commented.

"Very good, Sledge," Artie encouraged. "Children today don't realize how important reading is. If only we could get them to stop running around and exercising. Sickening."

"I came across this book," she mentioned, handing him a book. The king began reading, 'Rules and Regulations of a Shiny Knight.' Ah yes, this book was written over two hundred years ago by the righteous counsel of King Pinn. I got it from Merlot for a winter solstice present. He used to rest his drink on it." Sledge, looking for a passage, leans over and begins turning the pages. King Artie smells her hair. His eyes cross because of the flowery fragrance. "Gee, your hair smells terrific." She blushed, "Thank you, I just washed it last month. Look, look here. The book says here, in Chapter Seven, titled 'When Knight Falls,' 'Any knight accused of any naughty crime may have their sentence eradicated if he completes a given quest handed down by the king.' The king leaped up, his head hitting Sledge's chin, "My God. It's a brilliant idea." He excitedly hugged her. "You're a genius, Sledge," he yelped, finding himself looking deep in her eyes. "A beautiful, soft, luscious genius." The two can't help but embrace in a juicy, passionate kiss. She quickly pulls away, "No." He pulls her close, "Yes." He kisses her then he pulls away, "No." "Yes," she whispers, grabbing, and kisses him. After a brief ravish, Sledge stops, "Oh my God goodness, what about Chandelier?"

"Oh please, Sledge, I find your identical twin sister ugly and repulsive."

She shoots him a look of confusion, shrugs, then goes back to kissing the king.

Rather than sentence to death the two backstabbers he had come to love, the king used the loophole in the knight's handbook to spare their lives by sending them on a quest to find the Holy Grail.

The following day, King Artie wished the treasonous pair luck but specified they had only forty-eight hours to find the scared cup. "So, it is said, and so it is done. Are there any questions?"

"There's no way we can just order one… perhaps from the town of Woolworth?" Chandelier inquired.

Dancelot and Chandelier rode out of Camelrot and made it as far as the next town over. They found themselves in a pub trying to decide their best course of action in searching for the grail.

"Where should we start?" Dancelot asked.

"How should I know? You're the knight," she snapped. "I'm hungry. I want some bread-n-ale."

"We don't have much time. Why didn't you eat before we left?" he said, rolling his eyes.

"I wasn't hungry then," she fired back.

"Yeah, I'm sure those Bloody Mary's filled you up," he intimated.

"Oh, that's right, you're mister high and mighty," she huffed. "I'll tell ya what, the next time I have an adulterous affair; it'll be with a knight who can go all night."

"Yeah, well, you don't make it easy, woman. That raunchy booze breath could start the windmill on an old Dutch painting."

The pair spent the afternoon bickering and trading insults. They tolerated each other by throwing down pints of beer. By the end of the day, they were too drunk and tired to do anything. But they were now apologizing to each other and decided to get a room at the inn. The intoxicated couple soon became frisky and romantic with each other but,

Dancelot, because of too much alcohol, couldn't perform. He did his best to coax his member back to life with baby talk and shameless begging. The queen grew weary and frustrated, falling asleep on his chest. Sometime in the night, she vomited on him, and he moved to the floor.

The next morning the two awoke with splitting headaches. Right away, the blame game started, and the pair began fighting again. Dancelot had accidentally put on Chandelier's silken underlinen after arising in a mental fog. The hungover knight stood there in the puffy, frizzled garment, sniveling, "Well, how was I supposed to know?" But she didn't trust him. Down deep, her instincts told her he knew fully well what he did, and it was no accident.

With only hours left to find the grail, they knew it wouldn't be long before the king would send out the Triangular Knights to hunt them down. There was nowhere they could run and be safe. The adulterers decided that it might be best to return to Camelrot and put themselves at the mercy of the king. As they were preparing to check out of the inn, Chandelier came up with a brilliant idea. She would reveal it to Dancelot on the ride home but, before leaving town, she insisted they stop by the pub to get a little hair of the dog that bit her so she could cope with the journey back and Dancelot's god-awful singing with that irritating French accent.

King Artie sat on his throne, his eyes beaming as he examined the wooden cup in his hands. He couldn't help but feel skeptical. "Where did you find it?"

"In Glastonbury," Chandelier tossed out.

"In a church," Dancelot added.

"Actually, in a catacomb, under the church," she mentioned, making a cocktail.

"It looks so humdrum," the king commented.

"Yes, well, our Lord was a simple, ordinary carpenter so one would assume he would use a boring, common vessel," Dance stammered.

"Yes, I guess that stands to reason," Artie thoughtfully surmised as he inspected the cup in closer detail. "What is this? Here. On the bottom of the cup appears to be the letters JA."

In Dancelot's mind, he could see the big sign outside the bar they had stopped in. It had read "The Jackass Pub." Dancelot leaned over and quickly looked at it. "Hmmmmm, that is interesting."

"Oh, it's probably just a few dings or scratches. It is old," the queen chimed in. "Are we done here?"

"I know what that is," Pellie spoke up. He raced over from across the room to examine the cup. Upon further inspection, he looked up a Dancelot, staring deep in his eyes. "You son-of-a-bitch. You little son-of-a-bitch." Dancelot began to tremble in his curled booty shoes. "I can explain everything. It's not what it seems. Now let's try to be adults here." He held up his hands to calm the room, took a deep breath then promptly pointed to the queen as he screamed, "It was her fault! It was all her idea! Please, don't kill me! I beg of you!" Pellie approached him. He held out his arms, appearing ready to choke the knight as Dancelot cowered. Suddenly, the old man wrapped his arms around the scared chap and hugged him as he lifted him off the ground and twirled around. "You son-of-a-bitch! You did it!"

"What in God's name are you talking about, Pellie?" the king asked.

"Legend has it that the Holy Grail was brought over to this country by none other than Joseph of Arimathea," Pelican put forth.

"The one responsible for the burying of the Christ," King Artie augmented. "Thus, the inscribed initials JA."

"Precisely. It simply must be the long-sought Holy Grail," Pellie concurred. He picked Dancelot up again, spinning him around like a rag doll as the knight gave a nervous laugh of relief.

The king rose then spoke in a loud, reverberating voice, "I decree the death sentences for Queen Chandelier and Sir Dancelot abolished for according to the law once a quest, chosen by the ruler, has been achieved the prior sentence becomes null and void."

"Booyah!" Dancelot exclaimed.

"It is a grave mistake," a voice called out from the back of the room. Everyone gasped as the court turned around to find Morbid casually leaning against a pillar. "You see, my dear king, by allowing treachery and treason to go unpunished you open the door to an unlawful, chaotic Camelrot and a house divided certainly cannot stand. I won't have that in my kingdom."

"My dear boy, perhaps you have been asleep in the coffin too long today or playing in the garden and over did your pale skin with some fresh sunlight and have become, shall we say, a bit delusional." Everyone breaks out laughing until the king continues, "Need I remind you, my deathly chap, that this is and always will be my kingdom. A kingdom that abides by my rules."

Morbid arrogantly paces around. "Can we be sure that is indeed the true Holy Grail? Perhaps it is just a cheap ale mug from Godfrey Gout's Tavern?"

"Hogwash!" Pellie cried. "Mr. Gout closed his tavern years ago for religious reasons regarding serving alcohol. It's now a dry, respectable brothel."

Alone, in the center of the room on a stand, sat the Holy Grail. Circling it was Morbid, Dancelot, Chandelier, Pelican, Sledge and a hideous, wrinkled old maidservant, Hildegard. King Artie, holding a wine bottle, approaches the relic. "This cup was touched by none other than God himself. When lifted towards the heavens, it was promised to bring new life and that whosoever drinketh from thy Grail will rejuvenate back to their youthful days." He slowly pours some wine into the cup. Chandelier makes a move towards the wine but Dancelot holds her back.

"I think we've toyed around enough here. No one knows where the Grail is, if such a thing exists," Morbid insisted. "Enough with the games. These two must die and you, my dear father, must abdicate since you have demonstrated you are unfit to rule."

"Hildy, could I borrow you for one brief, shining moment?" the king pleasantly asked.

The old woman flashed a toothless smile accompanied by an awkward curtsy. The king gave an agonizing double-take as he looked at her repellant worn face. "Ouffta," he mumbled to himself as he held up the Grail in front of her, using the cup to block her face.

"For me, sir?" Millie inquired in a cutesy voice.

"Yes, yes. Please, partake and quickly," he said, avoiding eye contact. She bashfully giggles then guzzles the drink down, capping it off with a booming, hoarse rolling burp that lasted several excruciating seconds. "Very good hooch it is, your majesty."

"Just as I thought," Morbid roared. "A cauldron of scolding oil on this woman's head might help a little, but this, this is all a royal scam.

Insanity has stricken the king, and he is unworthy to rule. I motion that he be removed from the throne and... and..." Morbid looks at the stunned, aghast faces of the onlookers peering behind him. He slowly turns around to see the old maid magically metamorphosing into a young, gorgeous woman with long, flowing hair. Every guy's mouth in the room drops open.

Chandelier leans over to Dancelot and murmurs, "What the hell did you put in that thing?"

Dancelot whispers in her ear, "Eight thimbles of badger urine, some sheep blood, ginger, nutmeg and two pinches of saffron. A concoction once revealed to me by Thelonious, a recluse monk who dwelled in the forest of Gump along the banks of Tyra. Good stuff, huh? I'm ninety-six years old."

"Save me a snoot," Chandelier called out.

Morbid grabs the Grail, examining it. "My God, it's real."

"Yes," King Artie stated. "And with the holy goblet, I can unite all the kingdoms in the world under the righteous and godly laws of Camelrot. Where every human being is treated fairly with kindness and compassion."

Morbid grabs the king's sword, holding it to his neck. "Or, even better. I rule all the kingdoms of the world, and people treated like the pigs that they are. The Grail, please."

"Scoundrel!" Pelican's shaky voice quivered.

Chandelier moves over to Morbid and rubs his arm. "I've always liked you."

"My foolish child," snickered the king. "You think you can just waltz out of here with the Grail?"

"He knows nothing about waltzing," Dancelot chimed in.

"Oh, give me some credit," Morbid laughed. "You think I would take the Grail and leave? Oh no, my jester friends, the Holy Grail stays here with me in my kingdom."

"Camelrot is King Artie's kingdom! It's all of ours," Sledge reminded as she exclaimed. "We are family!"

"Well put, Sister Sledge," Artie nodded. "If you haven't noticed, my pesky bastard child, you're well out-numbered. There will be no kingdom for you and very doubtful you'll get dessert tonight. You're a selfish, bad boy with poor manners. Now, if you put down the sword, I'll give you a light punishment; some community service; cleaning up the mucky horse doo-doo in the royal stables and scrubbing the stained piss buckets."

"My days of scrubbing urine containers are over. I'm through with tinkle. It's taken me three years to get the pee-pee smell out from under my nails," Morbid sneered through his gritted teeth. "This kingdom is mine, and I'm going to take what's rightfully mine."

"Ha! You and what army?" Pelican jeered, inciting everyone around him to laugh at the pale arrogant fool.

"Funny you should ask," the boy heir grinned. "Why, the Duke of Wayne's army."

Suddenly, the doors burst opened as a group of knights piled in, wearing their black suits of armor, led by the Duke. "Well hello, pilgrims. I'm not gonna hurt ya. I'm not gonna hurt ya… like hell, I'm not."

"I sincerely hope you all don't mind dying?" Morbid mocked with his devious smirk.

Dancelot stepped forward with his chest out, "We would love it." Morbid shrugs, "Well, then… you're first."

Dancelot shrieks and then runs behind Pelican to hide. Morbid snatches the sword Exotica off of the table and tries to run it through the trembling, unarmed knight. The weapon, as if electrically charged, sparks, then flies out of his hand and onto the ground. It magically slides across the floor to King Artie who swiftly picks it up.

"Ha-ha. The sword's only use is for good, my little tulip," King Artie said in a sing-song tone.

"Well played," Morbid nodded. "I see I have no choice but to have the Duke kill you."

"It'll be my pleasure, missy," replied the Duke.

"Would you please stop calling me that? It's Morbid." he sighed.

Thinking quickly, Pelican tosses Dancelot a sword. Catching it, he stands frozen, unsure of what to do.

"Oh my God, his shaved legs are dead. His rhythm. He's lost it," Chandelier cried then leaned over to Pellie, "Does this fight come with an open bar?"

The Duke takes a stab at Dancelot, but he stylishly leaps onto the Triangular Table. The angry butcher of Wayne wildly swings his sword, trying to cut down the graceful knight. Sir Homey runs over and mouths down a rap beat. Dancelot starts to feel the beat, becoming more agile.

"By Jove, I think he's got it!" Pellie beams then and runs over to the window where he begins clucking like a chicken to the street below. It was signal he once set up as a distress call to summon the knights. Pellie, knowing he was too old to be a knight, wanted to bring something to the table.

Dancelot continued to dance, with remarkable skill, as he tussled with the Duke. The hand-to-hand combat forced the knight into a tap-dancing routine. With every shuffle-ball-change, he dodged the on-coming flailing weapon, traveling across the floor with what would become known in the dance circles as the "triple buffalo" maneuver. Pelican and Sledge could only sit back in awe and applaud the performance. During brief respites in action, Dancelot couldn't help but take a quick moment to bow.

Suddenly, the knights of the Triangular Table burst into the room. "We heard the distress clucks," Sir Loin cried. The knights of the Triangular Table charged the black knights, and a battle ensued. Morbid made his move towards the unarmed king. He faced off with his father. "I hope you won't mind a sword through your heart?"

"Not at all, my bratty little brat. As long as you won't mind a foot to your balls," King Artie responded with a kick to the groin.

"You're dead meat," Morbid squealed in a high-pitched voiced, giving the king time to grab a sword. In no time, the pair were swashbuckling.

Dancelot found himself cornered by a group of black knights. Out of options, he tried a little soft shoe number, throwing out a few wavy jazz hands to distract them. It was futile. To them, dancing was for princesses and queens. The Duke parted his soldiers, making his way up to the nervous knight, then held a sword to his scrawny, jasmine scented neck. Trembling, Sir Dancelot held up his hand and squeaked "Time out?"

"More like... time's up, my frightened French poodle," the Duke grinned as he attempted to jam his sword into Dancelot. The nimble knight dropped into a split, finding his face eye-level and directly in front of the Duke's groin. Seizing the moment and the sack, he reached out, grabbing a handful of testicles. "I'm having a ball. And you?" Dancelot quipped.

"Cheater," the Duke wailed in a high-pitched tone then swung his sword at his enemy's head causing Dancelot to duck and scamper away like a skittish mouse. On the other side of the room, Sledge grabbed cantaloupes from the buffet tables and fired them at the black knights, hitting several of them in the head and knocking them out.

The battle raged as Morbid and the king continued fighting. "I didn't think "your kind" could fight," the king baited.

"My kind? Are you implying I'm a peasant girl?" the clumsy bastard retorted. Morbid then pointed to the ceiling, "Look, there's... something." Foolishly, King Artie looked up, and Morbid knocked the sword out of his hand, throwing out a cocky "Ha-ha" as if a cherry on top.

"I will die before I relinquish my throne," the defenseless king hissed.

"You must dabble in the black arts cause you read my mind," the ruthless Morbid sneered as he reared back and swung his sword at the king's head. The weapon cut through the air but wound up hitting nothing because, magically, Artie had vanished, and instead, sat a plump beaver on the ground with the king's clothes on.

"What the devil?" Morbid wondered as he wound up again to kill the beaver. Suddenly, the beaver changed into a chimpanzee, also wearing the king's clothes. They are face-to-face like pro wrestlers. The monkey bops him on the head then flashes his teeth.

"You're trying my patience, monkey man," Morbid said festered. The chimp screeched as it jumped up-and-down. The villain, at wit's end, raised his sword to finish off the hairy king who was now covering his head with his arms. Before Morbid could chop downwards, he is blindsided in the head by a melon, dropping him like a drawbridge. Sledge shoots the chimp a thumbs-up. The Duke had cornered Dancelot. After knocking his weapon out of his hand, the Duke was now pushing the tip of the sword into Dancelot's neck. "How would you like to die, mister?"

"Is "old age" a choice?" the French knight responded in a Woody Allen manner.

"I'm not gonna kill ya. I'm not gonna kill ya. Like hell, I'm not," the Duke chimed with his John Wayne demeanor, preparing to strike him. Pellie, realizing the dire situation, raced across the room like a bloodthirsty wolf and jumped on the Duke's back, locking his arms around his neck. Unsure of what to do next, he bit the Duke's shoulder, leaving a bloody bruise along with a blackened, rotted tooth lodged in his skin. The stabbing pain sent the Duke into a frenzy; in a suffocating panic, he reared up and screamed, bucking about like an unbroken stallion. The old man hung on for dear life, digging his rough, unshaven, whiskered cheek into the enemy's neck while drooling down his back and making odd moaning noises. The Duke pushed back, slamming the feeble pest against the wall. And still, a persistent Pellie held on. Feeling claustrophobic, the Duke struggled harder to free himself, knocking poor Pellie into doors, over chairs and plowing into stone pillars. And yet, the pesky king's counselor refused to let go. The Duke could hear a tenacious Pellie snorting in his ear, like a wild forest boar, as rancid salvia dribbled down his back like sulfuric lava from Mount Vesuvius. The wrinkled old man's rank, putrid breath gushed over his neck as if a dam had burst that once held back a raging river of raw sewage. The rotten stench seeped into his nose, singeing his nostrils. Feeling like his face was melting off, the desperate Duke flipped the stubborn, elderly attacker onto the buffet table, sending scones and bangers flying. Everyone in the room was amazed to see Pellie's meat hooks still clinging around his foe's neck as they watched the Duke pounding the old geezer into a vat of figgy pudding. They had no idea that it was Pellie's foul breath that had sent the vat of figgy pudding of Wayne into a tizzy and summoned the beast within him.

Pellie refused to relinquish his grip. After another ten minutes of trying to get the dragon-breathed monster off his back, the exhausted Duke had had enough. Unable to carry the stinky wrinkled baggage any longer, he collapsed in a heap. With scant signs of life, he began clawing his way across the floor to escape the inexorable beast with the putrid mouth. Pellie quickly scampered over to the fleeing coward and pounced on top of him. Manhandling his scrawny foe, he rolled him over like a game, easy-going, subservient, paid-for wench. The foggy-headed Duke looked up only to notice the fierce, aged tiger inches from his face.

"Scurrying off, are we, ya little rat?" he hissed in the gagging man's ear. Pellie stared into his enemy's eyes as if to say "gotcha" while heavily panting through his toothless moldy mouth. The stinging, filthy aroma refused to dissipate, lingering in the dampness. Wheezing, the Duke struggled for words as the wretched halitosis stench blasted on his face like a stale, musty coal cloud that had drifted up from the intestines of Hell.

"You're a feisty son-of-a-bitch," Pellie huffed as spit droplets spewed out of his mouth, falling on the Duke's cheek, causing a painful burning sensation on his skin. The weary butcher of Wayne cried out "sweet mother of God" that was followed by a gurgling noise in the back of his throat as he desperately gasped for the slightest morsel of fresh air. Pellie, as he did with all of his subdued combatants, leaned over and bit his opponent's nose, gnawing on the facial appendage for a long minute as he growled like a rabid badger. The Duke felt no pain as the pungent pong seem to paralyze his face. Within seconds, his eyes crossed while his head dithered in a dizzying fog. There were several reflexive gags, and then, as a final act, he vomited on Pellie's shirt. His pupils rolled back just before he passed out.

The fight was long and brutal, but the king's right-hand man had prevailed. Ironically, it looked like old Pellie had enjoyed the tussle. Sitting on the Duke's chest, the elderly warrior pounded his own chest and released a howl that sent a rancid scent throughout the room. Several nearby knight's knees wobbled as they braced themselves on a nearby pillar, pinching their noses, hoping to avoid the foul, manure-like odor that hung heavily in the air. The old trooper groaned as he struggled to get back on his feet. He found himself straddling his adversary, his sagging, flabby bum inches from the Duke's pale, comatose head as he teetered back-and-forth. Perhaps, due to his aged muscles, Pellie let loose a rumbling burst of flatulence that seemed to shake the castle walls. The Duke's body jerked, in an uncontrollable, reflexive tremor then quickly became lifeless as if to welcome death. Pellie would later claim that the only reason he had passed gas was to ensure the Duke had passed on. Whether the gas release was accidental or purposely discharged, the Duke's days of ravishing and pillaging were over. (A few months later Pellie would discover his pants soiled concluding it most likely occurred during the brawl.)

That day, the knights of the Triangular Table fought bravely, beating back the Duke's army of thugs. The Camelrot kingdom spared as well as the lives of the unfaithful Dancelot and Chandelier, as long she agreed to an amicable divorce. Over the years, the ex-queen enjoyed the company of all the Triangular Table knights, finally settling on Sir Cumcise. Morbid thrown into the dungeon, later, became the plumber in charge all the royal loos. Pelican was knighted and given free dental work, after which, he found people tended to talk to him longer.

Merlot would visit Artie from time to time to check on him and ensure all was well. In his old eyes, he still saw his young protégé sitting on a stump, pestering him with questions like, "Why are people mean?" Merlot would smile and pat him on the head, "Evil is part of the world, my boy. But, fear not, you will be the once and future king that will slay this beast." The king always knew when his sorcerer was close. The wind would softly blow, leaves would rustle, and a bottle being uncorked could be heard - just as he knew Merlot had saved him on the day of the great battle by changing him from a beaver to a chimp.

King Artie unified England and went on to live a long happy life with his new queen Sledge and their two kids - one of which had buck teeth and the other was overly hairy and loved bananas. Every night he drank from the Grail believing he would live forever. Perhaps it was indeed the true Grail because the legend of King Artie has never been forgotten.

AMERICA IN A NUTSHELL

In 1620, a group of religious folks known as Puritans had conflicting interests with the church and state of England, so they decided to leave a life of fish and chips, and bangers, jump on a ship called the Mayflower, and head to a brand-new world. They labeled themselves as Pilgrims (mainly because it didn't sound so high and mighty as Puritans) and made it easier for them to make friends. Once arriving in the new world, they built log cabins and invited the Native Americans over for some turkey, creamed corn and a side of cranberry sauce. Because there was no stuffing, the Indians rebelled by mocking the Pilgrims who had joined in a rain dance ceremony and claiming not only that the white man can't dance but that they looked silly in those puffy shirts and knickers. This behavior embarrassed and infuriated the settlers. They plotted to slowly steal the Native's country by duping them with a bogus slogan; "Go west young Squatting Bear, go west."

    Colonies of convicts began to fill this vast new land. King George was quite content to ship the abundant bread-stealing scum out of their homeland. He rewarded them by implementing taxes on everything. The people angrily stamped their feet getting taxed for that as well. (The Stamp Act) This action teed off the subjects, so they threw a party in the Boston Harbor. Things got out of hand; intoxicated men wearing lantern shades on their heads began chucking creates of Earl Grey overboard. Within a few months, Paul Revere was riding through towns yelling, "The British are coming!" while townspeople screamed back, "Shut up, ye ole drunk. I'm sleeping!"

A group of people soon formed a Continental Congress. One of the elite members, George Washington, would often reminisce of picking cherries off a tree in his front yard. "One day, I finally chopped it down so that I could make a set of wooden teeth." Everyone would roll their eyes knowing old George's mouth was all bark with no bite. Later his wife's lips would become infected as a result of splinters. Ben Franklin, an astute man with brilliant ideas, wasn't taken very seriously. Every time he offered a suggestion, he was told to go fly a kite. He did and what he found shocked him. The states united, and Thomas Jefferson was able to unify the clan by drafting a Declaration of Independence. The declaration essentially told King George that they were fed up with his taxes and his attitude. More importantly, they were tired of having to wear silly wigs.

Soon British soldiers were sent to stifle the revolting colonists. A shot was heard around the world coming from Lexington. They first captured New York City. (Broadway had not been born yet, so we gladly forfeited the Big Apple.) Trenton and Princeton followed. Washington organized a small band of troops and crossed over the Delaware River. There were no taverns open so, cold and pissed off, they attacked the redcoats. After that, Washington treated the troops to a winter vacation at Valley Forge where his soldiers could bask in the snow and nibble on their boots to survive. (Talk about putting your foot in your mouth.)

The American Revolution raged on. Benedict Arnold fought bravely for the States until they named an egg dish after him, then he fought valiantly for England. The French soon joined in to lend the "colonist pigs" a helping hand. (We would return the favor by saving their derrieres when the great wars rolled around.)

After the war, by the way, we won; the thirteen colonies united and became states. Betsy Ross got into the sherry while knitting her husband Pete a quilt. Upon completion, the damn blanket looked like a flag, so she donated it to the new-found government. Washington was elected the first president, and a government established. We, the people, were happy that corruption could now begin in an organized fashion. Taxes would continue but, at least, they were our taxes.

Sometime in 1812, the Brits would return for another round of fighting. We were like, bring it on; we're a bad-ass country now. Francis Scott Key, who sang off-key, composed a song during the battle at Fort McHenry. This occasion was the only time in history that did not include peanuts, popcorn, and ice-cold beer at the end of the patriotic ditty.

The Louisiana Purchase obtained from Napoléon for a case of our best Chardonnay, some cotton balls and three barrels of cheese was the greatest land deal in history, and it was all about location, location, location. In no time, towns became cities and people begin to move into the middle of the country and wearing a dead raccoon on your head was all the rage. The stagecoach became the main form of transportation, and it made an unbelievable twelve miles a day. The coach was vulnerable to Indian attacks, hold-ups, and the fresh smell of horse manure.

In the 1850s a man named Willy Oltimer yelled: "There's gold in dem dere hills!" Nobody could find "dem dere hills" on the map, so they just headed West. A mad rush ensued to California. (During the onslaught, Willy got trampled to death.) Miners set up camp in the mountains and panned for nuggets. Jack asses would help haul loads into town where the gold got weighed and sold. Then the other jack asses would squander their money in local saloons. Most importantly, this brought people to the west coast where they could later make a good living as actors and singers while eating kale and Tofu.

In the South, slavery existed on the cotton plantations. This institution infuriated the North because it was morally wrong, but Rhett Butler didn't give a damn. Southerners could no longer tolerate the North's monopoly on industry nor their funny accents like "pak your cart," so they succeeded from the Union. To save the devastation of the Q-Tip market the North had to draw the line, the Mason Dixon Line, and soon, it would be an all-out civil war.

The bloodiest battles ever fought were during the Civil War. It was blue against gray, brother against brother, cat against dog, and chowder against grits. War ravaged on for four years. The turning point occurred when the Union defeated the Confederates at Gettysburg. It was the greatest battle of the war. (The second greatest fight was when a lowly private tried to pry a booze bottle out of General Grant's hand.) Sherman marched to the sea, burned Atlanta, collected the insurance, then waltzed back. He later got diagnosed as a pyromaniac. Lincoln set the slaves free with the Emancipation Proclamation and, after the war, celebrated by catching a play. (It was a shot in the dark if he was going to enjoy it.) After annihilating the country, we thought it was best to build it back up - we reconstructed it with carpet baggers and cheap Irish labor, that was thanks to a shortage of potatoes.

The choo-choo train linked the East to the West. Rugged individuals left the big cities to start a new life in the Wild West. Many men became ranchers or farmers and would often sing "Oklahoma" show tunes while working in corn fields as high as an elephant's eye. Gunslingers with names like "Doc" and "Cody" made a living by..., slinging guns. Small wooden towns with a feed store, stables and saloons were hopping with gamblers, cowboys, and prostitutes. (Sometimes even prostitutes who dressed like cowboys.)

By the turn of the century, the automobile slowly began to replace the horse. Henry Ford assembled a line, and the horse was elated. Roosevelt, a rough rider, carried a big stick that he used to beat Teddy Bears. The Wright Brothers took a bicycle with wings to the beach and made a successful flight at Kitty Hawk. Wilbur lost his brother's luggage, so Orville decided to go into the popcorn business.

In 1914 Germany decided to take over the world because Kaiser Wilhelm did not like a roll named after him. This action provoked us to send doughboys "over there" to straighten out the misuse of baker terminology. Shells flew, and mustard and ketchup gas filled the air. Soldiers were sent home with trench foot, trench mouth, and trench coat. After Germany was defeated, all was quiet on the western front. We said a farewell to arms by the signing of The Treaty of Versailles. The treaty pretty much stated, "Hey hun, stay in your own damn country and behave yourselves." Twenty years later they would misinterpret this.

After our brave soldiers returned home, they got a party. It was called the "Roaring Twenties", and it lasted a decade. People drank hooch, danced the Charleston all night, and woke up the next morning in rumble seats. Prohibition was in, but people were too drunk to realize what it meant. Elliot Ness had a Capone to pick with the mobsters. (Yes, that's a stretch.) Women wore flappers. Men wore women. And, everyone was worn out. The dames won won voting status, so that they could get rid of the men.

The movies started talking with Jolson singing Jazz. In 1929, the stock market yelled, "The party's over!" then passed out.

Times were tough as The Great Depression occupied the 1930s. People aimlessly walked around in a dust bowl mumbling, "Brother, can you spare a dime?" You couldn't even buy time. A penny for your thoughts was out of the question. And, putting your two cents in... forget about it. Even President Roosevelt couldn't afford new tires for his wheelchair. People waited in long lines to purchase a dollar loaf. Back then, that was a lot of bread for... bread, that they dipped into their dust bowl. The radio distracted them from misery. Ozzie married Harriet. Fibber played with Molly. Andy taunted Amos while Abbott fought with Costello and only the shadow knew, along with father, who knew best.

Japan bombed Pearl Harbor while on the other side of the world a tyrant with a cute little mustache, named Hitler, decided the world economy needed a boost, so he declared war on Europe then Africa then Russia. America didn't like a bully who goose-stepped, so we declared war on him. Thanks to Rosie the Riveter and war bonds production the economy in the States exploded, and unemployment was almost as low as a German U boat. The Fuehrer was also down because our marines landed in Normandy. Patton drove his tanks to Berlin, and France gave us three berets and a statue with a torch for liberating their country. We invented the big bomb which we tested on Hiroshima. The makeup exam was on Nagasaki. The bomb got an A, and the war was over. People celebrated to Bing's bassy ba ba ba boos, Frank's soothing bar room crooning and Dean's slurring. It all became a wonderful life as Bogart insisted that Sam play it again and, before anyone knew it, the decade was gone with the wind.

The 1950s were considered happy days. You can ask the Fonz. Kids were rebelling and listening to ghastly Rock and Roll music while smoking cigarettes that had no warning labels. The jitterbug was in, and teenage boys were lubing their hair with grease from their '57 Chevys. They wore leather jackets with gang names on the back like "The Screaming Bedwetters." The girls wore bobby socks and bunny hopped to malt shops to cuddle up to jukeboxes. James Dean was a movie star and not yet a sausage. Communist suspects were rounded up and unjustly used as test subjects for Hula Hoops. This era was known as "The McCarthy Error." King MacArthur split the Koreas then returned to the Philippines to get his pipe and sunglasses that he left in the jeep. Eisenhower built a great big highway system, and people now had no excuse to prevent them from visiting relatives.

JFK became elected in the early 1960s. Marilyn Monroe jumped out of his birthday cake and into his bed. Cuba threatened to send nuclear cigars over if we continued to make fun of Fidel's beard. Young men laid down their lives for a country no one knew existed - not even the Vietnamese. Thousands protested the war and the fact that Tiny Tim was allowed on TV. Civil rights were passed out, and so was Timothy Leary. The beehive progressed to headbands and beads; the Beatles invaded America while the long-haired hippies invaded drug stores. Everything cost more than sex because sex was free. People were so strung out that they often forgot where they put their LSD. Car companies were making a killing along with Charlie Manson. This certainly was the age of Aquarius.

During the '70s, everyone was into doing their own thing - together in groups with one another. Nixon was in the office during the day, and at night he was in hotel rooms. After his impeachment, it became Watergate under the bridge. (What's another stretch?) One was the loneliest number, an Odd Couple, Three's Company, Four Tops, five Jacksons and fifty ways to leave your lover. Somehow disco music made it big. People twirled on dance floors while flashing mirror-colored lights reflected off their stiff polyester attire and their powdered noses. Talk about hitting bell bottom. (Many soldiers after seeing this demise of the country wanted to return to Vietnam.) Donny had Marie, Sonny had Cher, Starsky had Hutch and BJ had the bear. Women wore tube tops, clogs and mood rings, that changed colors every five minutes. Men just wore sideburns and moustaches while they streaked and that's the naked truth. Jimmy Carter littered the White House floors with peanut shells while his brother passed out six packs before passing out himself. We loved to watch Archie Bunker's hate. And, it wasn't unusual to hear truckers on a CB radio say, "Rubber ducky, can you get me out of this decade?"

One of the most popular politicians stepped into the Oval Office in 1981. Finally, we had a professional actor in the White House. He was shot and took one for the Gipper... again. (The would-be assassin was a man who was insanely in love with a Foster child.) Reagan was nursed back to health by chomping on a bag of jellybeans. Soon he was strong enough to invade the powerhouse country of Grenada and suppress their three troops from threatening our homeland. Ronnie told Gorbachev to tear down the ugly, graffiti-marked Berlin Wall, or he would smack the ink blot stain off of his forehead. The Cold War was over, and people were warming up to Punk rockers with pierced noses, and spiked hair with music that pierced our ears. They slam danced in the street while rubbing belly button rings with each other. Nobody cared. The economy was good, and so was greed but, most importantly, we had Brat Pack movies and Pac-Man.

The nineties gave us the internet and porno was now free. The naked breasts would eventually lead to the dotcom busts. You no longer had to go out and meet sleazy women in bars; you could now save money and do it on the computer. With internet dating, you could be anyone you wanted. Grunge music was bigger than Ross Perot's ears, and we had a president, Bubba Clinton, who liked a little sax and loved a lot of sex. Impeached, Bill had a dress that stained his legacy. He not only fought in Kosovo but in the Oval office with Hillary. Kosovo was the easier battle. Besides that, nothing happened in the nineties.

Rolling into a brand-new century, we somehow survived Y2K, and another Bush became president. He moved into the White House while everybody else bought a second and third house. Whatever people didn't have they slapped on their Visa. Other credit cards purchased more credit cards. Wall Street, paved with riches, while nobody noticed the potholes. Gas prices went up to four bucks, then our stocks went to two bucks. The market crashed like a plane into the Twin Towers. We learned that, maybe, we were too free with our freedom and that somebody out there doesn't like us - even though we're a good country. We buckled down and got serious on terrorism and banned bringing shampoo on airplanes.

The United States has come a long way as it continues to make history in the 21st century. We've been through almost everything from muskets to Facebook. We are indeed the first democratic country in world history. People have the right to speak, tweet, and sadly, watch "The Kardashians." Well, sometimes we must take the good with the bad. It's either that or fake news. As the experiment continues, who knows how much more history America has left in her but, hopefully, we will continue to be a beacon of light that illuminates hope and freedom.

FROM LITTLE PECKER TO BIG PECKER

On a small prairie clearing, a group of Indian warriors circled a raging bonfire to celebrate the start of a boy's journey into manhood. The teenage brave was known as Little Pecker, so named because at the moment of his birth the forest seemed to come alive with the ra-da-tat-tat sounds of woodpeckers announcing his entry into the world. The native child was the son of Snorting Boar and Nibbling Groundhog, both members of the Poonani tribe. As the drums in the background played a rhythmic, sultry blues beat, several Indians, dressed as wild animals circled the boy. Hooting and whooping, they hit their hands against their mouths while stomping their feet.

Suddenly, the music stopped. The heavy-set chief stood up. He was known as Strong Buffalo Breath because of his severe halitosis, most likely a result of years eating deer meat, eagle droppings, and horse dung - which was thought to make one more virile. Elk urine was almost always used to wash the delicacies down. While flies swarmed around the leader's mouth, he began to speak.

"A super-duper day is upon us. The son of Snorting Boar journeys from the valley of youth to the mountain of manhood. Tonight, he will begin the sacred rituals of making him a strong Indian warrior." The drums pounded as the tribe chugged booze and chanted, "Yi, yi, yi, yi, yo, yo, yo yo da man! As part of the initiation rites, there would be three tests given to the boy to prove himself worthy of manhood.

The first trial was to tame "The Great Kicking Mule." The elusive burro lived on the American Southwest Delta plains, east of the sun and west of the moon. The vulnerable animal had gone insane and found itself seeking tranquility in the wild. Not only had the troubled beast spent much of his life carrying mining supplies but also carrying a secret, unspeakable past. After being sold to a gold miner named Slappy, the old timer began to groom the mule. It started with sugar cubes and extra bales of hay but quickly progressed into something more sinister. Slappy wasn't just looking for gold, he was looking for a piece of ass from the ass. After months of being groped and fondled against his will by the sleazy man, the animal began having traumatic nightmares. In these disturbing dreams, he'd see the wrinkled face of the straggly bearded pervert hoovering over him, grinning like he found a sixteen-ounce gold nugget. How the young borrow hated lying down at night, knowing the deranged monster was nearby. Many times, the debauched miner would find his way into the Red Eye whiskey. After a few snoots, his personality would change from a happy, go-lucky gold seeker who would laugh, jump up and click his heels together to that of a decadent sick-o who hid under the darkness taking liberties with a scared beast of burden. The edgy mule despised the lingering foul body-odor pouring off that filthy ole timer and the sweaty dirt stench that emanated from the musty geezer. It made his tail go limp. But the worst was when the stinky shady miner curled up next to him and he'd feel that heavy hairy meat-hooked arm drop over his torso, and his tobacco chawed, stale whiskey breath huffing into his pointy ear whispering the name Catalina, who was supposedly a young, pudgy Mexican sombrero weaver he'd once had relations with. The mule shivered every time he thought about it.

Pounding, horrendous memories of the grubby frisky gold miner would all too often reverberate off the walls of his mind and throw the tormented mule into a tizzy where he would uncontrollably buck and kick in hopes of releasing the taunting demons. One night, feeling dirty, disgusted and tainted, the mule snapped. In an irrepressible rage, his mind went blank, and he kicked and stomped his slimy shameless master to a bloody pulp. After the fatal beatdown, the molested mule dragged Slappy's lifeless body to the entrance of a shaft, lit his corpse on fire, and then collapsed the whole mine in, entombing the depraved miner for eternity. Yeah, he was upset. Mules were created to carry heavy objects and not for anything else, certainly not for devilish pleasing purposes. Why couldn't the miner use some of his gold flakes to buy a sheep and leave him in peace instead of wanting a piece? Was that too much to ask? As far as the mule was concerned, come sundown, he was off the clock. Needless to say, the vile occurrences left the poor mule unsettled, unnerved and scarred for life. Whatever happened on those gloomy forbidden nights, this mule was taken it to the grave. With good reason, the skittish animal became reclusive and untrusting of all humans.

With his homemade knife and trusty bow and arrow, Little Pecker set off to confront the mule. With a beaver-skin on his head, the flat tail dangling over part of his face, he watched from a tree that looked down over a slow-moving river where the mule appeared to be in a neurotic bathing scrub down as it splashed water on itself and mumbled "I'm so dirty, so dirty."

Like a prowling bobcat, the Indian boy crawled through the tall grass as he began his approach. At one point, the mule seemed to suspect something wasn't right. If some lonely cowboy or unhinged horny miner out there had thoughts of mounting him, they had another thing coming. Those days were over and, besides, he never even received a nugget or sliver of buckwheat cake for the disturbing escapades, which was the biggest slap in the face. The four-legged creature lifted his head and sniffed the air. Sensing trouble, he kicked his legs toward the sky as if to warn any would-be trespasser. Unimpressed, Little Pecker pooh-poohed the lame warning. Nothing scared him. He reached in his buckskin sack and grabbed an arrow then loaded it into his bow.

The brave brave fired an arrow that bounced off the ass' ass. The mule released a loud groan as his neck lunged forward, flashing his mule-white teeth. He was pissed. He looked around for the perpetrator. The small native stood quietly with his arms out and one leg in the air, pretending to be a desert cactus. The mule was no fool, he knew cacti weren't indigenous to this part of the country, and if they were, they wouldn't have a beaver pelt on their head. Fired up, the mule charged Little Pecker. The young warrior jumped on a rock and pulled out his tiny knife. The crazed beast stopped in his tracks and just stared at the boy. It couldn't believe his eyes, thinking to himself that this painted toddler was going to take on the great kicking mule with just a pocket butter knife. The burro started laughing as his donkey-white teeth glistened in the sun.

To Little Pecker, this was a sign of great disrespect. He was a warrior, a courageous warrior who was now being mocked by a mule. In a fit of rage, the small native boy let out a whooping yell then leaped onto the back of the animal, intending to use the Indian wrestling skills he had acquired as a child, to subdue the monster. The uneasy feeling of this human climbing on his back brought up bitter memories - sick and disgusting thoughts of "cuddle time" with the filthy gold miner. The mule went into a psychotic tailspin, kicking and whirling like a two-year child who flew in a fit when there was no more ice cream. His head began pounding as he recalled the abusive nights by the campfire. Suddenly, disturbing visions filled his mind, and he could see the old, scruffy man's dazed eyes and half-grin standing there in his flannel long johns with the back-trapdoor flap half-buttoned, leaning over and playing a set of spoons on his knees as he sang "Oh! Susanna." The mule felt a repulsed shiver from head-to-hoof as that horsey, cackling laugh reverberated in his mind. He pictured that twinkling gold tooth protruding from that sickening, gummy mouth while he was being petted and told, "This won't hurt. All the mules do it." It was too much for the beast to bare. The abused monster, exploding, reared into a bucking tirade, throwing Little Pecker high in the air only to watch him kiss the ground.

As the enraged equine prepared to stomp the boy into the great underworld, the small brave held up his hands to calm the animal then gingerly reached into his deer pelt satchel and pulled out a peace pipe. The fidgety mule cocked his head, unsure of what it was. Very timidly, so as not to startle the restless beast, Little Pecker packed the pipe with peyote then lit it. Slowly drawing off of it, he passed it to the snorting, suspicious mule. At first, the uneasy ass nudged it away with his nose, but the child was persistent, nodding as if to say, "It's okay." Cautiously succumbing, the mule leaned over and, without taking his eyes off the boy, took a quick puff. His hind leg twitched. The boy pushed the pipe at the mule, signaling "another round." This time the animal inhaled a little more. This smoking activity continued for several hours, with each puff getting bigger and bigger. Although at times, the animal would cough, he seemed to enjoy the mind-altering substance thoroughly. Soon, the mule's eyes became glassy. It leaned back, looking up at the sky, now lost in the clouds. Out of nowhere, the furry creature began to giggle, rolling on his back as his hoofs flailed in the gentle desert breeze. Little Pecker looked at him and, he too began to join into the chuckling frenzy.

Whenever the mule became overwhelmed with troubling thoughts of being inappropriately touched, Little Pecker would fire up the pipe of peyote to settle him down. It didn't take long for the abused animal to forget his troubled past. The kicking mule was now a laid back, stoned jackass. Nothing upset him anymore. As long as he was high, fondling and groping were just bygone activities from a long-ago time. The wacky weed seemed to bring the pair close together, and soon the animal and boy became friends. Puffing pals. Smoking chums. Toker buddies.

Little Pecker rode the mule back towards the village. Still loopy, they didn't realize they had been going in circles. When it dawned on them, they stopped and blasted up a little more peyote then giggled for an hour while munching on a few tumbleweeds. Upon finally arriving home, the tribe cheered the heroic brave for taming the wild beast. That night, a great feast, known as the Pow Wowapalooza, was given to honor the new hero's step toward manhood. Little Pecker now wore a special headband with a brand-new eagle feather to signify the completion of the first leg of his journey. He had also painted his face to resemble a coyote, but he looked like a sad circus clown. Squaws gathered around the brave and tickled him with peacock tails. During this ritual, the boy was not allowed to laugh for that would be a sign of weakness. To ensure he would not fail Pecker stuffed a porcupine down his pants and whenever he felt the urge to chuckle, he'd wiggle his hips and a sharp quilt would poke him in his testicles. He'd howl like an ailing wolf with its paw caught in a snare, but he didn't laugh.

The medicine man, named Doc Hooty Owl, had whipped up a concoction of cactus juice and deer blood for Buffalo Breath so that he may converse with the great, fat spirit, known as Breakin' Wind, to reveal the next task for the boy's journey towards manhood. After several shots of the intoxicating magical brew, the chief stood up and staggered around the camp. In between his stumbling he would pet tribe members on the head and slur statements like, "I love ya, baby" and "You're da bestest" while he'd point his finger at them and wink. After a few more slugs of the doc's cocktail, Buffalo Breath pulled up a log and sat down. He raised his hands to the sky and began to chant, "Hi-yi-yi-yi, hi-yi-yi-yi, mama-say-mama-sun-o-ma-cun-sun, obla-de, obla, da, doo-rah-ditty-ditty-dum-ditty-dum… Hey ya Breakin' Wind, oh great Breakin' Wind, we call on you from the mountains beyond." A loud rumble sounded, and a shadowy figure of a bloated moose appeared in a greenish cloud, bringing with it a foul stench. "Sorry about that," the spirit exclaimed, "I had little beans and franks for lunch." The disgusted Indians groaned as they turned away, gasping for a gulp of fresh air. "Soooo, what can I do you for today?" the hefty spirit asked.

Buffalo Breath called out, "Oh great, fat spirit of the wind that breaks, we call upon you to provide our young warrior, Little Pecker, with a test that will bring him into manhood." Thunder boomed, and everyone knew what that meant. They covered their faces and held their noses.

"Soooo, you want some sort of test thingy?" the spirit questioned back. The chief responded, "Sure, why not?"

"Okay, a test. A test, test, test" the spirit pondered.

A few more rumbles and the great fat spirit had an idea. "Alrighty, I got your test. I got your test, right here," The Indians leaned towards the spirit in excited anticipation. "Little Pecker must venture to ends of our ancestral lands, where the three rivers meet the four bushes and kiss Big Fluffy Bear." The tribe gasped in unison. They knew Big Fluffy Bear was not the kissing kind; a handshake was usually pushing your luck. Little Pecker sat dumbfounded. The chief recognized the boy's confusion and inquired to the moose spirit. "What kind of kiss you talking? A little one? A long, wet one? A make-out session? What exactly are you looking for?" These were all excellent questions. The spirit pondered for a moment. "Oh, just give the bear a peck. After all, Little Pecker is still a boy."

Kissing the bear may have seemed like an odd request. But there had been a severe drought for the past three years, and The Poonanis believed from their ancestors that this was the only way to lift the curse and open the door for the rain god, Drizzle the Great, to work his magic. Besides, what did they have to lose? The worst that could happen is Little Pecker is mauled and eaten. The tribe wouldn't mind having another spirit to watch over them.

The next day the boy and his glassy-eyed mule set off to find the big black grizzly. It took them a month longer to reach their destination because they stopped many times to smoke peyote, rendering them too lethargic to push on at a faster pace. Eventually, they reached the three rivers destination. Using the skills that Digging Groundhog had taught him as a child, he followed the bear tracks to a cave. Little Pecker and the mule cautiously entered the opening in the side of the mountain. Inside sat a large, plump black bear snacking on a river trout and nibbling on some recently picked berries. Startled, she looked up.

"What cho be doing coming on up in my cave hizzel? You best get on outta here or I'm gonna be tearing up a coupla fools who be creeping 'round where they shouldn't be creeping 'round," the bear warned.

"I'm Little Pecker," the Indian boy huffed as he pushed out his chest.

"I don't care about your problems," snickered the bear as she put down her basket. She stood up and tiptoed towards them, circling the pair. "Umm, umm, that's one nice ass you got there," she stated.

"Thank you," the boy responded, "I run five miles a day."

"I ain't talking 'bout choo, fool," the bear snapped. "I'm talking 'bout yo sexy lil' mule here."

An uneasy look of disgust appeared on the mule. He didn't like the way things were shaping up and he certainly didn't like her cocky attitude. The bear continued to circle, eyeing up the mule. "Um, um, um, yeah, that be one sweet ass. What choo want for it?"

"A kiss," the boy responded.

"A kiss? Ain't you somin'. I ain't kissing no fool, fool," the bear continued. "I'll kiss your ass but I ain't kissing no Little Pecker."

"If you wanna kiss my mule you'll have to kiss me first," said the boy. The expression on the mule seemed to say, "ain't nobody touching me." The bear got up into Little Pecker's face. "You ain't getting no sugar from me, little pecker man, so you best step off and bounce or I just might kick you to the wood pile then eat you like some little cracker, Cracker."

"Hey, ain't no reason to get up in my painted grill, bear" he fearlessly said as he held up his hands. "I don't wanna hurt you."

"Hurt me?" the chunky animal shockingly questioned then bopped her head back-and-forth as she emphatically stated, "Oh no, you didn't! Oh no… you…didn't!"

"I'm just saying if you wanna kiss my mule you're gonna have to kiss me first," the brave suggested.

"Is that right? Maybe I'll pay you no never mind and kiss yo four-legged friend without no never say so," she seductively commented as she shuffled around the mule, gingerly petting its head.

"I wouldn't do that," the native boy warned.

"Oh, I takes what I want," responded the cocky grizzly.

"Are you sure?" Little Pecker asked.

"Am I sure? Does a bear shit in the woods?" the bear huffed.

The Indian boy gave a half shrug, not sure how to answer.

'Well I do and if'n you trying stop me while I'm trying to makes me some time with your mule here I'll drop a deuce on your head, put you in a mound of trouble. A steamy mound."

The horny bear leaned over to kiss the donkey. The mule's mind began to whirl in turmoil as searing flashbacks of the filthy miner's scruffy beard rubbing up against him as he impermissibly mounted the innocent animal and yelling, "There's gold in dem dar hills!" Not again. Never again, he had vowed. As if contaminated with mad cow disease, the crazed mule began spinning and bucking out of control as the bear bellowed a loud, reverberating, high-pitched cry. Suddenly, he wheeled around and smashed a hoof on the snout of the bear, knocking her across the room and into a wall. The black beast was stunned. Dazed, she collapsed in a heap, suffering from a minor concussion. Little Pecker seized the moment, knowing it might be his only chance. He ran over to the bear, grabbed her by the back of the head and planted a kiss on her mouth. He pulled away, then thought to himself, "Hey, that wasn't half bad." With his hormones awakened, the teenage boy decided to dive in for seconds and soon found himself sucking face with an unconscious bear. The mule cocked his head, watching the lewd exhibition, wondering just what the hell was going on. Thoroughly disgusted, he kicked the horny Indian boy off the bear so that they could make their getaway. The two grabbed the basket of berries, knowing full well they would have the munchies later, then quickly scurried out before Big Fluffy Bear regained consciousness.

The story enthralled the Poonani clan as the boy sat around the fire recounting the events of smooching the uppity bear. One person compelled by the tale was a pretty, young squaw named Wet Beaver, who invited Little Pecker to her teepee for a hot cup of iguana tea. She wanted a private accounting of the bear story.

"So, tell me, how were you able to kiss this bear?" Wet Beaver inquired.
"Well, I was talking to it... then I... I..." Little Pecker fumbled.
"No, show me," she interrupted. "Show me what you did."
The Indian boy shyly smiled, feeling her attraction towards him. He was more than willing to impress her with his great bear story. Obliging her, he got down on all fours then began to spin about like the kicking mule. The squaw laughed and giggled at the silly spectacle. Suddenly, the young brave whirled around and booted her in the face. Wet Beaver flew, eventually landing in a balled-up lump. Little Pecker ran over to her, grabbed her by the back of the neck, and kissed her.
"And that's how I did it," the boy said to the half-unconscious girl.

The two had very little time to get to know one another. The next day Little Pecker was off to complete his final test of manhood. It would be his most challenging but rewarding task. He left his kicking mule behind to look after Wet Beaver and tend to her cheekbone injury. He talked to her every day, though, using smoke signals. Often, he would spend the last half hour of their smoke call sending puffs that read, "You hang up first." Luckily, he was on an unlimited call plan.

Little Pecker was to be sent out to retrieve the tribe's stolen sacred totem pole. Years ago, an Asian monk named Moo Shoo imprisoned in the China seaside city of Poon Tang for selling illegal fireworks escaped by weaving boiled chop suey noodles together, making a rope, and repelling down from his third story cell to his freedom. He was able to shanghai a dragon boat and sail to America where he found work on the railroad. The job was grueling and, eventually, he snapped and wound up killing his boss man by driving a spike through his head. (After being apprehended, the murderous monk claimed he was being railroaded and that all he did was apply an ancient acupuncture technique used to relieve headache pain.) But, before they could lynch him, he fled to the Wokawoka valley, just on the outskirts of the Poonani village.

One night, Moo Shoo, high on opium, snuck into the Indian village and stole their sacred totem pole. (One Indian, Crying Wolf, attempted to warn the tribe that the totem pole was about to be taken, but nobody believed him... as usual.) The ancestral pole was vital to the weekly rain dance ceremony. Ever since it had gone missing a drought encompassed the land, and the crop yields were dismal as the tribe bordered on starvation. Moo Shoo was not bothered by the lack of farmed food since he survived mainly on roots and prairie dogs.

On the top of Bald Eagle Mountain, Little Pecker came upon a hay hut shaped like a pagoda. He knocked on the door and, from inside, the boy heard a man call out, "Who there?"

The young brave answered, "Boo."

"Boo who?" said the china man.

"Why you crying?" laughed the boy. The door quickly opened. Angrily, the old china man yelled, "That not funny!" as his buck teeth glimmered in the sunlight. Little Pecker stood there with a stern look; Wet Beaver had adorned his face with war paint, preparing him for battle. She had added long whiskers believing it would make him look like a fierce mountain lion, but he really looked more like a timid Tomcat.

"Now what you want, kitty cat boy?" Moo Shoo snarled.

"I want our totem pole back," Little Pecker demanded.

"Yeah, right, that not happening," he stated as he took a puff from his opium pipe. "Now you go, dumb boy. Go back to your tiny wigwam and leave me alone. I no time to play games. I do laundry."

The China man went to shut the door, but Little Pecker's foot stopped him. He glared at the boy through his squinted eyes. His face turned to stone as his Fu Manchu mustache twitched. "Oh, you done it now, you pesky grasshopper boy. It's go time," the Asian sneered and then released a scream as he positioned himself into a kung fu stance, simulating a crane.

"Just give me my totem pole," Little Pecker demanded.

"Yeah, sure, right after I give you this," Moo Shoo said as he fired a front snap kick into the boy's solar plexus, knocking him on his buckskin butt. The brave was dazed and disoriented as he realized his final test for his manhood would not be easy. He slowly climbed to his feet and then held out his hand waving the old man on.

"You wanna dance, China doll?" Little Pecker egged him on.

"I not like dancing," Moo Shoo responded. "I much rather beat Indian big fat head in." With that, the china man went on the offensive, attacking the native with a flurry of kicks and punches. But Little Pecker was quick and blocked each move. As a child, he learned to fight by watching animals in the wild. He first started by leaping around his opponent like a bullfrog, screaming "rippet!" The oriental fellow was baffled, having never encountered such a lunatic. Next, the kooky kid got down on all fours and rammed the china man like an angry moose. Then, he began to growl like a bobcat and claw at his enemy's face.

Moo Shoo was somehow able to reach in his pocket and grab an old stale egg roll, which he proceeded to vigorously stuff into the boy's mouth with hopes of repelling his attacker. The young warrior had no choice but to disengage the battle so that he could spit the stale fried lump out of his mouth; how he detested cabbage. Soon, the two found themselves sword fighting with a pair of chopsticks. Little Pecker had always been good with a spear, but dinner utensils were his weakness. At some point, the tiny sticks broke, and the Chinese fellow hoped to end the battle by picking up a nearby Buddha statue and chucking it at the Indian boy's head. Pecker was too fast and agile. He ducked like a goose as the garden figurine crashed through the paper-thin wall. Then he decided to goose like a duck as he picked up a nearby bamboo stick and poked the monk in the bum.

"You shouldn't touch there," Moo Shoo glared. "That sacred land."

The brave let out a whooping Poonani war cry, just for fun, then dropped in the dirt. Calling on all his nature skills, he slithered like a snake, wrapping himself around the China man's feet then twisting around him like a boa constrictor. Moo Shoo, fearing slow suffocation, was able to unravel the boy by using an ancient Chinese secret of applying acupressure to an opponent's nipple and biting their ear. Little Pecker let out another Poonani cry… this time, not for fun. Pissed off, the slinky warrior hissed at him while shaking his bum like it was a rattle.

By now, the China man was infuriated, mainly because he had a snake phobia. He grabbed a bamboo stick and began twirling it as he yelled, "La ba sung di! La ba sung di!" (In Chinese this meant "May your scrotum be burned by the breath of a dragon.") Moo Shoo knocked the boy down but in doing so broke his weapon. Without thinking, the china man grabbed the boy's feet, and like a rickshaw, pushed him out the door, on his painted face, down towards the river. Along the route, he ran over rocks and banged into trees. He was a terrible driver.

The two warriors soon found themselves in the shallow water, tussling about like spawning salmon. Moo Shoo played dirty. He filled his mouth with water and spat it into the boy's face. It was known as Chinese water torture, a humiliating technique passed down from the Chinny-Chin-Chin Dynasty. Pecker moved swiftly and grabbed the Asian man's wrist and rapidly twisted his hands-back-and-forth. Moo Shoo, able to yank his hand away, noticed a horrendous Indian burn. The agile Chinese bully was able to position himself behind the boy and put him in a Kung Pao chicken wing chokehold – a maneuver he had learned in a temple from a Shaolin midget monk who looked up to every opponent he ever faced.

"Confucius say: Time for boy to meet untimely death," the Asian brute whispered.

The yellow man strangled the red man who was now turning blue. Gasping for air, it appeared Little Pecker would meet his demise at the hands of a totem thief. Suddenly, out of the woods charged Big Fluffy Bear. Huffing and puffing, like a full-blown cattle stampede, the six-hundred-pound beast blindsided the wiry monk. The bear heaved the China man up by the back of his pants and power lifted him over her head then body slammed him to the ground. "Oh no you didn't! That's my Little Pecker!"

she bellowed. Then, like a fiery wrestler, she jumped up and allowed her full weight to land on the whimpering monk.

"Now you best get your kung fu ass back to wherever it is you come from, or this Great Wall's gonna come down on your egg-fu-young face, humph," the big black bear huffed as she bobbed her head back-and-forth almost wanting another round.

Little Pecker walked up and looked down at his defeated buck-toothed foe. The brave pulled out his tomahawk and scalped off the China man's Fu Manchu mustache. Quoting Confucius, he said, "Hair today, gone tomorrow." (He and the mule would smoke it later in hopes of attaining the strength of his beaten enemy. It didn't happen, but the buzz was incredible.)

Moo Shoo was left on the bank to eventually crawl back to his pagoda hut and mend his wounds with herbal medicine and some ginseng tea. If only he had heeded the words he read from his fortune cookie that morning. It said, "Today is a good day to nap. Your winning numbers are 17, 22, 26, 33, 42, 46."

Little Pecker was grateful to his new friend. He asked the bear why she had helped him. The bear smiled then replied, "I guess I just done like the way you smooch. Umm, umm, them Indian boy kisses done make my fur stand up. Shoo-wee sugar, you gonna break some hearts with them juicy lips of leather hide." Pecker took it as a compliment and began to think the old bear was more of a cougar.

The brave thanked Big Fluffy Bear, giving him his homemade pocketknife and Kicking Mule's address. He attempted to hug the bear good-bye, but she grabbed him in a tight bear hug and kissed the boy as her thick back leg slowly lifted off the ground while the sun set over the mountain.

Holding the totem pole, Little Pecker stood before chief Buffalo Breath as the long-awaited ritual of manhood commenced. "You have shown great courage, Little Pecker, and have successfully completed the three tests of the Poonani tribe. From now on you will be called Big Pecker."

That night, a celebration ensued, known as "Ho Down, Go Down, Throw Down, Runaround, Take-a-chance Totem Pole Dance." Big Fluffy

Bear had been invited and spent most of the evening waltzing with Kicking Mule, who felt at ease in her arms. At some point, Big Pecker adjourned to his teepee with Wet Beaver to take his final test of manhood. The young squaw was truly amazed at the rise of Pecker and they celebrated… a few times. They took turns pleasing each other. None of them wanted to be thought of as just an Indian giver. Several months later Crying Wolf would run through the village warning, "The white men are coming." Nobody believed him.

THE PRANCING COWBOY

The sun was setting over the mountains when he rode into town. A short, pudgy man, slumped in his saddle, whistling a show tune that had been swimming in his head from a Burlesque musical he had recently seen in San Francisco. The happy, go-lucky cowboy rode a beautiful, stocky Shetland pony named "Baubles" who had a fruity, cinnamon-vanilla scent emanating off his silky groomed hair. He loved to prance - and so did the quarter horse. And both seem to enjoy a proper, bumpy trail.

The cowboy's name was Cissy Owens. One of the many things that stood out about Cissy was the carefree style in which he rode side-saddle. Dressed to kill, he was a chap who appreciated fine leathered chaps. His noir, charmeuse tunic, bought from a Wells Fargo catalog, gave him a feeling of freedom as the garment flowed seemingly in the breeze. His horse, was adorned with glistening buffalo-bone beads. Their look was all about contrast, all about minimalism, all about pushing the limits. A stark, neutral backdrop that showcased some brilliant accessories, done in vivid synthetic pigments. His lizard snip toe boots (by none other than Buck Blahnik, an up-and-coming designer out of Tucson) had been costumed-dyed turquoise to complement his dangling olive-neck bandanna. Chunky Southwestern jewelry, gleaming silver chains, and his cute little five-cup beige velvet hat seem to scream, "I'm here! Whatcha gonna do about it?"

Cissy tied up his adorable pony then skipped his way into the saloon. A quaint watering hole to socialize and gossip was always a treat for him. He enjoyed watching the rough, rugged men playing poker and telling wild tales of branding chickens and punching doggies. Cissy never punched a doggie himself, although he has been known to dish a little slap on a bum then playfully throw out, "You've been Cissy branded!" Moseying up to the bar, he ordered a Sassafras Spritzer. The stocky bartender handed him a warm beer. Cissy just smiled, and with a good ole' Texas lisp, he politely requested a straw.

A big-boned red-headed woman thumped down the stairs. Nell was the fifty-year-old flamboyant lady who ran the saloon. (Her husband, a cattle tycoon, left her the place after he ran off to marry his favorite black Angus.) The bovine beauty always took care of her customers, making sure they had drinks, a full belly, and a prostitute, with a full belly, to pass out on. Her face lit up when she saw Cissy sitting on the bar with his legs crossed. She puckered her lips and, with her hips leading, she elegantly waddled her way over to the cheerful cowboy.

"What brings you to town, Cis?" she asked while wrapping her brawny meat hooks around him and squeezing the little fellow until she heard a high-pitched squeal.

"Oh, I was hoping to catch a bubble bath and do some shopping. I need to find a few rhinestones, bangles, and beads to complement my complexion," he gleefully replied with a giggle.

Cissy and Nell talked throughout the night, reminiscing about their old days in San Antonio. They were ex-dancing partners with a long history. The two of them used to entertain in the "Trail Mix Saloon" which was adjacent to the infamous "Alamo." Their big showstopping number was "The Crocket Coon Skin Hat Shuffle." Every night, drunk cowboys hooted and hollered at the high steppin' stocking-laced pair, tossing coins at Nell while throwing spurs at Cissy. Nell later moved to Boulder where she opened a shoe store for pack mules called "Just Burrows" selling donkey footwear to any jackass that came in the place. Cissy ventured up north, to San Francisco, where he found gainful employment styling the beard hair on gold miners for precious metal shavings.

The bar began to liven up as Clyde, the gimpy one-armed piano player, began to pick up the beat on the ivories. (He had tragically lost his limb in a wild stampede. Someone had yelled free drinks, and the poor musician was nearly trampled to death as determined freeloading customers charged the bar.) After catching up with her old friend, Nell excused herself and made her rounds checking up on her drunk, horny patrons. Cissy ordered another drink, and this time, he didn't pull any punches. He requested a clean glass.

Suddenly, the saloon doors swung opened and in walked three rough-looking, dirty and smelly men. They were hairy, wore jeans, and smoked cigars. Cissy's mouth dropped in shocked when he noticed their boots clashing with their black hats. He rolled his eyes and giggled to himself. The men nestled up to the bar and began to chug shots of whiskey. Cissy just casually slurped his beer, making a disgusted face after every sip. The sounds of the off-key piano seem to take hold of him as he wiggled his bottom to the music. The men took notice of the fancy boy's bum shaking and began to murmur and cackle amongst themselves. Cissy simply ignored the wranglers, commenting to the bartender, "Whatever."

As the night wore on, a loose and tipsy Cissy, lost in the music, found himself two-stepping on the rickety hardwood as he shadowed danced with himself. Boot scooting across the floor, the raucous cowboys cheered him on with rude jeers and laughter. "Yee-haw, you go fancy boy!" one of them yelled. Oblivious to the ill-mannered behavior, Cissy did his best to remember his old dance steps as he'd count to himself. Every so often, the light-footed toe-tapper would make a mistake then quickly hold up his hands and say, "Wait! I got it! I got it!"

Nell loved to watch him. The bags under her eyes glistened as he spun and twirled effortlessly around the tables pausing ever so often to show off his patented tiptoe-toe stomp that he had mastered thanks to Dusty Rump, a transvestite Cabaret dancer he'd once worked with in Philadelphia. When Clyde began to play "Clementine" Cissy leaped in the air, threw his hands back, and let loose a high-pitched shriek. It was his favorite song and reminded him of the fun nights of sitting around the campfire crooning to miners who had put a gold pan on his head to add to the entertainment. His mother used to sing the old tune to him while they knitted Dooley's together. Nell wished she could join him but had thrown her hip out years ago in a barroom brawl while attempting to break up the scuffle between a gambler who had been making time with a cowboy's mare.

The three caliginous strangers were now drunk, laughing amongst themselves. There was no good; only bad, ugly, and uglier. Kit Dungy was the leader since his attire was darker than the others. Dungy was a gun-slinging thug that was rotten from his tobacco stained gold molar all the way down to his stolen soiled underwear. He was the only surviving member of the Peach Cobbler Pie Gang. He robbed trains, banks, and dabbled in hog rustling until some pig squealed on him. He was also known for stealing candy from a baby. When asked why he did it, he casually replied, "It was as easy as taking candy from a baby."

Dungy escaped from an Amarillo jail by convincing a dim-witted deputy that he was invisible. (A $10,000 reward was put on his head and a $5,000 prize on his legs.) He was wanted dead or alive in six states. (Four of the states would also accept comatose.) Rumored he was so mean that, one chilly night, he bit his horse on the tail for hogging his blanket and punched a donkey for snoring too loud.

Cissy basked in praise of the amused cowboys, believing them to be enamored with his dance moves. The hooting and hollering made him feel accepted like he was part of the gang. Bustling inside, Cissy twirled and spun his way to the back of the room. Lost in a melodic chorus of "Oh my darling, oh my darling," he accidentally tripped over a spittoon and fell into the arms of Kit Dungy. The piano music stopped. Everyone in the room gasped as a deafening silence filled the air.

"Beg your pardon, sir," Cissy giggled as he batted his eyes.

With a slight grin, the stone-faced hog rustler pushed his hat back. He placed his beer on the bar, turned, and stated, "Quite the little prancer, ain't ya?"

Flattered, Cissy blushed and said with a slight southern lisp, "I've been dancing since I was a yearling."

The three mean men burst out in laughter. Feeling embarrassed Cissy retorted, "I studied at NYU."

The amused men laughed harder.

Frustrated, the feminine cowboy snapped, "I could've gone professional if I didn't twist my knee on a tricky flutter leap, thank you very much."

By now the men had doubled over in uncontrollable titillation. In a tizzy, Cissy turned and began to storm away.

"You a fancy boy?" Dungy called out.

Composing himself, Cissy turned around and said, "Sticks and stones might break my bones, but names can never hurt me."

The quip caused the saloon to erupt in laughter. A shocked look appeared on Dungy's stern face. He reached over, grabbed his beer off the bar, and splashed it on Cissy's chest. The patrons gasped.

Stunned and wet, Cissy marched right up to the hostile bully and sniped, "That is going to chafe my leather. You know, this is a three-bit, full-grain moccasin cowhide vest."

Sensing trouble, the men behind Cissy pushed back from their tables, stood up, and scurried to a safe corner.

Nell ran over and got between the two men. "Now boys," she smiled. "We don't want any trouble. We're here to have a good time, right?"

Dungy turned to his boys and bellowed, "Well, whatta we have here? A steer and a queer. You stickin' on up for your girly friend here, Nell?"

In a huff, Cissy retorted, "I'm not a girl, thank you very much. But, you're a brute. A big hairy, bully brute. And, you smell like an unbathed gelding."

The room grew eerily quiet. The cowboys in the bar stepped back, giving their leader some room. Dungy stood erect but, before his face could turn utterly red with anger, Cissy leaped into action, reaching out and tickling bully's belly.

"Tickle! Tickle!" he cried out.

Dungy doubled over in laughter. He jumped on the bar to avoid further humiliation, but it was to no avail. The polished manicured nails dug into his tummy causing a frantic giggling attack. His two befuddled friends looked on, caught in limbo, as they watched the baffling display. Nell smiled as her eyes lit up.

"Stop it! Stop it! I'll kill you!" Dungy laughed.

"Tickle! Tickle!" Cissy playfully yelled.

Dungy lay on the bar with his legs kicking as he rolled back and forth. Cissy would pause long enough for him to catch his breath then the process would begin again. At one brief intermission, Dungy gathered up enough strength to cold cock Cissy in the face, knocking him back over the top of a table. With tears streaming down his face, Dungy sat up on the bar. He was out of breath and had wet his pants.

Cissy, clearing his head, looked up and snapped, "If you didn't wanna be tickled, you should've said something, silly."

The dark dressed man, with a stained crotch, jumped off the bar and made his way over to the cowering feminine cowboy. He reached down and picked the little fellow up by his neatly pressed shirt with ruffles. The two stood face to face.

"You plumb tickled the wrong man," Dungy said with a clenched jaw.

"And you have filthy wretched stinky breath," Cissy fired back.

The towering cowboy raised his fist but, reflexively, Cissy quickly slapped him. "I do not appreciate your vulgar, brute behavior," he scolded.

Cissy turned to walk away then heard a gun cock, causing him to gasp. He slowly turned back around to find himself staring down the barrel of a Remington six-shooter. Cissy never carried a gun because he didn't believe in violence. He was a dancer - a peaceful, sensitive dancer. While his brothers learned to rope cattle, wrestle, and shoot pistols in their youth, Cissy distanced himself from those activities. Often, he would play in the barn, using haystacks as a theatre platform, staging various musical ensembles with Beanie, the family cow, his pet sow, Hammy, and whatever chickens and hens he could coax into rehearsals. Designing cute little costumes occupied his nights and, it was undeniable, the lad was talented, sewing an unbelievable frizzy pig tutu. Young Cissy once directed a two-man play with his sheepdog, Rumba, and a young colt named Tango. The production fell flat and was deemed, more or less, a dog and pony show. His mother used to watch him through the kitchen window, twirling on the prairie plains, honing his skills while waltzing with a tumbleweed. When he finally came in, around sunset, she would often chase him around the house with a butter stick because he neglected his daily chores. The little fellow was usually too nimble for her, and she was never able to beat or churn any sense of responsibility into him.

With Cissy's life in jeopardy, he did what very few men would do in the situation. He stuck out his chest, lifted his chin then began to cry.

Dungy and his two cronies started to laugh as they mocked the bawling ballet boy.

Nell ran over and said, "Leave him alone. He never hurt nobody, unless he stepped on their feet while dancing."

Cissy looked up and innocently blushed, perhaps looking for a little sympathy from the rugged boys.

"We don't like his boot-lickin' kind," Dungy barked as he backhanded Nell, knocking the chewing tobacco out of her other mouth. This action infuriated Cissy as he reflected on all of the times the kindhearted woman had lent him her stockings for a show.

Every man in his life has one moment that defines his manhood. An instant that evolves him from swimming in some watering hole to walking on land. Cissy tweren't no crayfish, he was almost a man. In him flowed the juices of righteousness and justice and he had reached his limit. With the courage of a cornered wolverine, he stood up and faced his enemy. Dungy smirked, pointing his gun at Cissy's beating heart. The room was so quiet that one could hear ole' Nell spit on the floor, if she still had her chaw.

Dungy's squinted, dark eyes met Cissy's glare as the two squared off. The fancy cowboy held up his hands and tipped his little five-cup beige velvet hat to signify he didn't want any trouble. Then, with the quickness of a Sierra bobcat, Cissy, out of nowhere, suddenly burst into a song and dance number. "Mamma's little baby loves shortnin', shortnin', Mamma's little baby loves shortnin' bread."

Caught up in the moment, Cissy crouched down and began slapping his knees and bobbing his head as he continued, "Mamma's little baby loves shortnin', shortnin', Mamma's little baby loves shortnin' bread."

Dungy couldn't believe his squinted eyes. His mind raced as he tried to comprehend what the hell was going on. The brawny cowboy seemed frozen, unsure of what to make of the pint-size buffoon crooning out, "Put on the skillet! Put on the lid! Mamma's going to make some shortnin' bread."

Kit Dungy gritted his teeth as his face turned to stone. He had seen more than enough. "You done got some water on the brain, boy?" he snarled.

Cissy, seemingly lost in his own world, ignored him and continued with his folk ditty, "They popped up well and started to sing. Skipping round the room doing the pigeon wing." Cissy was now galloping in circles, spinning and twirling, bellowing out "Momma's little baby loves shortnin,' shortnin' bread, shortnin'bread..." In no time, the icy mood had changed to a cheerful glee, becoming infectious as the cowboys in the room joined in, clapping and singing off-key.

Kit Dungy stood there, with his mouth agape, tightly squeezing his gun, believing he was watching a monkey fall off his rocker. To add more coal to the fire, Cissy put his hands on his hips and began to whistle as he two-stepped around the confused gunslinger. Dungy was now at his wit's end. Fed up with the insane display, he fired his gun in the air. The place went quiet.

In a soft voice, Cissy whispered, "What's wrong? A little too shy to dance?"

Dungy grabbed the scrawny prancer by the shirt and growled, "I'm gonna rip your head off, fancy boy."

Cissy stood his ground and looked Kit right in the eyes. "Try it, and I'll scratch you."

"Boy, I'm 'bout to bury a bullet in your chest," Dungy answered back.

Without blinking, Cissy replied, "Really? Maybe I'll pull your hair, kick your knees, and bite your back."

Dungy had never been talked to like this before. He began to seethe under his skin. Nell could see the fire in his eyes. She raced over and got between the two of them. "He done don't mean nuttin' by it, Kit. He likes to perform his little songs to anyone who'd give it a listen. He got that performer blood in him. Loves an audience. Can't help himself. Go on; leave 'im be."

In a rage, Dungy backhanded Nell out of the way, knocking out the last tooth she had. "You need to reign her in, little hoofing cowpoke," he snarled and then rudely continued, "You can't be letting bison run free." Dungy's cronies roared with laughter. By now, Cissy frizzy bandana was in a bunch and he had had enough of the brute. He came at him hard, clawing at his chest and screeching like a wild bobcat caught in a fur trap. "Nobody hurts my Nell!" he hissed. "I'll get you good, you monster snake!" Kit just stood watching the crazy fool scrapping at his torso. The gunslinger could barely feel it, but it did help relieve the itching caused by some poison ivy he'd unwittingly contracted while dropping a smasher in the woods. After about ten seconds of the scratching frenzy, Cissy quickly became tired. Panting, he dropped to his knees, releasing several sobbing gasps. He softly whimpered, "You made me do that. I didn't want to."

Playtime was over. Dungy had had enough of the games. He gurgled a frustrated groan then lifted his gun to the little fellow's chin with the full intention of pumping the tiny dancer full of lead. Everyone watched in fear.

Cissy climbed to his feet while making exaggerated squeaky moans of pain. Surprisingly, he kept his cool with no sign of fear. Dungy pulled the six-shooter's hammer back. Things were looking bleak for the dancing cowboy. He blushed several times as he stared down the barrel of the Remington. Then, before anyone could blink, Cissy sprang into action, catching Kit totally off guard. He reached out, grabbed Dungy by the neck, pulled him in close then planted a kiss square on the mouth.

Kit Dungy had become jaded early in life when he lost his parents at a young age in a runaway stagecoach tragedy. The mother and father hated their kid, so they hopped on a stagecoach and ran away. The disillusioned boy ended up with the Brothers of Baldwin Missionary Orphanage where his days were spent washing floors, scrubbing pots and polishing Rosary beads. He professed that his only friend was a Saint Benedict statue, but the two of them rarely spoke to each other. He would later be tossed out of the orphanage for punching the head off the sculpture, claiming it looked at him the wrong way. Kit joined a cattle driver clan out of Abilene working the Chisolm Trail. He was often taunted by the cattlemen who would often practice their roping skills on him. His breaking point occurred along the Red River when the boys, during a night of wild drinking, teasingly hog-tied Kit and branded his left ass cheek with a longhorn symbol. After that, he always bathed in ponds wearing his long johns, making sure the back flap was always buttoned. Eventually, he moved further west and began his life of rustling and bank robberies.

No one knew what happened that day. But whatever it was it changed Kit Dungy. After Cissy's lips pressed against the gunslinger's mouth, they say he merely dropped his pistol, walked out of the saloon, and left town without uttering a word. Some say he was just too embarrassed, others, well, they seem to believe ole' Kit like the way Cissy hoofed-it across the floor and figured it's a shame to rid the world of a fancy dancer who put a smile on folk's faces. Nell seems to think it was a little something more. Kit liked that kiss, and he liked it a lot. The callous cowboy had never never been kissed by anyone before. Not by his mother, his father, or even the family filly. It was like his soul became unchained, and he was finally free to bury the anger and bitterness that bubbled from inside. It was a cowboy kiss that seemed to give him purpose and meaning, quashing all the meanness that lurked deep inside.

Nell tells her customers, "It was like pouring a canteen of water on a raging campfire. Hell, the man just needed to know he was loved."

For years after the incident, Cissy roamed from town to town, shopping and touching stern, cold-hearted cowboys in his unique way. He never believed in violence. That was never a dance step in his life's repertoire. In filthy barrooms throughout the west, Cissy two-stepped around, gliding and sliding across the floor, trying his best to spread a little cheer and lift some spirits.

One hot, muggy night in a Dodge City saloon sat a group of gamblers entrenched in a grueling poker game. Dutch Bass, commonly known as "Aces", threw down his cards, fuming, after losing another hand. He tossed down a four-fingered bourbon shot to numb the pain from all the money he'd been losing throughout the evening. The three other men playing dare not utter a word, knowing full well Aces was not someone with which one trifled. They just let him stew in his anger, brooding over every rotten hand he was drawing.

Cissy happened to be in the bar that night. While running through some new dance steps in his head, he couldn't help but notice the sour look strewn across Ace's face. That did not bode well with ole' Ciss. He wanted everyone around him happy, and he would do what he had to do to bring out a smile. Without a second thought, Cissy walked over and whispered something into the piano player's ear who immediately stopped tinkering the tune "Comanche Moon" and rolled right into "Clementine."

Cissy, donning his five-cup velvet hat, an eye-catching vest and garnishing a pair of sleek, cowhide leather chaps, began to embrace the music. He put his hands on his hips and, in a sassy fashion, strutted across the hardwood, moving slowly towards the gambler's table. The boys were intensely wrapped up in five-card stud and didn't notice the prancing cowboy. Cissy, trying his best to get their attention, took two steps forward and one step back as he shook his bum to the bouncy tune. Every so often he'd pause, toe-tap his furry grizzly bear boots in a circle, then throw his head back and wave his hands in the air.

Ace's eyes were locked in on the fanned cards he held up in front of his face. He ground his teeth, grunting over the pair of deuces staring back at him. He pushed his thin cigar over to the other side of his mouth in hopes of changing his luck. Suddenly, his concentration broke when he heard a soprano-like voice rising above the clunky ivory tickling.

"Light she was, like a fairy. And her shoes were number nine. Herring boxes, without topses. Sandals were from Clementine."

Through the thick, cloudy smoke Dutch Bass peered over his set of cards to see the stubby, fancy dressed cowboy coming his way. When Cissy caught Ace's fiery eyes, he tipped his petite hat down, at an angle, like a Cabaret dancer, and put his thumbs in his pockets, marching towards the table, allowing his hips to lead the way. He continued with the song in hopes of garnering a smile from the somber gambler.

"Drove she ducklings, to the water. Ev'ry morning just at nine. Hit her foot, against a splinter. Fell into the foaming brine."

Aces could not believe his eyes. Sashaying directly at him was something he'd never seen before and he thought he'd seen it all. He served in the Civil War and witnessed bloody carnage at Pea Ridge and Chickamauga. He had delivered a breached colt on the plains of Oklahoma, ambushed by Apaches. And, nearly hung, for hornswoggling and unspeakable sheep abuse. But, this little display, well, it just made his stomach turn.

Cissy, like an attention-starved puppy dog, just kept coming, oblivious to the world around him and enthralled in the gold miner ballad. "Oh, my darling, oh my darling. Oh, my darling, Clementine."

Dutch leaned back in his chair, centering his husky shoulders as he watched the swaggering buckaroo, flouncing, and dosey-doe-ing. Agitated, Aces bellowed out, "You toying with me, boy? Looking to play me for some kind fool?"

Cissy held up his hands like a mountain lion, making growling noises as he scratched the air, pantomiming that he had claws. "You are lost and not forgotten. Dreadful sorry, Clementine."

The clenching of Dutch's jaw revealed he was far from amused. Hell, all he wanted was a quiet night of drinking and a peaceful card game. And, to make matters worse, several months prior, Aces had found his fiancé in the arms of a rodeo clown who's name just happened to be Clementine.

"Hey Mister gambling man," Cissy said in a sing-song voice as he shimmied his shoulders. "Whatta ya say you turn your frown upside down and take a little twirl with me?"

Dutch Bass quietly sat there with an icy stare, pondering for a long minute. Finally, with a soft grunt, the gambler stood up, looked intensely at the prancing cowboy, then, like a curious prairie dog peeking out of a desert hole, the right corner of his mouth slightly raised and a half, twitching smirk appeared on his face.

Cissy's eyes widened as he beamed. He shuffled his feet and slowly turned around, shaking his hands in the thick, smoky air while singing, "And that's what it's all about. Yeah!" He finished on one knee with his arms spread open, hoping for a little admiration from the pouty stranger for his uplifting number.

As fast as a snapping bullwhip, Dutch drew his pistol and lambasted Cissy in the gut, pumping the stunned little fella full of lead. Cissy released a high-pitched squeal as the blast lifted the stumpy dancing boy in the air, knocking him six feet back and flat on his keister. Aces calmly put his gun back in his holster and sat down. "Start dealing," he muttered.

Cissy lay in a heap against the wall, making exaggerated whimpers. He looked down at his stomach and, through his sniveling, murmured "That was my favorite paisley buckskin vest." With an irritated expression he glanced over to Dutch and called out, "Somebody's got a pissy attitude," then passed out.

That day the light-footed, prancing cowboy learned he couldn't put a smile on everybody's face. "I reckon some folks just don't wanna have a little fun in life," he would later confide to Nell. As luck would have it, Cissy had recently started wearing a new type of alligator tummy tuck belt he had ordered from a *Butterick Catalog* to help conceal his pot belly and thwarted flab from jiggling around whenever he danced. The reptile hide was so strong that it prevented any penetration of Dutch Bass's bullet. Cissy would not become discouraged. "Gosh darn it, then life's just not worth living if ya' can't spread a little cheer," he'd often say. It would take seven or eight months for the stubby hoofer to build up the courage to get back on the horse and show off his dancing skills to saloon patrons. Sadly, he would get kicked by a Chinese railroad worker, body slammed by a blacksmith and thrown across the bar by a beefy prostitute. His claim to fame was when he was shot in the shoulder by none other than Billy the Kid, just for asking the young gunslinger if he enjoyed a good foxtrot. And still, he continued to dance throughout the west. He would later die from an infection as a result of stepping on a rusty nail during a shuffle, ball, change tap dancing maneuver. Cissy Owens was buried in a cemetery outside of Deadwood. His tombstone read "I'm down here. Whatcha gonna do about it?" Cissy's gleeful, nonviolent ways became legend and tales were told around a campfire of a fancy prancer who could two-step the hatred out of any bloodthirsty gunslinger. Heck, cowboys from all over the west would stop by to where ole' Ciss is buried and pay homage by dancing on his grave.

GRINDING TO THE AMERICAN DREAM

It was a sticky, humid day in New York City when a massive luxury liner glided past the towering Statue of Liberty and pulled into Ellis Island. The newly arrived Italian immigrants poured off the ship with tired smiles and beaming hopes of finding a better life. Among them was Ugolini Bonomo, an older man in his sixties who was short with well-toned, aged muscles that were covered by bushels of curly hair. He walked slowly since his knees ached as a result of numerous falls from slipping on banana peels that seemed always to litter the floors of the shabby one-room apartment he had recently left behind. The hunched man carried a battered leather suitcase in one hand and, in the other worn hand, he held the paw of a jittery monkey, who sported a tiny red bellhop cap. The pair strolled towards the check-in station to begin a new life.

For the last twelve years, Ugolini had scraped out a meager living by traveling the southern cities of Italy, churning a hand-cranked organ and singing opera songs in a scratchy, off-key baritone voice. Nobody paid attention to him and he often had to pay people to listen to him belt out a number. Eventually, he wisely acquired a cute, perky monkey to dart around with a tin cup and collect coins from amused on-lookers while he concentrated on getting his song lyrics right. The monkey's name was "Chimps", and he came from a traveling circus that mistreated their animals. Chimps was required to perform six shows a day as a trapeze act with a few drunk clowns while dressed in a puffy tutu. The name "Chimps" was a misnomer. Chimps was not a chimpanzee but a larger-than-normal chubby spider monkey... with an attitude.

In the old country, times were lean, and Ugolini would often grapple with his monkey sidekick over a stale roll a deli owner would supply for free if he promised to play his barrel organ on the next block down. Ugolini decided to try his luck in America. The land rumored to have gold-lined streets and promises of wealth and riches to anyone willing to work hard.

Ugolini's sister, Rosa, had moved to America seven years earlier and had found a residence in Little Italy on Mulberry Street in Manhattan. She bore a strong resemblance to her brother, except that his mustache was a tad bushier. She was well-known in the neighborhood for her uncanny ability to give timely precise fortunes by reading the lumps off various vegetables that her clients would set in front of her. Zucchini readings were her bread and butter, and her predictions were spot-on. She once warned a woman of an impending horse cart accident just by feeling the bumps on a fresh eggplant. Sadly, the client was a skeptic, refusing to believe anything about the black arts. Coincidentally, the following day she was trampled by a team of spooked horses pulling a vegetable cart. Even more, coincidentally, she lay in the hospital in a vegetative state. After a miraculous recovery, she went on a strict meat diet.

Rosa was excited to see her brother and get the news from the old country. The two united with hugs and kisses outside of Ellis Island while the monkey scampered in circles, stretching his legs from the long cruise.

"Wella, I seea youa stilla gotta thatta furry thing?" Rosa stated.

"Mya mustache, ita bringa me good luck," her brother responded.

"I'ma talking about thata littlea monkey thing."

"Heya, thisa monkey isa mya ticket to thea American dreama," Ugolini responded. "Everyonea lovesa the monkey."

"He's a noa good. Whena you gonna getta a reala joba likea streeta cleaner, huh?" the sister clamored. "You'ra back is stronga enougha to a lifta the horsea pooh piles."

"Shuta your mouth," the old man barked. "Wherea youa live? The monkey. Hea needsa nap."

Ugolini settled into his sister's small two-room apartment and quickly learned his way around. It was a bustling neighborhood – a prime area to make some decent money. A man-monkey musical team usually operate on downtown streets. The organ grinder would set up on a corner, wearing his instrument on a strap over his shoulder, and then support its weight with a stick while he played. Meanwhile, the monkey, tethered to a leash, would scamper around with a tin cup, collecting change. Audiences were dependable and enjoyed the hurdy-gurdy songs like "Dixie" and "Funiculi, Funicula." Sometimes the monkey would tumble, flip or do a playful jig for the amused people. Then, he'd stick his tin cup in front of their face, coaxing the dupes out of spare change. Chimps had the routine down pact. After ten to twelve hours on the street, the pair would arrive back home, and dump the loot on the bed to count their day's wages. On a good day, they could make up to three dollars, but that was a rarity.

The old street performer would pour the coins into a cigar box he found in a back alley outside a seedy brothel. Down deep, it bothered him that the prostitutes were able to smoke better cigars then he could afford, but he was at least grateful he didn't have syphilis. Chimps watched Ugolini stuff the box under the cheap mattress. It would be nice to have some of that loot to make him feel important, Chimps thought.

"Nowa youa getta to beda, sleepy head," Ugolini said as he shoved the monkey under the covers. Then he took off the little pet's hat and patted him on the head, "I don'ta wanta youa alla grouchy tomorrow ina fronta alla the paying customers."

Ugolini began to walk out of the room then spun around to catch the monkey flipping him off with his stubby middle finger. "A littlea wisea guy, huh?" he snarled. The old man flew off the handle and grabbed the little runt from under the covers and put him over his knee and began swatting it's behind, hoping to teach him some respect. Ugolini was never proud after he whacked the monkey's bum, but it had to be done to ensure discipline, and it happened all too often. The neighbors knew it also. Every night, they could hear old Ugolini spanking the monkey.

Ugolini insides swirled as he sat at the kitchen table staring at a nearly empty bottle of wine. "Whatta are youa looking at?" he slurred at the red vino. Since he arrived, there were long days on the street and money was barely trickling in. He had grown disillusioned that he hadn't yet achieved the American dream. They were barely scraping by. Every day was the same, grinding his organ while the monkey got all the attention. Sometimes the little beast would scamper off for hours leaving Ugolini to track him down, only to find him flirting with giddy dames enamored with his monkey tricks. Time was money, and he wasn't making any when his furry partner wasn't waving that tin cup.

One day, while out organ grinding, Ugolini's eyes fell upon a shy apple peddler. Her name was Becky, and she was beautiful in her unique homely way. It was love at first sight. Ugolini stood there frozen, contemplating how to approach this vision of beauty. Suddenly, she looked up, and with a beaming smile she exclaimed, "You are soooo cute."

Ugolini, playing coy, bashfully bowed his head as he nervously circled his foot in the dirt. The excited girl raced towards him. He perked up and smiled as he stretched out his arms for a warm and unsuspecting hug. She ran up to him then right past him and picked up the monkey who was standing behind him. As she twirled the furry mammal around, the monkey stared at the old man sporting a devious smirk. To add some fuel to the fire, the monkey winked as he snickered. Ugolini's face turned red as Roma tomato, as he boiled in his anger.

That night, Ugolini made a six-course meal for the monkey. He placed a Caesar salad, a loaf of garlic bread, a bowl of Pasta Fazool, Baked Rigatoni with sausage and a slab of tiramisu cake in front of his little partner. As he tied the napkin around the Chimp's neck the old man gently stroked the back of the monkey's head as he nicely asked, "Maybe tomorrow you introducea the pretty apple lady to old Ugolini." The monkey shrugged rolling his eyes as he began digging into the food.

Later in the evening as the man was tucking the monkey into bed, he repeated his earlier statement, "Yeah, nowa youa bea the good littlea monkey and say somea nice things to thata fruita girl abouta me. Thatsa whata friendsa do. Youa anda Ia, we alwaysa being good friends." The monkey ignored him as he reclined on his back and lifted his legs to his stomach. "Oh, youa wanna a littlea belly rubsa? Sure. Why not? Whatsa friendsa for?" The monkey snuggled in for his gentle stomach massage and would later demand a bedtime story.

Ugolini sat on a barrel excited over an anticipated introduction. His heart was beating fast knowing he would soon meet the girl of his dreams - an hour past, then another one. Frustrated, Ugolini went to find out what the problem was. In the street, he found an empty pushcart with no monkey or apple lady in sight. Ugolini roamed the city for hours in search of the pair until darkness set in. Distraught over his predicament, he was about to head to the police station to file a missing animal report when he heard some loud music rippling from the corner pub.

He made his way over and peering through window sat the backstabbing monkey with the love of his life. They were enjoying dinner as they giggled and laughed, sipping on glasses of red wine. The Italian man watched in disbelief while the monkey led the girl onto the dance floor. His wrinkled face dropping in disgust. With his heart pounding in rage, he seethed as he watched the couple Lindy Hop across the floor. It was a cold slap in the face to the Italian peddler. His mind raced but, down deep, there was no denying it. The monkey had game, and he was just a little man who used an animal to do his begging.

As Ugolini lay awake in bed, he heard the monkey stagger into the apartment. A flower vase crashed to the floor, and soft slurring monkey noises could be heard emanating from the front room. An angry, restless Ugolini turned on the light to find the drunken animal swaying in the hallway with lipstick on his fur and reeking of expensive booze as a cigarette dangled from his lips.

"You'rea sada sight fora the sorea eyes," Ugolini sneered.

The glazed-eyed monkey looked at his master as if to say something but then just vomited on the floor. His head loosely bobbed then he smirked then fell face down.

The next morning Ugolini was dressing the monkey for work. "I'ma put a leasha ona you," snapped Ugolini. "Thatta way I know whereas exactly you are and whatsa you'rea upa to." Chimps murmured a hungover groan. "Shuta youra little monkey moutha," the old man chirped. "Ugolini, he knowsa whatsa best for you."

One sweltering hot day, things reached a tipping point. The daily take had been poor and to top it off, Chimps had wiggled out of his leash and tied it to the tail of a bulldog. Ugolini eventually figured it out when he felt the dog relieving himself on his old man's leg. Ugolini spent half the afternoon searching for his monkey only to find the little varmint snuggled on Becky's lap as she petted him fondly. Ugolini flew into a rage. He walked up and grabbed the monkey and brought him out to the street.

"We've been out here alla morning and afternoon anda alla you gotta a show isa twoa pennies anda onea nickel." The monkey shrugged as if he could care less. "Heys you a littlea monster, you better getta youra heada in the game or I'ma gonea finda newa partner."

The monkey threw down his hat and squared off with the feisty old man. The little furry beast began clenching his dukes as he eyed his master. "Oh, youa wanna piece of Ugolini," the old man grumbled as he set down his Hurdy-gurdy. He hunched over like a bare-knuckled prizefighter and threw a couple of air punches followed by a quick shuffle of the feet. Unflappable, the monkey squared up to him as a street crowd gathered around. In no time, the monkey scurried up the front of the old man and wrapped his arm around his fat, wrinkled head then shrieked as he bit his nose. Ugolini was able to flip the beast over his shoulder and onto the ground. The two began to roll about, changing positions of dominance. At one point, they were able to get to their feet. With their arms wrapped around each other's necks and touching foreheads, they circled like Greek wrestlers, each pawing the other for the upper hand. And, within seconds, they were back to rolling around in the dirt.

Becky ran out and positioned herself between the two, stopping the brawl. "You two oughta be ashamed of yourselves," she shrieked.

"Wella thata littlea bugger started it," Ugolini responded.

"I don't care who started it. You two have worked together for a long time," Becky pleaded. "There's a lot of love here. Now both of you try and get along."

She was right. The pair settled down, and they got up and dusted themselves off. Ugolini picked up the monkey's hat and tin cup, which was overflowing with coins. The crowd had enjoyed the fight. The three of them all went out for lunch but, much to the old man's chagrin, Becky's attention was on Chimps, as usual.

That night, Ugolini begged the monkey to put in a good word for him with Becky. Chimps just sat there with his arms folded. The Italian man grabbed his satchel of money and poured it on the table. He pushed half the pile over to the furry animal. "Thatsa for a you. We fifty-fifty partners." Hey, come on. I do anythinga fora my pal." The monkey was no fool. He knew Ugolini was now kissing up to him. He wanted the girl, and the monkey was the only one who could open that door, but the old man was going to have to earn it.

The next day the two were back on the street but, things had drastically changed. The monkey was now in control and running the show. The sound of the organ reverberated through the busy Five Points neighborhood. Churning the handheld organ was none other than Chimps while Ugolini, wearing the small red cap, scampered around on his all fours waving a tin cup in front of surprised spectators. It was embarrassing. Humiliating. And that's the way the monkey liked it.

While Ugolini did an awkward clumsy somersault in front of the onlookers, he looked up and noticed Becky watching from the crowd. Ugolini had never been so embarrassed in his life – except the time when his mother made him balance a meatball on his nose at a family gathering. The monkey had made a monkey out of him and knew it. On the upside, they made more dough then they ever had before.

"I'ma through with a you!" Ugolini yelled as he threw down his tiny hat. "You'rea nothing buta disrespectful a little scamp, treating your Ugolini likea you have."

That day the duo split up.

The monkey moved to a flophouse and soon found gainful employment running numbers for a Five Point's gang known as the Bum Rum Boys. He was making good cabbage too. While in the mob, he climbed the ladder and started making illegal booze runs. And it wasn't long before

Chimps was strutting around town in a nice tailored suit, smoking a cigar and flashing greenbacks.

Ugolini had used his savings to buy a shoeshining kit. He set up his station on the corner of Seventh and Main. People would recognize him and ask where his cute little monkey was. He would always respond, "Whatta monkey? I never knowa a monkey."

One day Becky stopped by to check on Ugolini. She was concerned about his mental health now that he was on his own. She handed him an apple. His heart sang with joy as he gently caressed it for a long uncomfortable minute as salvia gathered on the corner of his mouth. He was ecstatic to have something she had touched. He smiled and then took several bites as if it were a piece of her heart she had given.

"Oh," she surprisingly said. "I was just hoping you would polish my apple so I could put it on the shelf and eat it for breakfast."

Ugolini slowly stopped chewing then handed the half-eaten fruit back to her. "I brung ya something else," Becky shyly said. She pulled out a little doll she had made and handed it to Ugolini.

"I like to make dolls in my spare time," she proudly stated. "Maybe it'll bring ya luck." The object looked so real that it was uncanny. The man gently fondled it for a long awkward minute as salvia gathered on the corner of his mouth while releasing a few soft, creepy moans. Again, he was just happy to have something she had touched. "Heys, yousa wanna takea a stroll?" he hopefully asked.

The shoe shiner shut down the shop early that day so that he could spend the afternoon in the park with Becky. They walked together while she talked, and he laughed. After an hour or so, she finally asked him why he was laughing. He had no answer, so he began to converse with her. While they were on the bench enjoying a hot dog, they looked up to find the monkey walking towards them. He was wearing a tailored pin-striped suit and smoking a cigar fatter than the hot dogs that Becky and Ugolini were nibbling on. Two chubby thugs flanked the furry animal on both sides as they strutted in sync. Coincidentally, they were just a furry as the monkey. Soon they hovered over the couple.

"Whatta you wanta froma mea, ya ungrateful monkey?" the old man snarled.

The monkey just smirked and blew several cigar smoke rings in the air. The cocky beast snapped his finger paw, and one of the thugs handed him a hundred-dollar bill. The monkey strolled over to Ugolini and tucked the C note into his wrinkled shirt's front pocket, then tapped him on the cheek as if to say, "Go get yourself something nice to wear."

Ugolini jumped up and pulled out the money, threw it down and spit on it. The monkey went crazy, circling and shrieking, taking the disrespectful action as an insult to his monkey-manhood. He yanked off his suit coat and hunched over with his paws in front of him ready to pounce.

"You wanna takea a shot at old Ugolini again?" he snarled as he stood up. "Come on, Mister Biga Stuff. I'ma gonna takea you down oncea anda for alla."

Ugolini wasn't playing games. He swung his arm and knocked the cigar out of the monkey's mouth. The angry animal screeched then charged his former owner, knocking him over the bench. The old Italian threw the monkey off then leaped to his feet like a spry Coon cat. He shuffled his feet and waved his fist cursing the short primate.

"I'ma gonna rippa your tail offs anda shove it downs your throat," he threatened.

He was just about to do the Linguini body slam on the little pest, a move he had learned on the streets of Genovese as a teenage boy during scraps after a neighborhood Bocce Ball game. But before he could pounce Chimps' thugs grabbed him. Thinking quickly, before the old man got pummeled, Becky stood on the bench and jumped on Ugolini's shoulders, thinking she would gain the advantage in height - not to mention she was the high school chicken fighting champ. Unfortunately, the organ grinders knees were not what they used to be, and he crumbled like feta cheese. While Becky sat on his head, his face barely peeking through the bottom of her dress, the monkey scurried around them making mocking noises while the henchmen chuckled.

That night, as Becky nursed Ugolini's wounds, she made him a bowl of eggplant soup. He loved it. It was the best soup the Italian ever had. He looked deep in her eyes, her face beaming and, without a second thought, he kissed her. She smiled and reached over and touched the old man's face, then plucked out some stray eggplant stuck in his beard. Suddenly, a grand idea struck him. They would open their own restaurant.

Ugolini scraped up his savings from his days as an organ grinder along with his shoeshining cache. It wasn't much. Becky had set some money aside from the dolls she had sold. They were still in need of cash, so they went to a local pawn shop. Ugolini put up his old hand organ for collateral and obtained a thirty-dollar loan. It still left them short of their restaurant dreams.

The couple walked alongside the Hudson River.

"We'rea gonna geta our restaurant and it'sa gonna bea the besta place in the whole world," Ugolini beamed. "People theya gonna comea from miles to trow downa youra food."

"Yeah, sure they will, Ugolini. Sure, they will," she responded then started crying.

The old man held her in his arms tightly. "I makea everything alright. You'll see," he said. "Hey, come on, I'll leta you worka in the restaurant, cooking day and nighta tilla your fingers falla off. It'll be a funa for ya. You'll see. Ugolini makea the world spina round and around."

The Dago Darlings, a mob outfit that controlled the lower east side of Manhattan, were sitting around their bar hangout drinking booze, smoking and gambling. Chimps sat at the corner table wrapped up in a game of five card stud with three other thugs. The monkey had done well for himself, lying, cheating and stealing his way to the top. He was living the American dream.

Suddenly, the door slowly creaked opened. The place grew quiet as they watched Ugolini shuffle in. He took off his hat and fiddled with it in his hand.

"IA comea to speaka witha the bossa man?" he softly mumbled.

The humble organ grinder sat across from a fat Italian man, Mr. Spatero. He watched the godfather eat his meatball soup.

"So, you're looking for a loan?" the godfather asked.

"Ia got mea somea biga plans," the organ grinder claimed. Suddenly, the godfather spits a mouthful soup back into the bowl. "Holy mugatsa, since when do meatballs have bones?"

"Mya girlfriend she makea the besta soups ina the wholea wide world," Ugolini proudly stated. "Asa matter-of-fact, we a gonna open a restaurant and everybody gonna come from miles around. But, we no havea the money to doa this. It isa why I'ma herea before you."

"I'll tell you what. You bring over some of your gal's soup tomorrow, and if I like it, we'll see what we can do to for you."

The next day Ugolini brought the soup over. The godfather was completely enamored by the scrumptious broth. One could say he was bowled over by the bowl, if one wanted to say something idiotic. Without any hesitation, he put five-grand on the desk and slid it over to the old man. "I wish you much success on your new business," the godfather said. "It comes with a forty percent interest rate to be paid each week. Don't be late. Bad things can happen."

Ugolini, torn as he walked out, happy he was getting the money but, bitter that it was coming from a criminal organization. He despised the mob and couldn't help but think he made a deal with the devil. The Italian worked hard his whole life, and these people just took from little people like himself. As he walked out of the hangout, he shot a glance over at the monkey slumped at the card table, eating a breaded lamb chop and sipping on a glass of Rye whiskey. Their eyes locked for a moment. Ugolini gave a disgusted look and spat on the floor. The monkey put his arm over his other bent arm as he lifted his fist in the air. It was the Italian "screw you" sign.

Within a month the restaurant was up and running. Becky had done an excellent job decorating the place, hanging her many dolls on the walls. Word had spread about the tasty food, and soon the place was packed every night. While Becky worked in the kitchen, Ugolini would walk around taking orders and talking with the customers. Patrons often asked about his little monkey friend. Ugolini would shrug and say, "I thinka he's a stocka broker or something."

Every Friday, a few of the mob boys would stop by and pick up the interest money from the loan Ugolini had secured. Although it was a hefty fee, business was good, so payback wasn't a problem, but he would be indentured to the thugs for a long time. Ugolini's relationship with Becky couldn't have been any better. While the pair only had one night to go out with each other, at least they had money to do things like bowl, dance, or enjoy a Valentino picture show.

The monkey was falling deeper and deeper in with the mob. His tasks had become more dangerous. However, he was no longer rising in the ranks, and was becoming disillusioned. They were treating him like a second-rate gutter rat. After a long day of zipping around town running numbers the little monkey's till came up light. When the mob boss questioned him about the shortage, the furry animal shrugged it off as if to say, "Forget about it." After the third time it happened, some mobsters brought Chimps into the back alley and gave him the once over three times. The beatings were a message to ensure the monkey knew embezzling was something the mob didn't look too kindly on, not to mention they felt it was dishonest to steal any money honestly stolen.

On the other side of town, Ugolini's restaurant was beginning to have troubles of his own. A food critic gave a scathing write-up on a pasta fa zool dish that happened to contain a dark curly hair. Ugolini claimed it was just a roach, but the critic knew a greasy follicle when he saw one. It was so disgusting that the snotty critic would battle nightmares for the rest of his life.

The scathing article in the Times leveled Ugolini's business. The number of customers dropped by half. (Certain people who enjoyed stray hairs in their meals, mostly Asians, who found it an American delicacy.) The Italian entrepreneur tried everything to boost business. He gave out two-for-one sausage coupons. He even brought in a street magician to entertain folks at their tables, but the only thing that disappeared was the money in the cash register and the magician.

For over a year, Chimps had worked his way up the mob ladder and was now in charge of the booze runs on the east side. He ran a small crew of underlings who would hijack truck shipments, steal the barrels of hooch and then deliver it to the speakeasies on the west side. After each successful heist, the little varmint would celebrate by tearing up the town, boozed off his rocker, and sporting an entourage of flapper girls. With his cocky gangster demeanor, he would throw around tips, tucking dollar bills in people's pockets while blowing a wave of smoke in their face from his expensive cigar. The chimp was the man about town and relished his position as a thug.

The boss wanted to expand his operations. So, he directed his thugs to step up the shakedowns of local enterprises. One of the businesses was

Ugolini's restaurant. As a result of the stray hair in the food incident, the old man profits had slowed, and he was barely making ends meet.

"Whatta ya mean yous nowa wanna fifty percenta of my profits?" Ugolini screamed at the chimp.

The monkey gave a half-smirk and shrugged as if to say that's just the way it's gonna be. He then confidently puffed on his cigar not realizing he was sucking on a sausage he had accidentally grabbed off of the table.

Ugolini reached his breaking point, and charged his old sidekick, but before he could wrap his arms around the hairy gangster, the monkey's gorilla apes stopped him. They hoisted him off of the ground with his legs flailing while he screamed, "Whatsa matter for you? I takea you offa the streets and a raisea you froma a little bambino monkey, and this is the way youa treata me?" Chimps felt no remorse, or at least he didn't show it. His current occupation was the big money. The American dream. No more dancing like a fool and begging for pennies to be thrown in his tin cup. He was going to be somebody.

The monkey was starting to have problems. He had been taking a cut of the shakedown money to support his lavish lifestyle. The booze, tailored-made suits and trollops came at a price, but he felt he had an image to keep up. He was burning the candle at both ends, and was beginning to screw up on his job, missing mob meetings and essential shipments.

Chimps' behavior didn't go unnoticed. Suspicion was growing with the boss, who now had some of his boys keeping an eye on the monkey. The mob boss brought him in for a sit down and started to pepper his underling with questions, hoping to trap the furry embezzler. Chimps stayed cool, and didn't say much except for a few grunts and shrieks, then buttered up the boss by handing him a banana, which he would smoke later. For now, the boss was satisfied. He sternly told his employee to quit monkeying around and handle business. To make sure the little sneak understood, he had his boys slap him around a bit. Maybe it was because the boys had eaten lemons earlier, but the beat down left a sour taste in Chimp's mouth.

Ugolini had fallen months behind on his payments to the mob. The mob boss had no choice but to send some of his boys to have a chat with the old man. Chimps, now a captain, would lead the group. When he arrived at the nearly vacant restaurant, Ugolini was in the back, rolling manicotti. Becky rushed back to tell him the gangsters had entered the food joint.

The disheveled chef appeared from the back room with his arm around Becky to ensure her of her safety. Chimps, smoking his signature cigar, approached with his paw out, signaling it was "pay up" time. Ugolini, under a lot of stress and teetering on his breaking point, huffed as he lifted his rolling pin and began waving it recklessly in the air. "Youa biga thorna in my side. Takea, takea, takea! Ugolini worka hisa fingers to the bone anda youa strolla in here with a youra little monkey paws stretching out to geta da money I makea witha my pasta anda meataballs. I raised you from just a littlea monkey, and nowa look ata you. Youra a biga hairy disgrace. Youra momma, she'da bea ashamed of you."

The comment cut deep into Chimps. He loved his mother, tragically killed while riding a pony in the circus. He shrieked, then ran around the restaurant jumping on tables and throwing plates. Then the monkey suddenly calmed down, straightened his tie and composed himself. He approached Ugolini and held out his paw for his pay off. The old man sighed then handed the monkey six meatballs, "That's alla I got for you now." The chimp examined the meatballs closely then held his hand back out. Anger and rage appeared on Ugolini's face. He huffed, then grabbed two cannoli's off the counter and thrust them at the monkey. Chimps smirked as he took the rest of the payout.

The mob boss exploded when Chimps handed him four meatballs and one cannoli. "What the hell is this?" he questioned. "Where's my money?" The chimp shrugged, perplexed as to why the boss didn't think they got a good deal. He gestured as if to say, "Did you want meat sauce too?"

"You stupido monkey!" he yelled as he slapped the confused primate. "I want you to burn that restaurant down. No money, no business. Capeesh?" Chimps began to shuffle out of the room with his shoulders slumped. He looked back at the boss, hoping he'd have second thoughts. "Burn it!" the big boss bellowed.

Chimps sat on a crate down by the docks, looking over the water. His mind was racing. He felt so lost that he had no idea he had been smoking a banana for the last hour. "What had he become?", he thought. Although Ugolini and he had a fallen out and gone in different directions, he didn't hate the man. The monkey thought back to Vienna. The little town where Ugolini had rescued him from a traveling circus where he was beaten and abused and forced to do handstands on the back of an elephant for unruly crowds that threw peanuts at him. He remembered how the old man trained him to dance and do tricks for money, teaching him to play the crowd and soak them for every cent they had. He was a good man, and Chimps was starting to feel some regret, but he also knew that with the mob, business was business and there was no way out but in a coffin. They'd never let him walk away.

It was around midnight when Ugolini finished wiping down the kitchen. Becky was supposed to pick him up but was running a little late. Suddenly, the old man could smell smoke. He quickly checked his ovens and stoves to make sure all was turned off. He raced out to the dining room to see the front of his restaurant ablaze in flames. Escaping with his life was all that mattered now. Without thinking, Ugolini dove through the window and fell safely onto the sidewalk. He then managed to roll into the street and out of harm's way. Not far from him Ugolini heard some laughing. Looking over he saw Chimps, along with a few of his thugs, holding a gas can. Just then Becky pulled up in the car.

Ugolini jumps to his feet and points to the monkey. "Youa! Youa stolea my dreams! Nowa I'ma gonna takea youra monkey lifea!" The monkey ripped off his coat and tie then waved the old man to come and get it. Becky screamed, "No Ugolini!" It was too late. The broken restaurant owner had reached his breaking point. It was time to end it all… for good. He charged Chimps who charged right back. Ugolini planned on using the "clothesline take down" his grandmother from the old country had once taught him but Chimps was a step ahead of him and went low. He flipped the old man over his shoulders into the night air, in a resounding thud Ugolini hit the ground. The monkey lifted his arms in victory and pounded his chest. He seemed to signal that there was more of that if his old master wanted to continue the scrap.

Ugolini slowly climbed to his feet. He raised his hands in front of him signifying that it was over as he mumbled "No maas, no maas." He reached in his pocket and revealed a shiny quarter uttering, "What'sa that, huh? What'sa that?" He began to twirl his fingers slowly. Chimps cocked his head as he watched the coin change positions. "Huh, youa likea," Ugolini teased. "Youa likea the shiny quarter." Indeed, the animal did. Money was his weakness, and he loved it feeling its hypnotic effect. Suddenly, Ugolini flipped the coin in the air. As the monkey's eyes followed it, the little Italian man rocked back and then planted his foot into the monkey's crotch. The greedy mammal doubled over, gasping for some cool air to relieve the throbbing ball pangs. "The monkeys seea. The monkey swoona. The monkey fall downa," Ugolini sneered.

Chimps put his hands in the air as if to say he had enough. Then, with a tear in his eye, he stretched his arms out looking for a hug. The gesture seems to touch Ugolini. Maybe the feud was finally over. He smiled then raced over to give his monkey a loving squeeze. As he grabbed his furry friend the monkey grasped the old man's ears, fell on his back and put his hind legs on his chest, pulling the grinder down only to flip him over. Ugolini did a double somersault then kissed the cement. Lying stunned and motionless on the sidewalk, he shook his head to clear out the fogginess. Chimp's laughing face came into focus as he hovered over the old man. Suddenly, the organ grinder got a second wind then popped up, throwing punches in the air, looking for something to hit, and ready to go another round. The monkey and the man built a head of steam and a collusion ensued. They grappled and the old dog put the monkey in a bear hug. Standing by her car, Becky watched the horrific spectacle until she could take no more. She dropped her bag of popcorn and ran over to put an end to the fight. She grabbed Ugolini and the monkey but became entangled in the melee until they all fell to the ground.

Becky fell away while Ugolini held the flailing monkey in his hands. It was time to end the turmoil. He moved towards the burning building, and without a second thought, he threw the monkey into the flames. An eerie silence filled the smoky air, broken by the soft crackles of burning wood.

The mob thugs looked on in shock as they watched their four-legged leader perish in the inferno. Ugolini took one last look at his blazing restaurant then pushed his way past the mob hoodlums and into the safety of the car. Becky had already made her way to the car where she sat in the front seat, tightly bundled in her coat, and weeping. They drove away somehow believing their American dream was still out there.

Life continued in New York at full speed. Immigrants were pouring in, all in search of the American dream. Many had made their way out west where new cities were beginning to bustle. One of them was San Francisco where dreamers had ventured to find gold and then decided to stay. On one of the corners was a lively bar that featured top-notch showgirls dancing in bubbly flowing dresses. But the big draw was when an old man would take the stage and softly play the hurdy-gurdy to the melody of an Italian song while a monkey would entertain the audience with a playful jig then run around and collect dollar bills in his tin cup. Ugolini had kept his name figuring he was safe on the west coast. Chimps, well, he would always be Chimps. The duo had come a long way from spare change.

In a small church, Ugolini and Becky held hands at the altar. She was wearing her homemade gown made from the fabric of the doll's clothes she used to sew. She also had set five beautifully dressed dolls in chairs next to her as her as bridesmaids. Ugolini, standing more erect, looked dapper in his tux that he purchased instead of renting. Next to him, stood his best man Chimps in his tailored-made suit and chewing on an unlit cigar.

"Do you take this woman to be your lawfully wedded wife?" the preacher asked.

"Sure. I don't seea whya not," Ugolini responded with a smile.

"And do you take Ugolini as your lawfully wedded husband to love and obey," said the preacher.

"He's my Ugolini," she bashfully stated in a soft tone.

The preacher then asked for the rings so he could bless them before they placed them on each other's fingers. Ugolini looked at Chimps who looked a little dumbfounded. He reached his little paw inside his pocket and pulled out a banana. He nervously smiled then reached in his other pocket and pulled out a bottle opener then looked at Ugolini as if to say, "I got nothing."

The old man turned beet red and got up in the monkey's face. "Whatsamatta for you, youa stupid monkey? Wheresa the ringa I gavea you?" Chimps snarled at him. "Oha, youa wanna piecea of Ugolini?" Chimps crouched down then waved him on. "Youa barking ata the wronga dog," Ugolini huffed. Chimps had seen this too often and got in his four-legged stance to take on the crazy fool.

Suddenly, Becky stepped between them to prevent any blood-letting skirmish. "Oh, you two boys," she giggled. The two were smart enough to realize that it was not a good thing to fight on the big wedding day. They had the rest of their lives for that. At the reception, Ugolini got down on one knee and with his hurdy-gurdy dedicated a sweet old Italian song to Becky. The off-key ditty brought a tear to everyone's eye. An occasion such as this was a time when people were vulnerable, so that's why Ugolini had sent Chimps around with the cup. They made a killing that day. Ugolini would later play a fast song and dance around while plastered from the wine, then fall on a table and pass out. Chimps would rifle through his pockets and grab what he could.

Becky continued to make cute little dolls that Ugolini sold at his new restaurant. He was proud of his talented wife, and every time he looked at one of her works of art, he'd reflect on the life-size uncanny depiction of the stuffed Chimp's doll she made. The same one she had concealed in her coat and slipped to Ugolini during the staged skirmish outside the big restaurant fire. The mobster never saw the sleight of hand as Chimps slipped into her coat as Ugolini pretended to wrestle with a monkey doll then quickly heave it into the fire. The pseudo tragedy of Chimp's death made him a free monkey – able to live a new life without the fear of mob retribution for leaving the gang. The life insurance on Chimps would give the three of them a fresh start on life. And, the insurance money from the burned down restaurant was enough to open a new and better establishment. And San Francisco seemed like an as good place as any to live the American dream.

THE FORGOTTEN VAUDEVILLIANS

During the early part of the century, people would entertain themselves by going to watch vaudeville acts. These acts would tirelessly travel from town to town performing one-night stands in packed theaters and burlesque houses. The routines consisted of everything from comedy, singing, juggling, magic, and yes, even tap dancing with a graceful prancing grizzly bear that could crush soda water bottles on his head. Among some of the top-billed acts were Bergen & McCarthy, W.C. Fields, The Marx Brothers, just to name a few. As much of a draw as these popular entertainers were there were a few exceptions that didn't quite measure up to the high-performance standard.

"Blowfish" Huey was a black trombone player from Tupelo, Mississippi. At the age of five, he picked up his first trumpet. He then used it to hit his older brother over the head for calling him stinky pants. After too many spats with his sibling, the horn was rendered useless. Recognizing the boy's instrumental talent, his father bought him a trombone. He could only play three songs because of extremely short arms. However, when he played his cheeks expanded to astronomical proportions. It appeared that he stored two cantaloupes, one in each side of his mouth. Huey toured the country for twelve years until one night in a brothel while performing a Louis Armstrong number, his head exploded. It was the only standing ovation he ever received while on stage.

Fran and Stan were eastern European immigrants who arrived in America in 1923. The Polinski brothers were three feet tall, and their specialty was tumbling. As a matter of fact, they were known as the Tumbling Twins—and they absolutely despised one another. Booked as an opening act, they would climb on each other's back and take turns throwing each other into the audience, even if there wasn't one. Trouble began when Stan's tiny foot clipped Fran's chin on a routine backflip. The two began brawling and rolling on and off the stage. It was a small scuffle that blossomed into a free-for-all that included the public in attendance. The twins miraculously escaped unscathed. Their career halted when, during a skirmish over who was funnier, Amos or Andy, the brothers tumbled out a six-story hotel window, still fighting on the way down. After that, the only rolling they did was in their grave.

Joey "Barefoot" Bunyon was the only shoe juggler in the country. At the beginning of his act, he would venture into the audience and gather shoes of all shapes and sizes from unsuspecting onlookers. Billed as "The Sole Man" he would toss loafers, sandals, galoshes, even slippers, high into the air. Sometimes he would even catch them on the way down. Usually five minutes into the sorry juggling display the crowd would boo, call him a heel then watch him get the boot off stage. For one midnight performance, he got hit in the face with a shoofly pie. Unable to see and disoriented, a wooden Dutch platform crashed down on his head rendering him unconscious and comatose for the next two weeks. Sadly, this was the only time he was ever given a round of applause. Tired of living on a shoestring budget, the shoe tosser quit and moved back to New York. He opened a foot apparel shop on Third and Broadway where he sold the footwear he had amassed over the years. Joey later fought in World War II as, believe it or not, a foot soldier, where he contracted, believe it or not, trench foot. He returned home as a hero and was decorated with a bronze booty.

Some very good magicians played the vaudeville circuit, unfortunately, Harry Klein wasn't one of them. Never good with words he billed himself as "Harry the Pretty Good Magic Guy." Just by getting on stage he could make a whole audience disappear. His best card trick consisted of pulling a card out of the deck, looking at it, then guessing it. Sometimes it would take three attempts while he muttered to himself, "Wait. I got it. Hold on. Let me try this again." All too often, he would pull a rabbit out of a hat—one piece at a time. Early in his career he used to make a colorful handkerchief appear in thin air. The trick was later terminated after his assistant, before the show, used it to relieve a sinus infection and the fabric became too stiff to work with. After misplacing his saw one night, he attempted to hammer and chisel an audience member in half. Upon being discharged from the hospital, the bandaged crowd volunteer filed a lawsuit and, any money Harry had saved, vanished into thin air. Sadly, his union wand got confiscated, and he was no longer allowed to perform. Broke and dejected, the inept magician got arrested for shoplifting an apple. It fell out of his sleeve.

Escape artists were always a big draw. People would pack into theater houses in hopes of seeing an artist kill himself. They loved when tragedy struck because, since it wasn't a full-length show, their money would get refunded. Lil' Anthony Gamboni began honing his act at the age of six when he would wriggle and jiggle his way out of his mother's clutches. Eventually, she would wait 'til he fell asleep to spank him. His career began when, as an ice delivery boy, he accidentally fell into a cold box. After hours of kicking and screaming he was eventually able to emerge from the tiny compartment. Although it was never locked to begin with it did give him a passion to try his hand at the art of escaping. On stage, he would be handcuffed, shackled, and have his shoelaces tied together then lowered into a water tank. In all his years, he never escaped once. (Because his father didn't believe in bathing, Anthony learned at an early age to hold his breath for days.) Only after his face turned the right shade of blue would they pull the waterlogged freak out of the tank. By then, the audience had become frustrated and left. With his fondness for water, Anthony later joined The Ziegfeld Follies as a synchronized swimmer. He got fired for padding his bathing suit. In his later years, he would be diagnosed with water on the brain and, supposedly, meet an untimely death. His passing away got prematurely reported, and the poor fellow was buried alive in a coffin.

The toughest job was that of the comedian. If a comic couldn't make an audience laugh, they would most likely be pelted with something from one, or all, of the four food groups. Shecky Leibowitz had the timing of a broken pocket watch. He couldn't even deliver a newspaper, let alone a joke. (Incidentally, that's why he lost his paper route.) Because he lacked material and, more importantly, wasn't funny, he would mostly emcee. Shecky did several "Knock, Knock" jokes but always forgot his next line after the audience rattled him by yelling, "Who's there?" Most of the time, whenever his mind went blank, his pause breaks got the biggest laughs. One of his many weaknesses were dealing with hecklers. His favorite comeback was "I'm rubber, and you're glue…" Often, he would screw that up by saying "I'm glue and you're rubber…" He tried his hand at a few impersonations to spruce up the lame act. While hunched over, he'd limp around on stage and say in a deep Yiddish accent, "Ou vey, holy moly cannoli, I can't live like a monkey in a basket." Then he'd look out to the audience to see if anyone would call out the name of who he was impersonating. He'd hear responses like "You stink! Get off the stage. Where's the hook?" Oblivious, Shecky would bellow, "That's Uncle Irving!" and, that's when food would start to fly. During one performance the hack comic thought insults would go over, asking a patron if that was a cabbage on his neck. Unfortunately, the man he verbally abused was an intoxicated Jack Dempsey - the heavyweight boxing champion. For the next two years, Shecky entertained doctors and nurses from a hospital bed.

Some acts worked with animals. George Burns started out using a seal in his vaudeville routine. Later, the slippery mammal went solo with his own radio show that aired opposite "The Shadow." A woman by the name of Gertrude Butterbutt came along in the late thirties. She did a song and dance routine with a chimp, named Hugo, dressed in a turquoise tutu and a tiny plaid dickey. Gertrude would sing "Sonny Boy" as Hugo would curl up in a ball and cover his head with his long monkey arms. On upbeat numbers like "Yes! We Have No Bananas'" and "Happy Days Are Here Again" the riled-up chimp would scurry back and forth on the stage with a banana in his mouth then climb the curtains, swing out over the awed audience, and hurl dung at their heads. Other times, he would sit down, pick fleas out of his fur, and nibble on them while making chimp faces at Gertrude who was trying to remember the lyrics to "Tea for Two." After grueling years on the road, Hugo began to hit the bottle incessantly. Drunk, the sauced chimp would forget his dance steps and his screeching often got slurred. He would hang out in seedy monkey bars, miss shows or simply blackout on stage. He was seen several times, backstage, trying to peel a Johnnie Walker bottle. The end was not far off for the duo. One night, at the Orpheum Theatre in Waterloo, during the big finale where Gertrude would rock Hugo in her arms and sing "You Must've Been A Beautiful Baby," the chimp interrupted her song with a series of belches in her face. It was the final straw. The act split up, and Gertrude went on to team up with a basset hound dog named "Valentino" who could howl up to twenty Bessie Smith tunes... the showstopper being "Empty Bed Blues." Eventually, Hugo, the chimp would develop cirrhosis and undergo a transplant surgery where he received a baboon liver.

Rasheesh Bungdhi was one of the oddest acts around. He was a regurgitator who swallowed almost anything he could get his hands on. He started with small things like nuts and seeds then progressed to coins, dice and cue balls. Once he choked the object down, he'd open his humongous mouth to show the item was not under his tongue or tucked in his cheek. Then he makes a loud grunting noise as he punched his gut. Soon his belly would roll several times, and after a few gags, he'd vomit article back out. The other acts that toured with him always made sure they locked their personal items in a trunk. Rasheesh was outspoken and known for putting his foot in his mouth ... literally. He was known for drinking a jug of water followed by a jug of kerosene. He'd expel the kerosene, lite it on fire then release the water in his gut to extinguish the fire. The trick was also performed in bars in which he was nearly arrested for arson. When the cop asked him for his ID, Rasheesh said, "Hold on a second," then began to grunt, punch his stomach, roll his tummy, gag a few times until his gooey wallet shot out. The cop let him go, figuring if he beat him who knows what might fly out of that mouth. The famous regurgitator would later die from choking on a fur ball after swallowing a Persian kitten named Dingleberry who eventually escaped through the dead man's rectum.

Finally, there were a few ventriloquist acts that toured the country. The worst of the worst was an act by the name of Kit & Kaboodle. Kit was so cheap that his so-called homemade dummy was just his right hand with eyes and lips painted on it, which he called Kaboodle. For the most part, the field he chose was not very wise since Kit had been born with a speech impediment. His stuttering could drag a joke on for several long grueling minutes. Many times, Kaboodle grew tired waiting to deliver his punchline and would fall asleep. The limp hand would send Kit in a screaming tizzy, and soon both of his hands were fighting with each other. Kaboodle never trusted Kit, claiming he just talked out of the side of his mouth. At one point, Kaboodle threatened to leave the act. Kit calmed him down by treating him to a manicure. Attempting to keep the act fresh, Kit put lipstick on his big toe, bringing his right foot into the show as a new character. Strangely, the hand and foot fell in love and would end up eloping leaving Kit to try his hand as a regurgitator.

    The golden vaudeville years are long gone but not forgotten - although some of the previously mentioned entertainers would like to forget them. It was no easy feat traveling from town to town, staring down a leery audience and sharing the talent they believed they had. Contrary to popular belief, the bad acts didn't starve. People seemed sympathetic and would generously chuck mushy vegetables, eggs and rancid meat at them, thus ensuring, at least, one meal a day. At least these performers got their protein and daily greens. But for five dollars a week these folks would stand up in front of armed hostile audiences and do what they loved to do—entertain. And, even the talentless bottom billers put smiles on people's faces. After that, they were run out of their town and told never come back.

FROM SAUCE TO RICHES

The roaring twenties were an exciting time filled with high-spirited, carefree fun and frolic. Things like the Charleston, big bands, rumble seats, flappers, distilled booze and all-night romping were all just a part of life. Prohibition was present throughout most of the decade, but not many people noticed - they were too drunk. Prohibition was a statement made by the Federal government that essentially said, "We don't want your money anymore, give it to the mob." Alcohol sales were the primary source of income for the city tyrants. This money was used to stimulate critical local businesses like speakeasies, gambling parlors, and brothels. In other words, the things that are vital towards promoting a thriving economy.

The racketeers that controlled the bootlegged alcohol and gambling houses were people like Al Capone, Vito Genovese, Jack "Legs" Diamond, Owney Madden, Lucky Luciano, to name a few. They took control of cities, paying off government officials and other highbinders just to line their pockets. It was utterly mob rule.

Not so well known were smaller, less famous gangster mobs like "The Pop Thugs" who confiscated millions of empty soda bottles from legitimate businesses only to return them to collect the deposit. "The Cracker Jack Kids," strutted around town sporting boxed-prized licky tattoos on their arm and were known for bullying small children out of penny store candy. Then there was "The Red Rascals" who crashed group gatherings like dance halls, bingo parlors and bridge clubs spewing ideas of common ownership of the means of production and the absence of social classes and money. The purpose of the Marxist mob was to spread communism and have people pay them to keep their political views to themselves. These shake down propaganda punks were hard to shut up and were eventually rubbed out by the notorious "Capitalist Pigs" who ran the west side. But the mob that made a name for themselves that nobody had ever heard of was "The Sauce Bunch."

The gang began its life of debauchery at an early age. The members first met at St. Bruno's Catholic High School in Philadelphia. The leader was a smart-aleck hoodlum named Tommy "The Gator" Nelson. Gator, derived from the word instigator, reflected his reputation among the faculty of clergy. He was a born leader who would get his classmates to do his dirty work like put fake mustaches on the saint statues, fill the Holy Water with bourbon and rig the nun's rulers to break on the first swat. Tommy dealt in scheming, practical jokes, and the planting of disruptive ideas into the impressionable minds of fellow naive students. Lester "The Milkman" Duncan would often carry out the dirty work for Tommy. Many times, during lunch, Lester would make his colleagues laugh so hard that milk would ooze out of their noses. He was a class clown who split his time between "goofing off" and staying after school. Sid "The Worm" Levine, notorious for not returning library books, was the brains of the pack. He could make mini explosives, usually out of stolen ingredients from Brother Brunson's chemistry class, that were often ignited, generally by Duncan or McDuff, in the holy lavatories of the school. Tubby McDuff, the enforcer, was as dumb as a chocolate chip cookie, which he would snack on all too often. However, Tubby was vital to the group because he had the muscle to instill fear into his classmates while stealing their lunch bags.

During their final year at St. Bruno's the wild pack of boys was expelled for cheating on their bible exam. Tossed out into the city, they were forced to make a living. The four cronies soon gained employment at a local spaghetti sauce factory. Their hours were long - sometimes fourteen-hours a day. It wasn't unusual for the boys to arrive home drenched in tomato paste and sweat (which was the secret ingredients in the sauce).

One day, while Tommy was walking home through Five Points, he noticed Mr. Stromboli sitting outside his restaurant, appearing down in the dumps. Tommy dressed in his usual knickers and cap strolled over to him.

"Ay, Mr. Stromboli. How's tings?" Tommy asked.

"Tings? Not so good, Tommy, my boy," the old Italian man sighed. "Business been slow and prices going up on everything; the pasta, dough, the sauce. I'm barely getting by."

Tommy reached in his jacket and pulled out a can of sauce he'd lifted from the factory that he was planning to take home to his ma. "Yous take this. It ain't much, but it's somin."

Mr. Stromboli's eyes lit up, "Mamma mia, you getta the good stuff."

"Yeah, sure," Tommy shrugged like it was no big deal. "I'll bring yous some more tomorrow."

"And I'll makes yous a nice, bigga, fat, ajuicy, apizza pie," Stromboli smiled as he pinched the Gator's cheek.

Tommy didn't see it as stealing. The cans he grabbed were dented and tossed out anyway. Each day the lad stopped by the restaurant, dropping off a few cans. In return, he'd get a nice, hot Italian meal on the house. The new sauce made quite a difference in Stromboli's business. The place became packed every night. Eventually, Tommy depleted the factory of its allotment of defective cans, and when he had nothing to offer the old man, Mr. Stromboli tucked a note in the boy's shirt pocket and said, "I'ma sure you cana find some littlea box just lying around."

Later that evening, Tommy assembled his childhood chums in the abandoned ammunition warehouse, which had been vacant since the end of World War I, now used as their clubhouse. "Guys, I'm tired of working day and night for pennies. I'm tired of coming home and stinking like a meatball. How 'bout you mugs?"

"Yeah, it's nuttin' but horse hockey," the Milkman stated.

"I ain't even making enough dough to eat any dough," Tubby cracked.

"What about yous, Sid?" inquired Tommy.

"The Worm" looked up from his *Velveteen Rabbit* book and replied, "What else are we going to do? We ain't got no diplomas."

"Ah, we don't need dem. Dat's for squirrels, anyway," Tommy sniped. "I got us a way to make us some real rhino. Yous all in?" Everyone looked around and nodded except Tubby; he was too busy looking for a lollipop he had hidden in his coat pocket earlier. That night, The Sauce Bunch made a vow to be the leading supplier of spaghetti sauce to the city. It became known as The Tomato Paste Pact.

For the next six months, The Sauce Bunch would sneak into the factory late at night and heist cases of spaghetti sauce. They began supplying Stromboli but quickly branched out to other Italian restaurants like Rome Sweet Rome, Your Momma's, Daisy's Dump-n-Dive, The Parmesan Palace, Applebee's Knees, The Wop Stop, Duck Soup-n-Sandwich, Mug's Meatballs, The Cannoli and Canary and You're Da Man-icotti! to name a few.

Tommy and the boys made a considerable profit margin, after all, the sauce was free so whatever they made went right into their pockets. In other words, the sauce was pure gravy to them. Word hit the streets, and Ma and Pa grocery stores began hitting them up for orders. In no time, The Sauce Bunch was moving multiple cases of product. Sid worked his way up to accountant assistant at the factory and was juggling the books to ensure that the tomato trail was untraceable. He chalked losses up to unsellable cans, ripped labels and lost crates. There was some truth to it. Trucks got hijacked left and right, and it was all being done by The Sauce Bunch since they knew the delivery routes. For a while, the high school dropouts were hitting on all eight and raking in the Italian bread. But, it wasn't enough.

It wasn't long before Tommy and the boys spread their wings to other kinds of factories. The greedy gang approached shady disloyal employees and offered a monetary incentive to provide them with cases of their finest product. Their operation acquired stewed tomatoes, peas, soups, coffee, peaches, and even Spam, which was a big mover for them. Sometimes if a client bought enough stolen goods, Tommy would stuff a Spam can in the guy's pocket, give him a light slap on the face and say, "The Sauce Bunch appreciates your business a whole bunch."

Within a year, the bunch had cornered the canned goods market in Philadelphia. If someone requested from Tommy, "Hey, can you get us any canned corn?" Tommy would wink and say, "You bet I <u>can</u>." Then, usually, that person would reply "Great" then ask Tommy why he winked.

Greed began to overtake the saucy boys and would inevitably lead to their demise, but for now, they justified their actions by telling themselves that they were helping to feed the hungry. Lester often commented, "We give people a little food to put in their belly, and they give us a little money to put in our pockets. Nobody gets hurt."

One hot summer's day, Tommy gathered his troops to propose a risky new venture. "Whatta yous boys tink about expanding out of canned goods?"

Sid dropped his book and exclaimed, "You don't mean…"

"Damn straight I do. I say we move into jar items," Tommy shot back.

"What about da Peanut Butter Boys?" Tubby asked as he licked the inside of a Spam can.

"Yeah, dey ain't gonna like us cuttin' in on deir jar business," Duncan stated. "Screw dem jar thugs. Deir small peanuts compared to The Sauce Bunch. Anyways, deir stuff spoils in half da time our stuff does." Everyone nodded and laughed—except for McDuff; his tongue was still lapping away at the Spam morsels.

The Peanut Butter Boys had started their criminal outfit down in Atlanta, near the peanut farms. Theirs was the same formula as The Sauce Bunch, stealing then selling on the open market, but they dealt strictly in jars and glass containers. They always felt they were too small for the can market. (The Peanut Butter Boys were smart enough not spread themselves to thin.) After knocking off their competition, "The Jelly Jerks" things heated up when the boys were unable to supply their clientele with a crunchier product and, in 1921, and were run out of town by the notorious Jif Junkies. The PB Boys lammed off and moved up north hoping to go legit with a dog washing business. Eventually, they fell back to the easy money of bootlegging jars of goods after several of them found fleas in their hair.

Finding a home in South Philly, they met up with an old acquaintance, Mikey "the Bug" (so nicknamed because his eyes popped out like a surprised insect). The Bug was the inside factory man down south who used to help supply them off of Peach Street. Before the Feds could close in on him, Mikey took his money and moved to The City of Brotherly Love, mainly because his girl liked a good cheesesteak hoagie. (He later regretted the move as her constant onion breath bowled him over daily.) He found employment as a stock boy in a pickle plant and soon began wheeling and dealing on the side. He rekindled his relationship with the Peanut

Butter Boys, who had now spread their northern venture into a variety of stolen items like jellies and preservatives, cherries, olives, mustards, and the Bug's pickle products - which they relished in. They ran a lucrative racket that supplied most of the underworld up and down the east coast.

Trouble began on a Saturday night in the fall. The Sauce Bunch had coerced a local mustard factory employee to cut all ties with The Peanut Butter Boys and start supplying them with cartons of the yellow condiment. Soon, The Peanut Butter Boys received wind of the takeover and plotted revenge.

Their first retaliatory act involved poor Tubby McDuff. Tubby was found in an ally covered in blood and mustard - with a hot dog in one hand and a glazed bear claw in the other. Goons had beaten him with wooden spoons and spatulas as he fought ferociously to finish off his doughnut before his demise. A note attached to his forehead read, "Stay out of the jar business cause yous can't handle da mustard!"

This violence infuriated The Sauce Bunch who began to boil then ultimately simmer. After stewing on it for a while, the members bubbled over and went on a vengeful spree, raiding The Peanut Butter Boys warehouses and smashing open scores of jars. The rival gang knew they had to make a statement and show The Sauce Bunch on which side the bread was buttered. They quickly retaliated by taking hammers to their enemy's stockpile of cans; even going so far as to rip the labels off. The Sauce Bunch found themselves with an abundance of damaged merchandise that was unsellable - even to The Salvation Army.

Weary of the turf battles, The Bunch planned a sit down with The Boys to quash the feud and prevent more blood and mustard shedding. The two gangs sat around a table at the "Guys and Molls" restaurant on the upper east side.

"You got the cans. Why yous need da jars?" Joey DeLuca huffed. (He was the high pillow of the PB boys and went by the nickname "Spiffy" because he always dressed in sharp glad rags.)

"We like jars better. People cut their fingers on cans, and we don't want that on our consciousness," Tommy fired back.

"So, you want the jars, and we'll take the cans?" Spiffy questioned.

"No, we want them both," the Gator dug in.

"You just said the cans cut hands, and you didn't like that," Spiffy interjected.

"What do I care if stupid mugs cut their thumbs off. It ain't my business," Tommy retorted forgetting what he had said before. "I'll tell yous what, you can have the baked beans line and we'll take the olives."

"I ain't no two-bit sucker," Spiffy fumed. "Nobody wants that malarkey. They'll throw it back in your face."

"How 'bout you just keep the jar business and we'll stick wit the cans?" Tommy suggested.

Spiffy thought for a moment, "That sounds good to me." They stood up and shook hands, both believing they had accomplished something, but everything was the same way as it was when they first walked in. It would take several days for the two gangs to realize this, and when The Sauce Bunch did, they felt flimflammed. Nobody snookers them out of the jar business. Nobody.

The Sauce Bunch plotted their next move. They were going to make nice with The Peanut Butter Boys and let them believe they were giving up on bootlegging cans and heading to Miami to open an umbrella stand on the beach. They invited their foes to the old warehouse for their farewell luncheon.

April 1, 1928 was a windy day in New York City. The Peanut Butter Boys had arrived at that warehouse all wearing swell gray pin-striped zoot suits and Bowler hats. Their dapper glad rags were meant to convey a message of "We're not some monkeys to be trifled with cause our clothes are tailored-made." The Sauce Bunch made them feel at home and kept any wisecracks to themselves. The PB Boys were impressed with the spread their rival gang had put out for them. They thought to themselves; maybe these guys finally realize who the big dogs are in this town.

The jar mob dug into the smorgasbord of food strewn across the table; clam linguini, tortellini, stuffed shells, penne with pesto and sausage, rigatoni, spaghetti with thick juicy meatballs, pasta fagioli soup. The Peanut Butter Boys were in heaven. The Sauce Bunch sat back and watched their guests stuff their faces while they nibbled on their Caesar salads and enjoyed some Cabernet. Little did the PB Boys know the food, mixed with a high-powered laxative, appeared to be ricotta cheese.

"Yous got some good chow here. Them tortellini are to die for," Spiffy spoke up, following it with a bellowing belch.

"Yeah, I'm sure Tubby would've enjoyed 'em," Tommy threw out.

"I heard about dat," Spiffy shrugged. "It's a shame what happened to that big-boned fella. He choked on a doughnut or something, right?"

"Yous know exactly what happened to him," Lester blurted out through his gritted teeth while Tommy patted his shoulder to calm him down.

"Yeah, well I guess accidents happen," Tommy commented. "Whatta say we all have a little chocolate-almond biscotti and some moist tiramisu?"

The Peanut Butter Boys threw down the dessert helpings, unaware it had been soaking in a horse tranquilizer all day. Tommy and the bunch watch as the PB guys' eyes begin to droop. Sensing they were now at a disadvantage, he bellowed, "We're taking over the jars and dere ain't nuttin' you and your mugs are gonna do about it."

Through his half-opened eyes, Spiffy managed to slur, "Forget about it. Everyting goes tru us. Everyting." Within seconds, he and his cronies were slumped in their chairs, fast asleep. Tommy stood up and said, "That jerk is right. When those laxatives kick in, everything is gonna go tru him." The Sauce Bunch let loose laughing and mocking the now passed-out mob. They picked up the remaining plates of food and dumped it on The Peanut Bunch Boys.

"Here ya go, saps," Lester quipped. "The foods on us."

The guys padlocked the doors as they left their patsies in the abandoned building which had no functioning bathrooms. A few days later a janitor noticed a wretched, foul stench emanating from the warehouse and, after prying off the locks, found a bunch of rubes, lying groggily on the floor, covered in linguini sporting filthy, soiled pin-striped suits. The place reeked like a Bronx sewage plant. It was a horrendous sight, and, unlike the recent St. Valentine's Massacre, this would come to be known as the "April Fool's Blow Out."

The soiled trousers were not enough to deter The Peanut Butter Boys who were now hellbent on revenge. One late evening, Lester Duncan was walking home from a shipment drop when a car pulled up next to him.

Four PB thugs leaped out and began to pelt the unsuspecting "Milkman" with cans of stewed tomatoes. Lester tried to throw his shoe at them in hopes of scaring the hitmen off. It was a feeble attempt, and the tin cans were too much of a lethal barrage. He collapsed on the sidewalk, covered in red tomato paste. He was later found being licked by a horde of feral cats. The next day the newspapers read, "Milkman Canned for Life."

The Sauce Bunch had dwindled in size, and the two remaining members were beginning to doubt if the bootlegging business was all worth it. They had made good money off the cans, and it was greed that made them reach for the jar line. And, because of that, two good hoodlums, Tubby and Lester, were now dead.

Tommy had just had his shoes shined at his favorite stand on the corner of Sixth and Broadway. He enjoyed his conversations with the polisher Stumps McGill, a World War I vet who tragically had both his arms blown off at the Battle of the Marne in France. Word was Stumps got sloshed the night before the engagement and passed out on an ammo stockpile. In the heat of the bombardment, the hungover lush was accidentally stuffed into an 80-millimeter Howitzer then fired towards the German trenches. He fell two hundred yards short but appeared to be unscathed. He got up, and while staggering back to his line, the murky-headed, shell shocked doughboy stepped on a British anti-tank mine. One of his arms they found in a Belgium schoolyard playground where kids were using it to whack each other in the head. The other limb is still unaccounted for but is perhaps on some Kaiser soldier's wall. He had a unique way of shining shoes. He would lick the leather then rub it dry with his bum. Tommy would flip him a can of Spam and say, "Thanks for the spit shine, Stumps" then shake his foot good-bye. The shoe shiner always felt gypped by the stingy Gator and, over time, would cut back on the licks to the leather.

As the leader of the Sauce Bunch walked away from his weekly shoeshine, a Rolls Royce Silver Ghost pulled up behind him, and two fellows jumped out. Holding Tommy at gunpoint, they forced him into the vehicle. They drove him to The Peanut Butter Boys headquarters.

Inside, they tied him to a chair. Spiffy entered the room togged up in a brand-new suit.

"Hey, I like your new rags," Tommy sneered. "The last one yous wore kinda stunk to high heaven."

"So's your body when it's rotten in the Jersey landfill," Spiffy shot back then slapped Tommy across the puss a few times for cracking wise until blood trickled out of the corner of his mouth. The Peanut Butter Boys weren't playing games. They humiliated Tommy by dressing him up in a skimpy flapper's outfit. Holding him at gunpoint, they made him Fox Trot with Peepers, the gang's bulldog, mocking his clumsy steps as he hoofed it across the floor with the panting, slobbering mutt.

The gang decided to get rid of their competition once and for all. Tommy was tied up and thrown in a car where two thugs, Leo and Duke, would drive him out to the Jersey Shore, fit Tommy with cement shoes and toss him in the ocean. The Gator vehemently insisted that he didn't look good in cement shoes. "It clashes wit my tie. You sure you ain't got nowhite linen spats?"

On the way out of town, Tommy put a bug in the ears of his captors, hoping to get them thinking. "You patsies like da ponies. I got a sure ting in the seventh. Dis bangtail can't miss."

"Ah, bushwa. Sure, you do," Duke shrugged.

"I got one too," Leo added. "You lying at the bottom of the ocean with a salmon up your ass."

"I'm serious," the Gator assured. "I got a guy on da inside putting some laxative powder in the jockey's pastrami sandwich an hour before post. I'm sure you mugs remember what da stuff is. It ain't pretty."

The two gangsters looked at each other, remembering the horrendous *"April Fool's Blow Out."*

"You know for sure he's doing this?" Duke asked with curiosity.

"As sure as your motha works the seventh street brothel," Tommy fired back.

Benny knew he must be on to something. His mother had worked the brothel for a long time. Greed quickly overcame the two jar boys.

The smell of fresh horse manure waffled in the air as the three men lingered around the rail, gripping their ticket that had "Lollygagger" to win.

"This is a sure ting," Tommy confidently stated.

The gates flew open, and the racehorses charged out. Caught up in the action, Duke and Leo began cheering as they egged on Lollygagger to pick up the pace, unaware Tommy had climbed up on the railing. As the horses flew by, the Gator leaped onto the back of the galloping horse "Misty Moonshine" and clung to the surprised Mexican jockey's neck. He looked back to see Leo and Duke, frozen, with their mouths agape, watching the backside of the horse trailing away. He flipped them the bird and, as if that wasn't bad enough, Lollygagger, who had been slowly trotting, stopped directly in front of the two Peanut Butter boys and dropped a deuce on the track. It was determined he had eaten the pastrami sandwich.

Tucking a can of pinto beans into the jockey's top pocket, Tommy bribed Juan to jump the fence and take him into town. For their trouble, he brought the pair into a local gin mill and ordered a few drinks to wet their whistle and thank them for lift. By late afternoon, Misty had passed out under a table, and Juan, holding a bottle of tequila, was following the cigarette girl around, making weird moaning noises while whacking the gasper gal's caboose with his riding crop. After ignoring several requests to take a bounce by Wiggins, the hefty mick bartender, the creepy sloshed jockey was hoisted up by the seat of his puffy silk knickers and tossed into the back alley. Juan would awake the next day strewn out on a pile of rancid garbage with his knickers stolen off his body and his riding crop sticking out of his ass. Someone claimed they saw Skeet, the skid rogue wino, wearing a pair of shiny knickers, but he was never proven the culprit. When Juan inquired about his missing horse, Wiggins claimed he hadn't seen it. But, oddly enough, Philly Cheesesteaks were now on the menu — which was never listed before. Wiggins also claimed that Tommy had jumped the tab and Juan was now responsible for the bill. The jockey attempted to pay it off with a can of pinto beans, but the mick wasn't having it. Juan spent the next two weeks washing dishes. He would later marry the cigarette girl and work his fingers to the bone to provide her with the good things in life, never knowing that while he was working long shifts Wiggins was out painting the town red with his wife.

Following the ordeal, Tommy met up with Sid at a nickel bookstore. Not to arouse suspicion and remain incognito, "The Gator" arrived dressed as a bellhop, which precisely made him look out of place, drawing more attention to him. The Worm sat at a table hiding behind a book called *"How to Date A Paper Doll"* while pretending to read.

"It's over, Tommy. We're through," Sid stated, peering over his book.

"Listen here, you worm, I ain't goin' down without a fight," Tommy sternly exclaimed.

"Come on Tommy; we had a good run. Let's leave it," Sid surrendered.

"Why you gutless four-eyed sweet tart. We're going to bring down these Butter Boys den we can walk away wit our heads held high," huffed the Gator.

"So how you plan on doing that?" the Worm inquired with skepticism.

"We're gonna turn over our can business to Dutch Schultz and his boys," Tommy said with a devious smile.

Tommy set up a one-on-one meeting with Joey "Spiffy" Delucca on neutral turf.

"You should be at da bottom of the ocean now," Spiffy stated.

"Yeah, well, you got circus clowns working for yous who couldn't hit a horse in da ass with a snow shovel," Tommy smirked. "Now let's get down to business."

For the next hour, the pair talked over a few scotches and finally agreed. "So yous wanna turn the cans over to me?" Spiffy commented. "Just like dat?"

"As long as you let Sid and me walk away. Untouched. No monkey business," the Gator replied.

"Done. But I wanna see you mugs dust out of town," DeLuca warned.

"Yeah. Sure ting. I have one last truckload to deliver to Dutch Schultz," Tommy declared.

"We'll take care of Schultzy," Spiffy assured. "I want you to scram on a train tonight, taking a powder from here. And, why you're at it, I think you should lose the silly bellhop costume too."

Tommy had indeed met with Dutch regarding his bootlegged cans. Schultz never realized how lucrative the business was and appeared very interested in a piece of the action. But first, he wanted to sample the goods. Tommy told him he was turning over the business to his new partner Joey

DeLuca and his boys but would have them send over a can of their best sauce. The following day a can arrived, and when Dutch Schultz opened it, several spring-loaded snakes popped out and scared the hell out of him. A note in the canister read, *"If you want my cans you'll have to pry them from my cold, dead hands, signed Joey "Spiffy" DeLuca."*

Spiffy and The Peanut Butter Boys delivered their truckload to Schultz later that afternoon having no clue some spring-loaded snakes had caused ole Dutch to piss his pants. Within minutes, the gang was all gunned down by the Schultz mob who then took over the can and jar business. DeLuca's bloodied, limp body lay on the street clutching a tuna can with a spring-loaded snake stuffed in his mouth.

The Gator and the Worm were pulling into a train station in Madison, Wisconsin. It would be their new home. With the loot they made from the canned underworld, they used the money to buy a dairy farm, even though neither of them knew anything about cows. Their first attempt at milking a cow was disastrous. Sid put a bucket under the teats, and when nothing came out, he had his partner crank the tail around thinking that would start a flow. Poor Tommy was booted in the head by the perturbed cow, hurling him into a nearby pig pen. Pissed off, the Gator squared off with the unruly cow, believing he could whack some sense into the beast like he used to do on the streets of Brooklyn to deadbeats who owed him money for his cans. But as soon as he slapped the cow, it rammed him and knocked him on his ass into a mushy pile of manure. Tommy and Sid soon realized getting milk, churning butter and making a little ice cream wasn't easy for a couple of hard-boiled city boys. After draining all their sauce money into their new venture, they decided to do what they did best - being lazy mobsters.

They noticed that cheeses were a luxury that most people couldn't afford. They decided to change that. Using their bootlegging mobster skills developed over the years, they met some employees in a local cheese factory and soon they were getting heisted crates of cheese and selling it on the black market. Tommy and Sid enlisted a small group of guys to help with the cheese distribution. This sinister gang of wedge peddlers became known as "The Cheese Clan."

The organization grew and soon the clan was supplying Swiss, American and Pepper Jack cheese throughout the upper Midwest. Things were good for a while, and the partners were raking in some good dough. But then, the Gator, as usual, became greedy and "the Worm" wanted no part of it.

"I tink it's time to expand out a little more," Tommy mentioned.

"Are you nuts? We're on easy street now," Sid sternly stated.

"I'm tinking... and I'm just tinking here. I'm tinking lunchmeats."

"Lunchmeats! That's crazy talk," Sid exclaimed. "You know The Deli Dogs have that market locked up. You heard what they did to "The Ham Hooligans." I can see branching out to goat or cream cheese, but lunchmeats? Whatta the hell do we know about salami? Or porchetta for dat matter?"

"What about crackers?" Tommy suggested.

"Come on, Tommy. Tink! The Cracker Chumps has run dat racket for over twenty years. Then you got The Saltine Squad to deal wit," Sid snapped, then continued. "And don't ask me about bagels 'cause you know 'The Jew Crew' runs that territory."

That was The Gator's problem. He always wanted more. The cheese wasn't enough to fill his basket. He knew The Worm could no longer cut the cheese. He had checked out, tired of wheeling and dealing blocks of dairy product. The pressure had gotten to Sid. He became paranoid and developed a case of the heebie-jeebies. He began hiding hunks and blocks and wedges throughout his house hoarding it in fear that a cheese famine would hit. There would be no famine and Sid would sink more and more into a depression, unable to cope with the life of crime he had led.

Maybe it was all the books he had read that was throwing him into a dark descent. Tommy only believed that comic books were good for the mind and was now becoming leery about trusting his partner anymore. He got wind that the Worm had given some handout Cheddar to a homeless guy coming out of a soup kitchen. This situation didn't sit well with Tommy, who was all about the profits, fearing Sid was turning soft and may, at some point, run his mouth and bring about some unwanted heat on the clan.

One rainy Sunday morning, Tommy stopped by to bring Sid a book a cop had once thrown at him. The Worm sat in a corner, mumbling to himself as he played a board game called "Hokum" using cheese balls as player parts.

"Whatcha doing Sid," he inquired.

"They're watching me. All of them. They're watching everything I do," the Worm murmured.

"Who's watching you, Sid?" Tommy reluctantly asked.

"You know who. The cheeseballs look at them," Sid garbled as he slowly swayed back-and-forth. "We can't trust them."

"No, no we can't," The Gator said in a soft tone.

As Tommy stood behind Sid, he reached in his pocket and pulled out some stale string cheese. The Mozzarella was so old and tough that a team of oxen could've used it to pull a Studebaker out of the mud. He wrapped it around his hands several times making sure it was taut.

"Everyting's gonna be swell, pal-y. The bee's knees," Tommy said as he dropped the string cheese around Sid's neck. The Worm just stared blankly at the cheeseballs as if he knew what was waiting for him. He felt a jerk then tugging on his neck. He gasped for air as his legs kicked a few times, but Sid had accepted his fate and didn't fight back. His cheaters fell off his face, breaking when they hit the floor. The last wisp of air leaked out of his lungs as he laid slumped in the chair. The bump off finished.

Tommy went around the house and gathered up all the hidden cheese to sell, even though some of it was over five years old. Being the cheap son-of-bitch, he was, he didn't want to pay for any funeral costs, concluding it would be easier to bury his friend in a rickety Brie crate. Unable to fit Sid's whole body in the flimsy wooden box, Tommy quickly became frustrated, deciding to throw his old partner in a sinkhole in the backyard. Too lazy to fill the pit up with dirt himself, he had Petie come over and complete the job. Petie was the dim-witted bag boy at the local grocery store. It would turn out to be a grave mistake.

The pair stood overlooking the lifeless body contorted in the ground.

"What happened to him?" Petie asked.

"Ah, he's just sleeping," Tommy assured.

"Why don't he sleep in a bed?" questioned Petie.

"Some people enjoy a hole," Tommy answered.

The curious bag boy was quiet for several seconds then blurted out, "Why he wants dirt thrown on him?" The Gator replied, "He gets cold at night, and the dirt keeps him warm. He'll dig himself out like a mole in the morning when the sun comes out." The naïve bag boy shrugged then tossed a heap of dirt on the curled-up body. It took Petie a few hours to pile the soil on Sid, and when he was done covering the body, he went to Tommy to get paid for his time. Tommy patted the kid's head then stuffed a wedge of blue cheese in the boy's shirt pocket and said, "Good work there, chief. You cover dat big fat noodle good?"

"I guess so. I think he'll be warm tonight," Petie responded without batting an eye.

"Beautiful stuff, kid. Remember, you didn't see nuttin'," Tommy smirked then lightly pinched the bag boy's cheek, "Enjoy dat wedge. Hey, when you get off work tonight swing by the gin mill and grab me some giggle juice. A bottle of Gibson Rye. You can earn yourself another wedge."

"I'm kinda busy tonight," Petie responded.

"Busy. That's a good one, kid," Tommy laughed. "How can you be busy? You're just a bag boy."

The degrading label stung and ate at Petie like a hungry maggot. Teed off, the pissed bag boy mumbled curse words under his breath as he left. He felt stiffed. His back was hurting from burying that lump in the hole and all for a lousy hunk of cheese. A cheese he couldn't stand. Tommy should've been able to guess he was a Gorgonzola guy. He thought about going back and demanding some money for his shoveling, or, at the very least, some aged Gouda. It wasn't about the cheese payment. He figured if he really wanted some cheese, he'd lift it from the store where he worked. The problem was he had asked Beatrice Peckerschmidt, the bucktooth cashier, out on date and was hoping Tommy would duke him a few bucks to pay for a meal. Petie was broke and hated being on the nut. He was pretty sure when the bill came the waiter wouldn't accept a wedge of cheese as payment. Petie was steaming, feeling like he been tossed aside like some pushover dupe. Nobody treats a bag boy like that he thought and stewed.

Petie filled his last bag with cornmeal, two round beef steaks, and some eggs. He told Beatrice he had to drop off a bottle of tiger milk at a man's house then he'd meet her at the restaurant. The cashier quipped, "Don't drink it all before you get there." Even though it was a stupid comment, Petie would typically find it funny and laugh along with her. When she giggled her neck would protrude out like a broodmare, and her buckteeth looked like they were coming right at him. In between the giggles, she would suck in deep, wheezing breaths, then continue with her laughing as salvia droplets spewed from her mouth dousing whoever was nearby. Petie was dizzy on the dame and usually found it sweet, but his mind was elsewhere as he contemplated how he was going to pay for the dinner if he only got another wedge of cheese for his delivery.

The Gator let the bag boy into his house as Fats Waller played on the gramophone in the background. Petie looked around and couldn't help but notice how well Tommy lived.

"Here's your bottle of hooch," the boy mumbled. "That'll be sixty-two cents."

"Thanks, kid. Sixty-two cents, huh?" Tommy said as he puffed on a cigar. "I'll tell you what. I like you. You do good work."

The mob man walked over to his Marion Davies painting hanging on the wall. He pushed it to the side revealing a wall safe. After going through the combination rotation, it opened. He reached in and grabbed a stack of bills then shut the vault. Petie became excited and began to have some regrets about his previous emotions.

Tommy quickly counted the lettuce in front of Petie's nose, folded it, then stuffed it in his pocket. "That's for the speakeasy tonight. Now, let's take care of yous." Petie's puss dropped in utter disappointment. The Gator opened a cigar box sitting on his walnut china cabinet and pulled out a wheel of cheese. "Yeah, you like dis, weak sister? Wait'll dat flavor hits your yap," he said, running the cheese under the bag boy schnozzle. "Now that's a whole wheel, kid. You deserve it. Don't spend it or eat it all in one place."

"I got a date tonight with Beatrice Peckerschmidt," Petie proudly stated.

"Peckerschmidt, huh. She got nice gams?"

"I guess so," Petie blushed.

"She a hoofer? A hotsy-totsy hoofer?" questioned Tommy.

"No, she's a cashier where I work. And she ain't no flat tire either," Petie stated. "I'm real keen on her."

"Well ain't you the drugstore cowboy. That shebas gotta be some kinda dumb dora to date a bag boy," Tommy jabbed.

"I ain't going be no bag boy my whole life. I got dreams."

"Sure, you do, kid." Maybe someday they'll promote you to box boy." Tommy jeered, laughing at his joke. "Let me get you a little something to help yous make some whoopee tonight, you swanky lounge lizard."

Tommy went in the other room then emerged holding a small wicker basket with an assortment of cheeses. "I don't give one of these tings to everybody. Now look here, you got your Cheddar, your Parmesan, your Colby, some Pepper Jack, and some Baby Swiss. Ya can't go wrong, kid. She'll love it. Oh, and give your little floozy one of dese." The cheap bootlegger grabbed one of his cigars and stuffed it in Petie's shirt pocket saying, "Dames love a good fat Havana."

Petie was flabbergasted. Beatrice would never smoke a cigar. She only likes to chew on them after dinner. Feeling insulted over the cheese wheel gift, the incensed bag boy scoffed, "I hope you enjoy the Rye, sir." Then he stormed out.

The Gator poured himself a big stiff drink to dip his bill then put on some Mill's Brother on the phonograph. Gulping his hooch, he looked at a framed black-and-white photograph of The Sauce Bunch boys sitting on crates of tomato paste swiped from a warehouse. "Top of the world," he mumbled to himself. The Gator smiled to himself, realizing the extraordinary journey on which he had been. As he went to pour another drink, suddenly, there was a pang in his stomach, nearly doubling him over. He assumed it was the codfish he had for dinner that he had marinated in the bathtub gin. Within an hour he began sweating profusely. Soon his muscles became sore, and his jaw tightened. As he tried to make his way over to the phone, he collapsed on the floor. His arms and legs became rigid as they convulsed. In a matter of moments, the Gator was having trouble breathing, believing he had drunk a Mickey Finn. Then, the door opened and in walked the bag boy.

"Did you enjoy the Rye?" Petie asked.

Tommy gasped for breath as he urinated in his pants.

"Nobody pays me in cheese," Petie grumbled. "Nobody."

As white foam dribbled out of his mouth, the Gator struggled to squeeze out his last words. "Bag boy" he murmured before closing his eyes. Petie kicked Tommy's body to ensure he was dead, then reached down and grabbed the lettuce out of the stiff's pocket. "Yeah, well, this boy just bagged him some dinner dough."

Beatrice looked beautiful in the swanky restaurant. Her peepers and protruding teeth seemed to capture the light from the candle on the table.

"Momma uses it to kill rats that come in the house," he commented.

"What's it called?" she asked.

"Strychnine. It doesn't even smell."

"Did you ever kill a rat?" she said with a giggle.

"Just one," he shrugged. "One cheap little rodent."

"Aww, poor little thing. You should've just given it some cheese and sent it away," Beatrice commented.

"That don't work… at least not with me," he snickered.

"Now I'm in the mood for some cheesecake," she stated, then laughed as her head rocked back-and-forth across the table and her buckteeth jetted out towards his face. It was cute for now but, Petie knew, if it ever became too annoying, he had the solution in a cabinet at home. The bag boy quit his job at the grocery store, replacing The Gator in the cheese underworld. He built a large empire, branching out into lunchmeats, crackers, and even dips. His gang became known as "The Hors d'oeuvres Hounds." Sadly, they would would eventually be rubbed out by the infamous "Pâte Palookas."

MENACE OF THE REICH

In 1942, Adolph Hitler's niece, Geli Raubal, showed up on der Fuhrer's doorstep with her son named Hans. She informed her uncle that the boy had high hopes of becoming a Nazi soldier and wondered if he could find him a position in the Third Reich. The Fuhrer was in a good mood. Dr. Morale had just given him a vitamule injection, a concoction of vitamins and amphetamines, which seemed to provide the dictator with the stamina of a young horse. (This was evident whenever he received good news on the front. He would drop into a handstand and kick his legs in the air like a wild stallion then treat himself to a sugar cube.)

Adolph was happy about his new arrival and whole heartily embraced the family member. Anyone with his Aryan bloodline would most assuredly be welcomed. The child was someone he could mold into a great Wehrmacht soldier and, who knows, maybe even, someday, rule over the fatherland.

Hans was twelve years old but looked sixteen but acted like he was eight. His image was that of a redheaded, freckled-face, chubby, little boy far from the ideal of the blonde, blue-eyed Hitler youth. He was a bit of a loner, shy, with a penchant for strange behavior. Nobody knew what was wrong with the kid; they just knew something wasn't right. Some speculated it was the handful of paint chips he nibbled on daily as a toddler, and others chalked it up to the young lads acquired taste for diesel fuel. It wasn't uncommon to hear the word "Stutthafenwitz" whispered around the roly-poly kid, which essentially means "oddball."

Most of Han's days were spent playing with Hitler's German shepherd, Blondie. While the chancellor was plotting military strategy, Hans would crawl around on the floor, biting the dog's tail and trying to suckle the hound. Other peculiar behavior observed was Hans racing around the room, pretending he was riding a motor scooter and chirping, "Ya Vol! Honk! Honk! Ya Vol!" as he zipped in between the legs of the irritated field marshals who's' only recourse was to just smile at the bizarre kid and try to kick him away when Hitler wasn't looking. The Fuhrer didn't pay much attention to the unusual actions; he was busy with little things, like conquering Europe.

Hitler had devised a clever strategy to invade England. Laid out before him, on a table map, were figurines of well-positioned platoons, tanks, battleships, and his infamous wolf pack submarine fleet, surrounding the isle of Britain. The foolproof plan was sure to win the war for Germany.

That night, while Adolph was asleep in his bed cuddled up with Blondie and his girlfriend, Eva, stowed peacefully under his bed, Hans was in his bedroom shaving his legs. After a while, the boy became hungry and waddled to the kitchen for a few Krapfens – a pastry similar to a jelly doughnut. The dessert was gone. He knew the culprit had to be Hermann Goering; the fat bastard was always on the prowl for leftovers. Bored, Hans roamed the house and soon found himself in Hitler's planning room. He noticed the little toy-like tanks and ships on the large table map in front of him. It was playtime.

Hans began rearranging all the pieces on the paper terrain while making gun and explosion sounds. After putting several submarines in his mouth, he picked up one of the tiny planes and ran around the room; giggling and yelling, "Vroom! Vroom! Ich bin ein Flugzeug! Ya Vol! Ya Vol!" At some point, the hyper lad tripped on Blondie's dog bone and fell, swallowing a sub. (The next day a small Wolfpack model was found in the toilet by Hitler's maid.) When Hans was through playing, he tossed the pieces back on the map. He had had enough; playtime was over.

The following morning, Adolph was excited to show his field marshals his ingenious battle plans to conquer Europe. As he unveiled the new campaign, the generals gasped when they saw the reformatted map.

"Forgive me, Mein Fuhrer, but perhaps you have made und eensy mistake," General Manstein stated. "You have several troop battalions und many panzer divisions set to invade Russia."

Hitler's eyes darted around as he studied the map. He didn't recall this part of the planning, but he had also never doubted himself before – except the time when he was an artist in Austria and was unsure of whether to paint a blue or red pony.

"The Fuhrer does not make mistakes," Goering interjected, unaware there was jelly on the corners of his mouth. "The plan is flawless." The team of officers apprehensively smiled and nodded in agreement.

"Und vas is the name of the operation, Mein Fuhrer?" Goebbels asked.

Hitler pondered. He hadn't thought of a name. Suddenly, Hans ran into the room, dressed in one of Eva Braun's flowered Austrian folk skirts. The dufus danced and twirled chirping, "I'm Barborosa. Look at me. I'm Barborosa." Nobody dared say anything, but down deep, they knew this kid was a jeep with no wheels.

"The operation is called "Barborosa," Hitler responded.

One day, while Hitler was reading over some intelligence reports on the French Resistance, he noticed raspberry stains and chocolate smudges on the papers.

"Hans," the incensed Fuhrer yelled, "Und get your assnzy in here!" The strange boy galloped into the room, pretending he was on an invisible unicorn. He was wearing knickers and a World War I soldier's helmet with a pointy top that drooped down over his eyes.

"Whoa, Helga," Hans called out as he pulled up in front of Uncle Adolph.

"Vas is dis?" Hitler questioned as he held up the papers.

"Pee pee, pooh-pooh, ca-ca," Hans responded. Hitler had no idea what this meant, but it sounded foul. The agitated chancellor rolled up the papers then hit Hans over the head with them as he yelled, "dummkopf!" Hans leaned over and growled at the Fuhrer, acting like he was a Hungarian wolf - or maybe Curly from "The Three Stooges."

Hitler had little tolerance for the insane insubordination. Something was wrong with the kid. Referring to Hans, he once told Eva "the cuckoo is stuck on that boy's clock." No matter, the dictator had no time to deal with this peculiar nuisance. After all, he had countries to bomb and people to exterminate.

"Hans perhaps you should spend some time in my Hitler youth, ya? It will make you a good German soldier for za fatherland," the Fuhrer remarked. "Und how's zat sound? You want to be a great little loyal Nazi soldier, Hans?" Hans smiled and enthusiastically nodded then began to goose step around the room chanting, "pee pee, pooh-pooh, ca-ca." Hitler just looked at the kid and rolled his eyes, releasing an exhausted grunt then mumbling "cuckoo boy."

Hans was proud to be a member of the Hitler youth. They gave him a whistle, which he was ordered to blow whenever he saw a Jew. He accidentally swallowed that first whistle but didn't realize it until, several days later, after he had devoured a plate of sauerkraut. The gas caused a whistling to emanate from his butt. A pack of barking German Shepherds quickly surrounded him.

Hans was not very good at recognizing a person of Jewish descent. One time, he approached the owner of a bagel shop and asked him his name. The old man replied, "Abe Goldsteinberg." Hans moved closer to the man, eying him from his feet to his Yamaka. He stared past the man's protruding nose and looked suspiciously in his eyes, then coldly stated, "You're lucky, ve're not looking for any Swedes." Hans started to walk away, but something bothered him. He quickly turned around and snapped, "Und clean that cream cheese off that big star on your shirt."

"Oy vey," the bagel shop owner replied. "So, I'll cleaningzy cheese off my shirt."

"Ya," Hans said as he confidentially stuck out his chest. "Und let me know if you see one of those Jews."

"Indeed. Mazel tov," Abe responded with a nod.

"Ya, you you muzzel your top too," Hans sternly said before goose-stepping off.

Hitler received excellent reports about Hans. Nobody had the guts to tell the Fuhrer his nephew was a complete idiot. Adolph decided to step up the boy's Nazi training by placing him under the wing of Joseph Goebbels, who oversaw Germany's propaganda.

Han's first assignment was to write a speech for Hitler's 53rd birthday to reinvigorate the German people and raise their spirits after a year of setbacks for the Third Reich. It was Goebbels' brilliant idea to have this blood relative craft a memorable rousing oration. Hans wrote for six days straight. However, most of the writing was a one-act play about a group of farm animals that lived in a barn outside of Dusseldorf. The idea had been swimming around in his head since he was a ten-year-old boy and worked as a plow hand one summer. (A farmer would tie a plow to the boy and let him trudge around the fields until the soil was ready for planting wheat, thus saving much wear and tear on the ox.)

Goebbels reviewed the speech, which was the one-act play. At first, he was confused at the irrelevant pile of nonsensical words and completely baffled over what farm animals had to do with the struggles of the German people against the outside world. However, as he reread the script several times, symbolism seemed to jump out at the propaganda master. The stallion must be Hitler because of its strong stature. The sheep were the German people who would follow the Fuhrer to the ends of the earth. The chickens were the Italians that had recently switched sides. And the pigs, well, obviously, this could only mean the Jews and Slavs. His assumption; Hans, like his uncle, was a genius. Not one word of the speech would be changed.

Hitler did not have a chance to read over the notes because he was busy all morning working on dramatic poses in the mirror. Things hadn't been going well on the Russian front, and he had hopes that the uplifting speech would put the German people at ease. Standing erect and confident, the Fuhrer towered on the balcony of the Reich Chancellery in front of a large crowd of people. Like a proud lion, he began his stirring oration.

"The cow goes 'mooooo,'" he began "Und all the hens say, "cluck, cluck."

Hitler paused for a moment as he nervously leafed through the papers. Clearing his throat, he continued, "Und vhere is my hay? I have not had a bale of hay for over a day. I'm sad to… say."

The mass of people began mumbling amongst themselves. "Vas is dis?" they asked one another. "Der Fuhrer noodle has gone soggy," others grumbled, implying their leader has lost his mind.

Sweat began to pour from Hitler's forehead, drenching his tiny mustache. He took a deep breath and proceeded, "Und from the farmhouse, the dog barked, "Voof! Voof!" Hitler, completely baffled, attempted to rouse the crowd by holding his arm straight out and yelling, "Voof! Voof, to za Fatherland!" Everyone just quietly stared at him, trying to comprehend the lunatic's words. As the Fuhrer continued the insane ratings about talking barnyard animals, the people were dumbfounded and growing weary. They wanted an update on the Stalingrad battle; instead, they received some burble about sheeps having tea with goats.

One by one, people began to disperse, shaking their heads in discontent. Panicking, the Fuhrer cried out anything that came into his crazed head. "The homeland is under siege! The Aryan race will prosper! The Allies will meet defeat! You can betting ze boots on zat. Betting ze boots!" Ignoring the rambling maniac, the crowd continued to walk away. "Ve vill vin! Our army is unstoppable! The Fatherland must prevail!" Hitler nervously looked around, "Hey, come back. Und free strudel for everyone!" As a last-ditch effort, he flew into a snazzy Charleston-like jig using Jazz hands, but it was too late to stop the mass exodus.

Hitler, along with Himmler, the head of the Gestapo, stormed into Goebbels's office. The propaganda specialist stood up, "Heil, Hitler!"

"Shuten ze mouth!" Hitler yelled as he rapped the man across the face. "Und who wrote that piece of garbanzy?"

"Your nephew, Hans, Mein Fuhrer" Goebbels quickly stated.

"Liar," Hitler snapped as he bopped the man on the head with a stapler from his desk.

"Ve vill ask you again," Himmler interjected. "Und who wrote the speech?"

"It was Hans," Goebbels assured him.

"So, you are saying Hans wrote the speech?" Himmler harshly questioned.

"Ya vol," Goebbels answered.

"Liar," Himmler yelled as he slapped the man's face.

"I swear, Herr Himmler, it was Hans," Goebbels pleaded.

"Liar, liar your pants zey are on fire!" Himmler shouted as he slapped his colleague silly then tousled his hair to add more insult to injury.

Hitler sent for Hans. The young man entered the room, wearing only boxer shorts and licking a paintbrush.

"Hans, did you write the speech I read today?" Hitler inquired.

"Nein, I wrote a one-act play about little friendly barnyard animals" Hans beamed. Hitler's face turned to beet red. He smiled at Goebbels as if to apologize then quickly spun him around and gave him a swift, goose step kick in his ass. "Dummkopf! Out! Out! Out of ze officenzy!" Goebbels, in tears, sniveled as he rubbed his bottom. "I didn't do anyzing," he softly mumbled as he slinked out of the room.

"You, Himmler," Hitler snapped, "Take the boy."

"Und vhat should I do with him?" the SS officer asked.

"I don't care. Make a Gestapo agent… or somezing out of him," Hitler barked.

Himmler thought it would be best to toughen up the boy – to make a good Wehrmacht soldier out of him. Perhaps the little idiot was smarter than anyone gave him credit for. He would put him to a test. Recently, a British spy, code name "Jarbo," had been captured in Munich for attempting to steal the latest dental technology that could help the Brits straighten out their teeth.

Jarbo was laidback and not easily rattled. He had forgotten why he was sent to Germany but was sure, sooner-or-later, it would come back to him. The secret agent was locked up in an undisclosed room. Hans was brought in, by Himmler, where he informed the boy that Jarbo must receive a thorough interrogation. "Do everything within your power to retrieve any information about the invasion of Europe by the Allied forces."

Hans enthusiastic about his new position, saluted the head of the secret police, accidentally knocking his hat off, then responding, "I'll have him singing like one of those cabaret singers who sings in the cabarets. Ya vol, Herr Himmler."

"Ya, ya, whatever," Himmler said as he rolled his eyes. "Just getting ze invasions plans."

Jarbo was tied to a chair when Hans entered the bare room. The Gestapo boy stared down at his foe. The British agent smiled, flashing his crooked, brown teeth. Hans pulled a Vienna sausage out of his pocket that he had been saving for lunch and began to circle the man while smacking the meat tube in his hand with hopes of intimidation.

"I say, ole boy" the agent inquired "Is that a Bratwurst or Kielbasa?"

"Shutting ze up!" Hans said as he slapped the sausage across the man's face. "Za remarkable zing about meat is zat it leaves no marks."

"Jolly good, but it can leave a nasty grease stain?" Jarbo casually responded.

Hans quickly jumped in front of the agent's face, "Ve have vays of getting grease out," he snarled. "Now tell me about za plans."

"Well, we like to have two bedrooms, a tearoom next to the loo. Tea for loo and loo for tea," the agent quickly sang. "My wife would like a large kitchen with a pantry, but, by Jove, I'm not sure we could afford that. The ol' bulldog has cut back on the secret service salary and…"

"I don't care about za plans for your new house!" Hans retorted as he bopped the spy's head with the sausage. "Vas about ze invasion?!"

"Bit loose with ol' sausage, aren't we mate?" the spy nipped.

"Ya, und you don't vant me to break out za meatballs," Hans coldly replied. "Tell me about zis invasion."

"Oh, yes, yes, yes, the lovely invasion," Jarbo lit up. "It's going to be big. Ships, boats, bicycles of all shapes and sizes, and bombs, lots of bombs. Boom, boom and all that silly rigamarole."

"Ah ha, now ve are getting somewhere," Hans nodded as he leaned in close. "Und vhere is this attack going to occur?"

"I'm terribly sorry, old chap," Jarbo replied, "I'm not privy that sort of information. I'd be more than happy to tell you the location of Piccadilly Square or Richard's Pub, that is if you fancy a good shepherd's pie."

Hans grabbed a chair, sat down and staring intensely into Jarbo's eyes replied "Tell me about zis pie" as he wet his lips.

The interrogation continued throughout the night. By the time morning arrived, the two had become best friends. Hans had even untied the man because the spy had promised to give him a ride around the room on his back, which he did, then showed young Hans some rope tricks. Hans had forgotten all about the invasion. He was more interested in hearing fascinating stories about King Arthur and the Knights of the Round Table. Jarbo was more than happy to spew out enthralling Middle Age tales if

Hans would answer some of his questions, like, the location of munitions factories and other little things like the development site of the V2 rocket.

Hans told the British spy everything he knew about Third Reich secret operations and troop movements, and in return, Jarbo intrigued him with stories of Lancelot, Sir Galahad and the quest of the Crusaders.

Hours had passed when Himmler checked in on Hans. He found the young Gestapo embarrassment tied to a chair with a sausage in his mouth. Jarbo was long gone but was thoughtful enough to leave a note behind that read merely "Enjoyed the day with the slow chap. Cheerio."

"Did you find out vhen and vhere the invasion would be?" Himmler angrily asked, pulling the sausage out of the boy's mouth.

"Nein, Herr Himmler, but I know vhere ve can get und good shepherd's pie."

Baffled, Himmler stood there, stone-faced. Strangely, a smile appeared on his face. Hans smiled back. Himmler then began laughing. Hans joined in with some giggles. Himmler continued grinning as he gently patted the boy's head. Then, suddenly, he yelled "Dummkopf!" as he whacked Han's over the head with the sausage, causing the boy to release a high-pitched whimper then shoot a quick growl at the stern general.

Himmler had brought Hans back to Hitler telling him that the boy had a lot of untapped potential and thought his talents might best be suited for the air force because the kid enjoyed putting his arms out and racing around making Messerschmitt noises. Hermann Goering quietly sat in the room, nibbling on a crumpet, dreading taking over supervision of the retarded monster.

"Mein Fuhrer," Goering suggested, "I believe the boy is Volf pack material. Ya, I zink he belongs undervater… for long periods."

Hans began racing around the room, with his arms out and making machine gun and bomb whistling noises.

"Look at him," Hitler said as he ruffled the boy's hair with his hands. "I zink the Luftwaffe could use a man vith his enthusiasm." Hitler kneeled in front of Hans. "Und vould you like to drop za bombs on London, Hans?"

"Ya, ya, ya bombs. Boom!" Hans yelled, scaring Hitler and knocking him back on his ass.

Hitler stood up and composed himself as he pushed his stringy hair out of his eyes. "You little…" Hitler gritted his teeth as he forcibly pinched the boy's cheek, practically ripping off the skin. "Little monster boy."

The winds of war had turned against Germany and, the Wehrmacht troops stalled outside of Stalingrad. The allies had a successful D-day invasion and were sweeping through France. Rommel had lost his stronghold in Africa. And, the invasion of Italy was about to begin. The Third Reich needed a miracle.

Instruction began for Hans on how to fly a Stuka – a dreaded bomber also known as the Junkers 88. The blundering boy had wrecked three planes before even getting in the air. Hans was known as the "Runway Putz." The instructor eventually just sat Hans in a chair and had him pretend he was flying. The boy managed to wreck eight chairs. (A week earlier he had totaled Goering's Mercedes while driving it to pick up the general's laundry, his mistress and some Chinese food.)

The Germans needed a wartime boost. Intelligence reports came through from a double agent stationed in Britain. He was known only as "Lederhosen" and had received information that Winston Churchill was speaking at a Friars Club meeting on the morning of December 15th. If the Nazis could snuff out this figurehead, it would be a significant blow to the morale of the Brits, perhaps even bring about a well-needed ceasefire.

Goering was fully aware it would be a suicide mission, but he didn't want to lose any good pilots, so he decided to send Hans. After all, the menace was a drain on the Nazi war effort; besides, he was still teed off after catching the little brat soaking his bare feet in his bowl of sauerbraten while eating his leftover sweet-and-sour pork.

Briefed on his assignment, Hans would take-off in the early morning hours, fly northwest, one hundred feet over the channel as to avoid radar, pass the white cliffs of Dover, continuing to London for the raid.

With preparations in place, Hans sat on the runway, then eventually got up and sat in the plane. He flipped his goggles down over the leather American football helmet, ordered from a Montgomery Ward's catalog, and waited patiently in the cockpit. Given the go-ahead, Hans yelled out the window, "I'm a Wunderwaffen!" which meant miracle weapon. The young lad smiled and gave Hermann Goering a thumbs up; the general responded by giving him the finger. Young Hans was off on his first mission for the Fatherland.

Hans would go by the code name "Die Buffoon," mainly because the mere mention of the name "Hans" gave the generals such anxiety that it made it difficult to concentrate on the task at hand. High in a sky, of scattered clouds, The Buffoon looked down enamored by the small villages, tiny cottages, and roadways that lined the land. He soon began daydreaming, wishing he were a wandering sheep dog prancing around the countryside looking for new and magical adventures.

"Buffoon. Come in, Die Buffoon," the cockpit radio echoed. It was Field Marshal Goering checking on the status of the bomber assassin.

"Ya, und Buffoon here," Hans replied.

"Und vhere are you, buffoon?" Goering asked.

"I am in the sky heading towards a puffy cloud," Hans assuredly responded.

"Nein, dummkopf!" Goering shot back. "Vas is your coordinates?"

"I think I can see my house," Hans answered.

"Listen very carefully, Buffoon," Goering said through his clenched jaw. "This is und critical mission, so you need to pull your head out of your kaputenzy und concentrate. Do you read me, Buffoon?"

"Ya, ya. Pull head out of kaputenzy," Hans confirmed.

On the morning of December 15th, Prime Minister Churchill took to the stage. It was 10:00 A.M. so he had already slugged through his first bottle of bourbon of the day. The war had taken its toll, mostly on his liver. He had received word that Montgomery had won a significant victory at Tikrit and had turned the African campaign around. It was cause for celebration and Winston was drunk - at least, more drunk than usual. At the podium, he began his speech.

"The war is progressing at a progressive rate," the prime minister slowly slurred as he gnawed on the wrong end of his cigar. "The Allied forces are doing bloody well as we continue to fight the evil Nazi regime in the air, on the water, across the land, and in our bathtubs."

The prime minister teetered back-and-forth as his eyes began to blur. He incoherently started to mumble as he stared blankly at the audience, "What are you looking at? Shut up! You wanna fight me? I'll kill every bloody one of you!" His angry demeanor quickly changed as he stepped out from behind the podium, his bloodshot pupils ogling a hefty, puffy-cheeked woman in the front row.

"And what's your name, love?" he garbled with a perverted sneer. "How's about an itty-bitty taste of the ole bulldog? Little snippet of Winston." The poor plump lady, blushed, her face aghast with fear, sat paralyzed, watching the drool drip out of the corner of the prime minister's mouth.

In his own world, Hans was zooming through the sky, entertaining himself by singing Octoberfest songs. "Ack ta Liebe Augustine, Augustine, Augustine. Ack ta Lieben Augustine, all is kaput." Whenever he forgot the words, he threw in a few "Om pa, pas." He had no idea where he was, nor did he care. He was enjoying the beautiful day.

"Die Buffoon" Goering was back on the radio. "By all estimates, you should be directly over ze target." Hans looked down. Baffled, he opened his jelly-stained map.

"Can you see London?" Goering inquired. Hans located London on the map. Pointing to it with his finger he said, "Ya vol. It's right here."

"Dropenze bomb," Goering ordered.

"Dropenze what?" Hans questioned.

"Ze bomb, you buffoon! Dropenze bomb," Goering yelled.

"Die Buffoon dropenze bomb," Hans complied.

The prime minister swayed on stage. "Come on, love, give ole Winston a big, fat kiss, you luscious plump pile of pretty pudding," he muddled as he stumbled towards the frightened woman with his flabby arms out.

Suddenly, a loud booming noise was heard, shaking the room. At first, the audience assumed the city was under air attack, but the sound was just ole Winston falling off the stage. The building wasn't bombed, but he was.

Hans opened the bombardier doors and released his cargo of explosives. The bombs were a direct hit, leveling an ammunition factory, an army barracks, a supply convoy, the Gestapo headquarters, and the Fuhrers car. Even the Allies couldn't have done more damage. The map Hans had brought with him was a treasure map he had pulled out of a comic book, and his compass had rendered useless after he had sucked on it for several hours believing it was a candy treat. He had been circling Berlin for the last six hours.

Goering sat silently, stewing over his German chocolate cake. "I don't care if ve vin the war," he solemnly said. "The only zing I vant is for that thorn in the side of the Wehrmacht to perish. I vant him dead like a dog und his body brought to me so that I may piss on it."

Several Messerschmitt scrambled and ordered to shoot Hans out of the sky. They pulled up next to him to find the pilot giggling and licking his compass. The young lad noticed them and gave them a thumbs up and a wink. The Luftwaffe pilots responded by firing a barrage of bullets into the belly of Han's Stuka. Hans thought this was an odd reception. He soon lost control of his plane and began losing altitude. Perhaps they had mistaken him for a duck, he surmised.

With his airplane now on fire, Die Buffoon had no alternative but to bail out. This was not the time for roasting marshmallows – although it did cross his mind. He remembered where the ejection button was because he had mistakenly hit it thinking it would start his plane. (Incidentally, he flipped twice in the air before hitting the runway pavement. He repeated this six times before actually learning that it was the wrong button.)

Grabbing his parachute, Hans successfully ejected from the smoking, disabled bomber. He sailed through the thin air, his chubby body dropping like a lead Zeppelin. Before Hans left the house in the morning, he had grabbed his Hitler Youth knapsack because it contained necessary survival gear and more importantly, some rations of raisins, chocolate bars and two carrots. Hans had the knapsack strapped on his back, which he didn't realize until he attempted to pop his chute.

Remembering a scene with Mickey Mouse in a Disney cartoon, Hans acted quickly and unfastened his belt and pulled off his pants. He tied his shirt to his trousers and wrapped the belt around his hands and the knickers. He let the shirt go, and it ballooned out above him. The makeshift parachute somehow worked. Hans, like a chubby butterfly, began to flutter safely to the ground.

Hitler pompously stood on a stage watching a military parade. He was proud of his Third Reich soldiers who stopped before him to accept his infamous Nazi salute. Then, the Fuhrer, as usual, jumped into a verbal tirade to rile up the German people.

"Ve are on the verge of victory," he screamed. "Our volf pack is courageously fending off the American led sea attack of our Fatherland. Our Luftwaffe is protecting our sacred skies from the villains who vish to harm our people und destroy our cities. Und our panzers are busy preventing the onslaught of a Russian invasion who vish to conquer the great Deutschland und rape our vomen und kill our children. It is the Jews that have caused this unwarranted injustice und ve vill exterminate all these problems. Ve vill never surrender!"

The crowd cheered as Hitler held up his head, firing another Nazi straight-armed salute. The applause quickly began to die down as the audience noticed an unidentified object plummeting from the sky. It was Hans, clinging to his pant legs and puffed shirt.

His naked, flabby body is whistling in the wind, like a dive bomber, while his lower limbs frantically kicked, hoping to find land soon.

Hitler, unaware of his descending nephew, sensed he was losing the attention of the people, so he continued with his ravings. "Und ve have never lost a battle! Und ve have never smelled defeat! Und ve vill never have a weight of the vorld on our shoulders again!" the tyrant finished with his proud chin up and a rigid pose he had practiced in the mirror for days.

Somewhere in mid-rant, Hitler felt a great weight on his shoulders – literally. It was Die Buffoon. The faces of the aghast German people watched in shock as Hans' naked body balanced on top of the Fuhrer with boy's pale bum resting on the leader's head. Unsure of what it was,

Adolph began running around in circles, swatting at the lumpy mound of flesh draped on him, thinking it was a giant bumblebee. Die Buffoon sat on the Fuhrer's shoulders, clapping his hands and repeating, "Hansi go kaput! Hansi go kaput!"

Somehow, the skinny dictator was able to flip the troublesome oaf off of him. After catching his breath and realizing who this attacker was, he began stomping the jackass with his Jackboots as he yelled: "dummkopf!" By now, the masses of people were in mass hysteria, laughing at the crazed, infuriated Fuhrer. Hitler looked out at his people and screamed, "Stop laughing at me! Stop it, I say!" It was too late. The people couldn't stop if they were in front of a firing squad. Hitler's face grew red, and he stormed off, without even goose-stepping. He was later seen, sobbing, in the corner of his office holding a copy of "Mein Kampf" to his chest and petting his loyal German Shepherd.

As if the ordeal wasn't humiliating enough, Adolph Hitler would also discover that when Hans abandoned his plane, the Stuka crashed into his favorite Alpine retreat, burning it to the ground.

Hitler had reached his breaking point with the boy. Just as he was preparing to put Hans on a train to a quiet little town named Dakar, Rommel intervened and, feeling compassion for the boy, volunteered to make a tank commander out of him. It didn't take long but, somehow, Hans was able to single-handedly destroy an entire Panzer division, a fuel depo and the General's stable which contained his prize horse named Augustus. A week later the great unflappable Desert Fox committed suicide.

Towards the end of the war, Hitler and Eva Braun hid out in an underground bunker awaiting the arrival of their escape plans from Martin Bormann. Within the documents would be a meticulous, well-laid out route, with the necessary contacts and safe houses, to get the pair to South America. Hitler anxiously paced the concrete floors, mumbling to himself. Finally, he received the good news that the courier had made it through all the chaos in Berlin. The bodyguards hustled the courier into the back room to where the failed leader of the Third Reich sat with his head in his hands.

"Und za courier is here, Mein Fuhrer," the bodyguard said.

Hitler released a sigh of relief then seem to gather himself. He looked up and, standing in front of him, was Hans, sporting an innocent dorkish smile on his face.

"Guten tag, Uncle Adolph," he said in a gleeful, sing-song voice.

Hitler's mouth fell open, and he dropped his cup of tea on his lap burning his testicles. He thought for sure, with the bombs dropping, the constant shelling, the gun fire and the city in ruins, that the half-witted child would surely be dead. This news was worst the surrender at Stalingrad.

"Und look vas I brought you," Hans said with a giggle as he held out an apple in his hand.

"Vas is dis?" Hitler asked in a stern voice.

"I thought you might be hungry since zere is not much food around. So, I brought you an apple," Hans proudly stated as he handed the fruit to the Fuhrer.

Hitler examined it, believing the little moron may have picked up a red painted grenade. He stared at the apple for a long minute then very gently inquired, "Und vhere did you get das apple?"

"Why I traded a man on the street for it," Hans replied, flashing a big grin.

Hitler's mustache twitched back-and-forth as he tried to remain calm. Afraid to ask his next question, he took a deep, long breath then slowly uttered, "Und vhat did you trade for zis apple?"

"Zat dirty old leazer briefcase Herr Bormann ask me to watch for him," Hans casually responded, proudly holding up his chin.

"You mean za leazer briefcase that Herr Bormann had put all za top secret plans for my escape with all za secret contacts? Zat leazer briefcase?' Hitler responded in a calm voice, doing his best to remain composed.

"I zink so. Can you believe someone would be dumb enough to trade me a beautiful, juicy apple for an old briefcase?"

"Yes, zere are many dumb people in the world," Hitler agreed with a slow nod then… "Dummkopf!" Hitler bellowed out as he turned as red as the as the apple then bopped the dimwitted boy in the head with the Luger he had been holding. Hans reflexively recoiled then growled at the Fuhrer like a mad dog. The perturbed German leader looked up and began shaking his fist and cursing like he was giving a fiery speech at the Reichstag. It made the young lad laugh at his silly uncle. In a rage, the furious Fuhrer began to pistol-whip the boy with a luger. Hans rolled on the floor giggling, believing Uncle Adolph was trying to tickle him.

The Allied Forces and the Red Army were closing in on the bunker. There was no chance of escape for anyone. Hitler's worst nightmare had come into fruition; Hans would be spending what little time they had left with him and his newly married wife.

Later that night, a worn and haggard Hitler walked in on Hans playing with a luger that he had left lying around. He snatched the gun from Han's hand and yelled, "Vas are you doing, dummkopf boy?" Uncle Adolph then reached into his pocket and pulled out a magazine then loaded the pistol. "Und now you play with it," he snarled like a crazed lunatic, handing it back to the boy. He ran around making gun sounds with his mouth as the leader of the Third Reich sat in his chair staring blankly at the annoying kid, gritting his teeth and mumbling under his breath. Hitler was reaching his breaking point as he watched Hans spin around, singing an old folk song, "Ach, du Lieber Augustin, Augustin, Augustin, Ach, du Lieber Augustin, Alles is hin." Just as Hitler was about to make his way over and strangle the boy, he had an eye-opening epiphany. He realized how he could turn the tides of war and restore the Wehrmacht to greatness. Why didn't he think of this before? It was so simple. Suddenly, Hans, amid a giggling twirl, tripped over Blondie the dog and the gun went off. The clumsy klutz looked up to see Uncle Adolph, standing in the middle of the room, with a bullet hole in his forehead. The Fuhrer stood there with a blank look on his face; his eyes fixated on Hans. Clinging to death, he mustards the strength to mutter his final words "dummkopf" before falling flat on his mustache. Eva raced into the room. "Und Hans vhat have you done? How did zis happen?" The bungling boy re-created everything that had just occurred. In no time, Eva Braun stood in the middle of the room, with a bullet hole in her forehead. Her final words would be "dummkopf" before falling flat on her face. Hans looked around. Noticing all was quiet, he put the luger into Uncle Adolph's hand then scurried out of the room.

While awaiting the arrival of the Allied Forces, Hans passed the time by finger-painting a Hitler-like mustache on Eva's upper lip and Groucho glasses with bushy eyebrows on the Fuhrer. It was later revealed, by Adolph Hitler's niece, that Hans was an illegitimate son from an incestuous relationship with none other than Hitler himself. Goering captured, and in prison, was informed that Hans would be testifying on his behalf during the Nuremberg Trials. The general quickly swallowed a cyanide capsule. After the war, Eisenhower awarded Hans with a medal of valor, which the boy promptly put in his mouth believing it was a candy treat. Hans would later write a book about his wartime excursions titled *Der Tyrann und der Dummkopf.* It became a worldwide best-seller, and Hans became a rich man.

EPILOGUE

BEHIND THE BOOK

I had been working on the book for about a year or so. I think. In front of me was a stack of pages that had stuff on them. The truth be told, I didn't know what I had. I'd been nibbling and picking at various stories and wasn't pleased with anything. There were notes, paragraphs, jokes, ideas, fragmented sentences, and words that may or may not be present in a typical Webster dictionary. In all honesty, I didn't remember writing any of this. On the upside, the mound of papers did resemble a manuscript of some sort.

I knew at some point I had to do one of the hardest things I'd ever done in my life which was to go back and read this gibberish to see if there was somehow a book in there. Anything's possible. I knew I couldn't do it on my own, I'd need help. I buckled down and made a stiff cocktail. Thank God for good friends. I began making my way through the cluster of stories. I had an uncanny hunch that finishing the drink would be easier then finishing the manuscript.

Upon reading the compilation I was rather surprised. I wondered from where this insanity arose. I had a good childhood. I skipped all the drugs and ate most of my vegetables. This could not have spewed out of my mind. Did I write this buffoonery? From a wild west cowboy that dances instead of fighting to an organ grinder that goes toe-to-toe with his monkey. A sexually abused mule? Surely, I didn't write such absurdity; I would've certainly made it a donkey, not a mule.

I received a call from the publisher who told me how excited she was to read my book. I said, "I'm still trying to figure out what the book's about." She laughed. I like it when people laugh when I say something funny.

"So, you'll drop it off on Friday?" she replied.

"Drop off what?" I asked, and she laughed again. I liked her laugh.

"The book," she casually threw out.

"The book?" I questioned.

"Your book," she pushed back.

"My book?" I said, hoping to annoy her enough to drop the subject.

Yes silly," she responded back. "The book you've been writing for which we paid you a ten-thousand-dollar advance and set a due date of February 7th."

"That would be this Friday," was what my ears heard coming out of my mouth, but it was like my mind refused to let that sentence in. "No, I'm sorry, we're full up here. We don't just accept heart-stopping news. Not without a reservation, which gives us time to process and make a stiff cocktail."

"Oh, stop your clowning. Save that for the book," she chuckled then told me she'd see me this Friday. God, I hated that deep, horsey, cackling laugh of hers.

My back was to the wall. That night I did what any good author would do. I meandered over to the liquor cabinet and made a stiff drink then followed that with a Xanax. This behavior became a repetitive habit throughout the night to help me brainstorm. At some point, I began to feel woozy and figured a nice stroll in the fresh air might revive me and open up my creativity.

The crisp night air rejuvenated me as I staggered down the street. The snow had been rapidly falling, relieving the pressure I was feeling. Each fluttering flake made me forget why I was strolling through the darkness. I had no idea where I was going. I just wanted to escape the responsibility of being an author.

I don't know how long I'd been shuffling aimlessly when I noticed a short figure in the road ahead of me. Through the blizzard, I could see the figure waving me towards himself. As I neared the little fellow, I noticed his features were that of a dwarf-like troll. A beard sat beneath his puffy rosy cheeks, and his eyes were big, taking long exaggerated blinks with a twinkle that displayed a trusting kindness. In a way, it reminded me of my prom date, but maybe it was just the facial hair.

"I was afraid you weren't coming," the dwarf man said.

"Who are you?" I inquisitively asked.

"Come, come, come. We mustn't dither," the figure insisted.

I felt compelled to follow him, watching him waddle as he walked. We trudged through the snowstorm. I remember looking back and seeing my footprints, but they were the only ones. He led me along, and we soon found ourselves in a dark forest. Along the way, I asked many questions like who he was and where we were going, but the little man remained quiet. Eventually, the woods opened up, and we came upon an enormous shimmering castle. The ivory-white walls, embedded with diamonds and rubies, had two rising towers on the corners made of a shiny green jade.

"Holy jamoly, what is this place?" I asked.

"Why it's Terradiddle," he casually answered. "The castle of knowledge."

"Damn, you got a sweet place here," I commented. "Hey..., what's your name anyway?"

"Chumfersnittzel," the dwarf man said.

"How about I just call you 'Chum'?"

"I would much prefer Chummy," he stated.

"Chummy it is," I shrugged.

A blazing fire crackled in the large fireplace as I sat there chatting with Chummy over a cup of tea made from surface dust of the planet Troubadour in the seventh galaxy of Voricon he claimed. Yeah, sure it was. It made me chuckle. He was a kind and gentle dwarf troll and seemed to know a lot about me. His warm demeanor allowed me to open up, spilling out my reservations, and insecurities as a writer.

"I don't know if anything I write has a purpose," I sighed.

"Indeed, it does," he assured. "Your words make my belly laugh."

"You've read my stuff?" I said, taken aback.

"Every book, article, script, story, and blog," he mentioned with a smile. "You are a very talented wordsmith."

"Thanks, Chummy. I wish I could believe you. The reason I was out walking in the snow was that I have a book due very soon."

"Oh, jolly splendid," he beamed. "I do so look forward to reading it."

"That's the thing, my friend. I've lost it. I have no ideas, no passion, and no strength to produce a manuscript. I have nothing."

"I think you just don't know what you have," the kind dwarf consoled. "Come. Come. Follow me. Perhaps I can provide you with some inspiration." I guzzled my tea. A warm feeling zoomed over me as my body tingled with an unexplainable excitement and ecstasy. Instantaneously I had gone from feeling low to high. I hoped Chummy would provide me with a couple of those mysterious tea bags as parting gifts.

He led me through the castle, as we weaved through various rooms with different decor. One made of all glass, another all stone, and even a chamber of all mirrors that made it difficult to judge its size. The tour ended when we arrived in a large open dwelling, appearing to be a sort of library. Shelves lined the walls containing books that seemed to go on forever.

"What in God's name is this place?" I asked in astonishment.

"The Library of Written History," he replied. "Everything ever written throughout time fills these halls."

"You gotta be joking," I beamed. "Are my books in here?"

"Indeed. In our latest century humor section, next to Woody Allen and, I believe, Dave Barry."

"Hmm, not bad company," I nodded with a sense of pride. "You mind if I browse the place?"

"I think it would behoove you," Chummy smiled as he bowed and rolled his hands out in an inviting manner.

I poured through as many written texts as I could read. The keepers of the castle were known as Lolliwobblers, and there were many of all different shapes and sizes. One Loliwobbler, Teeky, would periodically check on me, bringing me sprinkled crumpets and tea that undoubtedly had magical properties that could keep me awake, allowing me to pour over thousands of these historical chronicles. At some point, Chummy wandered in and startled me. "Anything to tickle thy fancy?"

"There are some amazing stories here," I exclaimed. "Where in the world did you find these?"

"We, the Lolliwobblers, were the first group of beings placed on the planet to be the keepers of all history. Terradiddle houses the library of all stories throughout time. Scrolls, manuscripts, books, etc. You name it; we got it."

"Wow. I mean… wow," I muttered flabbergasted.

He continued the tour leading me down a golden spiral staircase, bringing us into a large room where hundreds of nerd-like translators, known as Whizettes, sat. They were chubby, furry creatures with fat round noses and long buckteeth who wore thick bottle-lens glasses. Deep at work, they sat at tables vigorously writing and meticulously transcribing ancient tablets and tales into readable documents to categorize into their appropriate decade in time.

I spent what seemed like weeks, months, maybe even years browsing through the library archives that contained stories from every era. Unbelievable anecdotes that occurred throughout history, and as far as I knew, had never been told. I set aside thirteen stories that, for some unknown reason connected with me. I thought the world must come to know of these accounts. But, more importantly, I needed something to hand into the publisher. They paid me good money to provide them with a book and, by God, I was going to keep my word, even if they weren't my words.

"Chummy, do you mind if I take a few of these stories with me?" I asked, then added, "I'd like to share them with the world."

"What a jolly splendid idea," he responded with delight. "I believe the world will love them, simply love them."

"And, you know what? It helps me out too," I commented.

"Indeed. That's why I brought you here," he said with a sly smile.

"What I would give to write like this. These stories have everything, excitement, intrigue, knowledge, and humor. It's everything I dreamed of writing but couldn't get it out. I'm just a hack who talks about someday writing that great book."

"You have written a great book. You just don't know it," Chummy reassured. "Believe, my little foolish fool. Believe in your talent. Believe it to be true. It is vast and will serve ye well."

"Thanks, Chummy. You give me hope," I humbly responded.

"Time will reveal the truth. Never spend time, invest in it. Now, it is time for you to return," Chum continued. "Take your stories and release them to the masses. You will make us proud."

Chummy placed the stories I had chosen into a leather saddlebag which I slung over my shoulder. Standing before me, the bearded dwarf tweaked my nose, knocked me on my head two times then pinched my cheek telling me it was the formal Lolliwobbler goodbye. I did it back to him, and he smiled because I added an extra knock on his noggin. Chummy then did a quick shuffle dance, released a whooping purring yelp then clapped his hands three times. Out trotted a zebra-like animal with stripes of purple and gold, pointy ears and, below his bushy velvet eyebrows were deep blue eyes that threw out a radiant, beam of amber light. He also had a long tail that spun around when its head jetted forward. On his hoofs were tiny wings that most likely helped the creature speedily glide over land.

"What is this thing?" I queried in amazement.

"It's a Zephendackyl, of course. It will bring you back to where you belong."

I was happy to see the animal for I was not in the mood to walk home. I petted its nose then climbed on the thing's back. Chum pulled out a small silk satchel and dipped his fingers in it. As he sprinkled some glistening powder over my head, he uttered a nonsensical chant, "Goopy, loopy, doopy doo. Sheckel, Meckel, heckle pie."

And with that, the Zephendackyl galloped out of the castle into the cold, snowy night, his eyes lighting the path that lies ahead even though it seemed to know it exactly where it was going. I just hung on and enjoyed the ride as the wind whisked through my hair. The winged hoofs lightly touched the ground, appearing to soar in the air. We raced through the forest, zipping along while trees sailed by until finally emerging into a clearing at which point, the creature seemed to kick into a higher gear tearing across the snowy plain.

Through the thickly falling snow, I could see mountains ahead of me. All was well until I noticed in the distance a ledge that dropped into thick darkness. This crazy Zephendackyl was headed right for a cliff! Terror gripped my body. I froze with no choice but to hold on and put my life into the hands of fragile fate. I closed my eyes, calling upon a God I have ignored for many years. I hugged the animal's neck as the carefree beast leaped off the edge, seemly launching for the moon.

I awoke with my head on the desk, staring at an empty bottle of vodka. Through my blurry eyes, I noticed a neat stack of papers on my desk. Shaking off the fog in my head, I looked it over and, much to my surprise, they were the same stories I had taken from Terradiddle Castle. I began to doubt I was ever there. That's crazy talk. Maybe I wrote them in my drunken stupor. It wouldn't be the first time. I was afraid to read it or was just too hungover. Either one was a valid excuse. That's when I had the bright idea to have my friend Buddha read it. As long as he said, "It's okay" I'd know it was good and feel that I could hand it off to the publisher. Little did I know he'd pass the manuscript off to a homeless bum.

"So, these stories are actually from this Terradiddle Castle library?" the publisher skeptically asked. "Is that what you're saying?"

"I'm not sure," I hesitantly and honestly replied. "Did you like it?"

"I loved it," she beamed. "I peed myself at least seven times,"

"Well then, of course, I wrote them," I confidently stated. "There's no such thing as Terradiddle Castle."

I was hoping the stories did come out of some deep dark corner of my mind, but I didn't know for sure. Maybe I did get them from Terradiddle Castle. And perhaps, they are real stories that happened sometime long ago. That would be funny.

A smile starts on the lips, a grin spreads to the eyes, a chuckle comes from the belly; but a good laugh bursts forth from the soul, overflows, and bubbles all around.

— Carolyn Birmingham

CPSIA information can be obtained
at www.ICGtesting.com
Printed in the USA
FSHW020716291119
64603FS